JUST ANOTHER KNIFE CRIME
(or Identity Crisis)

DAVENPORT & LEPAGE BOOK 1

by
Judy Ford

Bernie Fazakerley
Publications

COPYRIGHT

Just Another Knife Crime

(or Identity Crisis)

Published by Bernie Fazakerley Publications

ISBN: 978-1-911083-84-9

DEDICATED TO

The people of St Luke's Church, Dunham-on the-Hill, and especially the organisers of the regular book sales at which I have been permitted to sell my output.

A Church for All
A Church at the Heart of the Community

CONTENTS

CONTENTS

1. PROLOGUE

'Ho-o-o-old, and rest. That's better! Very good. That really conveyed the feelings behind the music.' Dr Piers Claughton, tutorial fellow, organist and choir master at Holy Cross College, bent over his pupil and rested his left hand gently on his shoulder for a few moments in a gesture of approval. 'I think we'll call it a day now. Carry on practising the fingering on the piano, and I'll see you again next week at the usual time.'

'Yes, Dr Claughton. Thank you.' Gabriel leaned forward to gather up the pages of sheet music from which he had been playing. He stowed them carefully in the music case that he had been given for his thirteenth birthday three months earlier, before swinging his legs over the organ bench and getting to his feet. He enjoyed his weekly lessons with the middle-aged don, who had a knack of giving just the right balance of encouragement and criticism to spur him on to greater efforts without implying that his playing was inadequate. However, the knowledge that his mother would be getting a report on his progress when she took her morning coffee in the Senior Common Room the next day gave them an element of risk that sometimes made him uncomfortable. Casting his mind back over the last two hours, he was confident that, on this occasion, there was nothing that she could interpret as indicating a lack of diligence or aptitude on his part.

He got up and Dr Claughton took his place in front of the manuals, placing a new sheaf of music on the stand and pulling and pushing stops in readiness for beginning his own practice. Christmas always came early in Oxford, because of the need for carol services and other celebrations to take place before the undergraduates left for home during the first week in December. He had a concert of seasonal music looming and his performance needed to be perfect.

As Gabriel made his way down the steep steps from the organ loft, a familiar melody from Handel's Messiah reverberated through the chapel. Without thinking, he joined in with the soprano line, 'For unto us a Child is born …'

He reached the foot of the stairs and stepped out into the passageway that divided the chapel from the Hall, with its kitchens and store rooms. This was the rear entrance of the college, a narrow tunnel running through the building from Al Qahtani Quad (previously more prosaically known as the Back Quad, but recently renamed following refurbishments funded by a generous benefactor) to Goose Lane.

'And the government shall be upon his shou-ou-ou-ou-oulder. And the gov-'

He broke off as, turning to the left to make his way out, he saw a cluster of people in a uniform of white tunics and black trousers. The white hats and striped aprons indicated that they were some of the kitchen staff, taking a break from preparing dinner for the students and fellows of the college. Gabriel approached them in silence. They were standing across the door to the outside world, blocking his exit. As he drew nearer, one of them glanced his way and then turned back and continued chatting with his colleagues.

'Excuse me,' Gabriel said politely. 'May I go through?'

Instantly, they all turned and stared at him. There were three of them: two men and a woman, all dressed alike and all with cigarettes in their hands.

'Excuse me!' mimicked a youngish man with a shaved head in an exaggeratedly posh, rather camp, accent, 'May I come through?' Then, dropping the mocking voice, he continued, 'and what're you doing here then, anyway?'

'I've been in the chapel for a music lesson,' Gabriel explained nervously.

'What? They having bongo drums in there now?' scoffed the other man, a lanky redhead with big hands, which he was now moving up and down in front of him in a parody of playing African drums.

'No, I'm learning the organ,' Gabriel replied, knowing that they were making fun of him, but unable to think of a way of extricating himself from the conversation. 'With Dr Claughton.'

'Oh, listen to him!' The young woman stepped forward and leered at him. 'He's been playing with Dr Claughton's organ!'

'Oooh! You naughty boy!' the first man screamed, mincing towards Gabriel with one hand on his hip and the other waving his cigarette aloft in a gesture worthy of a 1970s comedy show.

Gabriel backed away. 'It's alright, I'll go round the other way.'

But they were all around him now. He was trapped.

'So, Dr Claughton likes them exotic, does he?' demanded the redheaded man.

Gabriel stared back at him in perplexity. What did he mean?

'Pays you in bananas, does he?' the woman joined in.

'No, he doesn't pay me. Mum pays him – for the lessons,' Gabriel replied, bewildered by the banter, but still anxious to be polite.

'Hoo-hoo-hoo!' taunted the redhead, lifting his arms in imitation of a gorilla and pretending to scratch under his armpits.

'Look! He's got a handbag!' The woman pointed down at Gabriel's music case.

'Let's have a look!' The shaved-head man grabbed the case and wrenched it from Gabriel's hand.

'No! Give that back!' he protested. 'It's mine! My dad gave it to me.'

Somehow, the whole group moved out into the lane, propelling Gabriel with them. The music case was open now and precious sheets containing the pieces that he was supposed to practise for his next lesson were dropping into the muddy gutter, filled with dead leaves and discarded cigarette ends. Gabriel bent down to retrieve them, but the redheaded man took hold of him and forced him back against the wall of the college.

'Don't you talk like that to us,' he growled. 'Where did the likes of you get this sort of stuff?'

'He's right,' the woman backed him up, coming up and putting her painted face uncomfortably close to Gabriel's. 'It's no good you claiming this stuff is all legit. I'll bet you pinched it from one of the students.'

'N-no! Honestly!' Gabriel pleaded. 'It's mine. My mum bought it for me. Please! Give it back! I'll be in trouble if I can't practise.'

'What d'you think?' Still pinning Gabriel to the wall with one hand, the man looked round at his companions. 'Shall we give him his handbag back?'

'Nah!' The woman shook her head. 'Hand it in to the porters as lost property.'

'Good idea,' agree the shaved-head man. 'If it really is his, he can claim it back, can't he?'

'OK.' Gabriel looked from face to face with pleading in his eyes. 'Give it to the porters, but let me pick up the music it's getting all messed up.'

The redhead stared at him, as if he was debating what to do next. The other two leaned against the wall and took slow drags on their cigarettes. Time seemed to stand still …

'Stop that!'

Gabriel's tormentors swung round to stare across the road at a voice that seemed to come from nowhere. It was loud and strong, a deep, man's voice, suggesting that its owner must be large and muscular.

'Let him go!' the voice came again. Gabriel still could not see where it was coming from, but more importantly, his captor had relaxed the grip on his shoulder a little. He slid out from under the huge, hairy hand and started to run. He was vaguely aware of a human shape running in the other direction, a big man, taller even than his father, but his whole mind was focused on putting as much distance as he could between himself and the three bullies.

His chest heaved and his legs began to ache as he forced himself to keep going through the network of narrow streets. As he reached busier roads, passers-by stared at him as he dodged and weaved to avoid bumping into them. He was flagging now, but still desperate to reach the High and the sanctuary of the bus that would carry him home. He rounded a corner and …

'What's the hurry, young man?'

Gabriel gazed up at the police officer with whom he had collided as he swerved to avoid crashing into a bicycle chained to the railings outside a bank. She smiled down at him, but held his arm in a firm grip that forced him to a halt. He stood there panting, conscious of his heart pounding against his ribs and his leg muscles protesting at the punishing exertion to which he had subjected them.

'Well?' It was another police officer, a man this time in a different uniform with three stripes on the sleeve. 'Let's hear it! What's the tearing rush?'

Gabriel stared, craning his neck round to see the man's face as he fought for enough breath to answer the question.

'My – my – my –,' he panted at last, gesticulating across the road with his free arm to indicate the bus stop, which had been his goal. 'My bus,' he gasped at last. 'My mum. She'll worry if I'm not back for dinner.'

He felt the grip on his arm relax a little. Was she going to let him go? 'Well, leave more time for it next time,' she said in a voice that reminded him of an occasion when one of his teachers had stopped him for running in the corridor at school. 'You could cause an accident, racing along the pavement like that.'

'Yes ma'am,' Gabriel muttered as she finally let go of his arm.

He started to move off, but the other police officer barred his way. 'Not so fast, young man. I'd like to know what you've got in there.' He pointed down at the pockets of Gabriel's duffle coat, one of which was bulging noticeably.

Gabriel felt his heart, which had just been getting back to normal speed after his exertions, speeding up again as he tried to remember what he was carrying. The bulge was caused by the knitted hat, which his mother had insisted on him wearing when he left home that afternoon, but was there anything else in there – something that he wouldn't want other people to see? He pulled out the hat and held it out towards the police officer, who took it and felt it all over as if expecting to find something concealed between the double layers of knitting.

He handed it back with a dissatisfied expression on his face. Then he delved with his own hand into each of the pockets of Gabriel's coat, pulling out the pair of gloves that the boy had not had time to put on before the dramatic encounter in Goose Lane. 'What's your name?'

'G-Gabriel. Gabriel Sibanda, sir.'

'The angel Gabriel, eh?' There was mockery in the voice. 'Well, let's see if you *are* so angelic, shall we? Take that coat off and stand up against that wall with your arms and legs spread so I can check the rest of your pockets.'

Gabriel stared back in momentary disbelief and then started following the instructions. He undid his coat and slipped it off his shoulders. The police woman took it from him and put it over her arm, smiling weak reassurance as if she were uncomfortable with the turn of events but did not like to protest. The man was clearly in charge.

'Go on!' he barked. 'I thought you were in a hurry.'

Gabriel stepped over to the wall of the bank. A few feet away, customers were queuing for the ATM machine. He could feel their eyes on his back as he stood facing the wall with his arms raised and his feet spread apart. The policeman patted him all over, reaching into his trouser pockets and taking out the contents for inspection. Satisfied at last, he stepped back and instructed Gabriel to turn round.

'OK,' he said in a much lower voice, 'that's all – this time – but you mind how you go!'

'Yes, sir,' Gabriel mumbled back.

'Better put this back on.' The woman officer helped him back into his coat. 'I'll see you to your bus.'

'It's OK, thanks. The stop's only just over there.'

'Still, I'll just see you safe over the road.'

2. CRIME SCENE

'Your phone's ringing!' Monica called out, putting down her spoon and reaching out for the smartphone that Alice had left lying on the breakfast table. 'Shall I get it?'

'No, it's OK, I'm here now,' her partner of four years called back, coming in from the adjacent utility room where she had been loading the washing machine so that it could complete its cycle while they were both out at work. She took the phone from Monica's hand and swiped the screen to answer the call.

Monica returned to her organic muesli and oat milk, listening with interest to the one-sided conversation.

'No, I haven't set out yet. … I see. … Yes, that makes sense. … OK, I'll expect you in a few minutes then.'

'Andy?' Monica enquired.

'Got it in one,' Alice grinned back, sitting down and pouring herself a mug of coffee. 'There's a suspicious death been reported in the centre of town – right outside one of the colleges. Andy's been called to attend and he's picking me up on the way. He says there's no point cluttering up those narrow streets with any more vehicles than we have to.'

'A suspicious death?' Monica felt a pang of regret that she was no longer part of the Oxford CID team. 'Does it sound interesting or just a rough sleeper getting hypothermia or a druggy taking an overdose?'

'Andy says it was a knife attack. The uniform who got to the scene first reckon a falling out between drug dealers – maybe a turf war between rival gangs. The victim is a black male, which would fit with that sort of thing. It sounds like it'll be pretty routine – lots of graft and probably nothing to show for it at the end of it all. You won't be missing much, if that's what you're thinking.'

'Oh well! At least you seem to have established yourself as *DI* Lepage's favourite bag-carrier,' Monica smiled, emphasising the newly-promoted officer's rank sardonically. 'It can't do you any harm being the boss's blue-eyed girl.'

'I wouldn't put it like that,' Alice protested. 'And besides, Andy isn't actually in charge. We've been merged with DCI Davenport's team. She's the boss.'

'She's not turning out to see this suspicious death though, is she? She's delegating, the way DCIs are supposed to, which makes Andy Lepage the boss, as far as you're concerned, and you should make the most of being in his good books. Why don't you put in to do your sergeant's exams? I reckon he'd back you.'

'I'm not so sure I want promotion. We don't need the money and I'm happy where I am. You've got enough ambition for both of us. It's only a pity you had to go back into uniform to get your inspector's post. But then, if you'd been more patient, instead of jumping ship in such a hurry, you might have got the DI job instead of Andy, when DCI Porter finally retired – again!'

'Oh, I don't know. I'm enjoying it more than I thought I would. The hours are certainly better. At least now if I'm working nights, I know that I'll be getting time off in the day – no more burning the candle at both ends to solve a case before the trail goes cold! And when I come in at the start of my shift, I don't find all the unfinished jobs from yesterday still staring at me on my desk the way I used to in CID.'

'But that's what I like about being a detective,' Alice protested, 'getting a case and being allowed to run with it. When I was in uniform, I never seemed to see anything through to the end – all those kids I brought in for possession, all those drunk and disorderlies on a Friday night! I never got to see what happened to them in the end. And then, after a bit, I started seeing the same faces cropping up again and again.'

'And now probably one of those kids you nicked has turned up dead because he tried to sell his stuff on someone else's patch. Let's face it, even in CID most of what we do is just fire-fighting; it doesn't make a lasting difference.'

'It does to the victims,' Alice argued, 'if we find out who did it, that is.'

Monica got up and carried her empty bowl and mug over to the dishwasher. 'How *are* things in the old firm now that Andy's in charge. I bet he's a bit more laid-back than Porter used to be.'

'Well, maybe a bit less driven,' Alice conceded, 'but still very determined. He's always looked up to DCI Porter – like somebody else I could mention!' she teased. It was a standing joke between them that Monica had once been madly in love (from afar) with the man who later became her boss. 'He's very fair and doesn't pull rank.'

'I reckon he's got a tough job, taking over from a hero like Porter,' Monica observed, emptying the dregs from the coffee jug down the sink. 'Jonah must be a very hard act to follow – not to mention how difficult it is managing a team of people you used to work alongside. I reckon I've got a much easier job in Abingdon, where nobody knows me.'

'I hadn't thought of it that way,' Alice murmured thoughtfully. 'Maybe you're right. I had noticed one or two of the guys can be a bit … well, not really taking him seriously. I wondered if they didn't rate him because he's black, but you'd have thought being in a wheelchair like Jonah was more reason for thinking he wasn't up to the job, and none of them would have dreamed of answering back to *him*.'

'Andy isn't really black,' Monica told her. 'I've seen him out with his mum. His whole family's white.'

'Do you mean he's adopted?'

'That's what I thought, but I asked him about it.' Alice smiled to herself at her partner's impudence. It was typical of Monica that she could not rest with an unanswered question in her mind. 'His mum had an affair with a Nigerian student – over here on a Commonwealth scholarship or something – when she was only a teenager. He buggered off back to Africa at the end of his course and she was left holding the baby.'

'Wow! I never knew. And I'm not sure you ought to have told me,' Alice added as an afterthought.

'Why on earth not? He told me straight out when I asked. He didn't try to hide it.'

'No, but … I don't suppose you gave him much option. I know what you can be like when you want to know something.'

'Well, he didn't seem to mind, and it's too late to worry about it now.' Monica picked up her uniform hat and coat and headed for the door. 'Anyway, I must dash. Text me if this dead body of yours keeps you working late.'

She flung open the front door energetically and then had to take a step back as DI Andy Lepage, who had put up his hand to knock only a moment before, almost fell into the hall on top of her.

'Hi Andy. How are you?'

'Fine thanks. How are you getting on in Abingdon?'

'Great! It's nice to have a new challenge.'

They both stood there unsure what to say or do next. Glancing over the top of Monica's head, Andy was relieved to see Alice hurrying towards them with her coat over her arm.

'It's OK, Andy,' she called. 'I'm ready now. Let's go.'

11

Arriving in the narrow back street quaintly named Goose Lane, they pulled up behind a police squad car and walked over to the cordon of blue-and-white police tape that stretched across the road from the honey-coloured stone wall of Holy Cross College on the right to the boundary of Lichfield College on the left. The sun had risen, but on this dull November morning, it was still only half light and the lamp over the back entrance of the college cast weird shadows on the yellowish paving and grey cobbles. They were greeted by PC Callum McLaughlin, who held up the tape to allow them to step under it into the crime scene.

Andy looked round. The wall on his right rose to twenty feet or more and had stained glass windows that began about halfway up. That must be the college chapel, he concluded. There was a door in the wall further on, beyond the end of the row of windows, and a tall, grey-haired man was standing just outside it in conversation with another uniformed police officer.

'That's the Principal,' McLaughlin told him. 'He came out wanting to know what was going on.'

'And what has gone on?' asked Andy. 'In your opinion?'

'Looks like just another knife crime to me, sir,' McLaughlin shrugged. 'Black youth stabbed to death in the street. Probably just a falling out and someone pulled a knife on him. The usual black-on-black stuff. A couple of women found him on their way in to work this morning – kitchen staff at the college. They called an ambulance, but the paramedics say he'd been dead some time, so it probably all happened last night.'

'I see,' Andy said calmly, while Alice treated the young PC to a hard stare, which he completely failed to notice. 'Well, I suppose I'd better go and have a word with the Principal, and then interview the women.'

'They're inside,' McLaughlin informed him. 'There's a WPC looking after them.'

'A police constable,' Alice corrected him. 'We're all supposed to be equal now, remember?'

McLaughlin pulled a face and looked towards Andy, who refused to offer the male solidarity that he was seeking.

'Thank you, constable,' he said stiffly. 'That's all for now.'

Sergeant Ben Timpson made introductions. 'This is Professor Giles Winthrop,' he told them. 'He's the Principal of Holy Cross College. Professor Winthrop, this is DI Andy Lepage and DC Alice Ray. DI Lepage will be leading the investigation into what happened here.'

Andy dismissed him with a brief, 'thank you, sergeant,' and then turned to address the professor. 'I'm afraid we're going to have to keep this area sealed for some time while our forensics team go over the crime scene. Will it be a problem for you to keep this door closed until we're finished?'

'It's not ideal,' Winthrop answered, pushing back strands of hair that had dropped over his face to reveal bushy eyebrows and pale blue eyes, 'but I suppose we can manage. I'll get the porters to put up notices telling everyone to go round to the main entrance. The biggest problem will be deliveries. Usually, the vans park here to bring our kitchen supplies. When do you think we can have this entrance back in use?'

'Hard to say, sir. We'll work as quickly as we can, but I think you'd better assume that it'll have to stay sealed off for the rest of today at least.'

'I see,' the Principal nodded, pursing his lips. 'Well, unless there's anything else, I'd better go and start breaking the news to the rest of the college. If you need me again, I'll be in my lodgings. Any member of college will be able to show you.'

Seeing Andy's answering nod of acquiescence, he turned to go. Then, a moment later, he swung round again. 'I don't suppose you can tell me who he is?'

'No, sir. We don't know ourselves yet.'

'You don't think he's a member of the college?' Professor Winthrop persisted anxiously.

'We really can't speculate on that, sir; but if you hear of anyone who's gone missing since yesterday, please let us know.'

'Yes. Yes, of course. Right! I'll let you get on.'

Andy watched him making his way through the entrance and along the short passageway to the quadrangle.

'Do you think it could be someone from the college?' Alice asked.

'No way of knowing at the moment. I suppose we'd better have a look at him and see if that gives us any clues.' Looking round, Andy saw that Ben Timpson had taken up a position a few yards away, next to a litterbin overflowing with fast food wrappers and discarded drinks cans. He caught his eye and the sergeant signalled to him to come over.

They gazed down at a crumpled figure lying partially propped up against the corner where the bin met the wall of the college. Beneath him, a dark stain extended across several paving stones and over the edge of the kerb into the gutter. Such a lot of blood! And yet there were no wounds visible on the body itself.

It was, as PC McLaughlin had reported, a black man, not as young as Andy had expected, well into his twenties or even early thirties. Not a member of a teenage gang, then. Maybe a drug dealer who had encroached on someone else's turf? But equally well, an overseas student or a visiting academic. Had the Principal had someone in mind when he asked whether the victim was a member of the college?

'Any ID on him?' Andy asked, crouching down to look more closely at the man's face. Alice was struck by how much darker the unknown man's skin was than Andy's, and reflected that he would probably stand out just as much in a line-up of police officers in, say, Ghana, as he did in Oxford.

'No sir,' Ben shook his head. 'The paramedics looked in his pockets, but nothing!'

'You'd expect his ID to be in his jacket,' Alice suggested, 'except that he hasn't got one on. It's a bit odd, isn't it? Going out without a jacket or a coat at this time of year.'

'You're right,' Andy agreed. 'Maybe the killer took his jacket.'

'To hide his identity, d'you mean?'

'Or simple robbery. It could just be someone after this wallet and his mobile phone.'

'If that's what it is, it's going to be virtually impossible to find who did it,' Alice observed.

'Oh, I don't know,' Ben put in. 'It depends how professional they are. If it's just some opportunist kid, they may try to use his credit cards or sell the mobile and give themselves away.'

'Well, the first thing's going to be to find out who he is,' Andy said, getting up. 'We'd better go and talk to the women who found him. You never know, they may even have recognised him.'

'Ever the optimist,' Ben grinned back. 'If they did, they never said anything about it. Come with me – I'll show you where they are. Stella Gilbert's sitting with them. D'you know her? She's only just finished her training, but she's very good – very empathetic. We thought they'd probably prefer a woman.'

He led the way into the dark passageway, passing the door into the chapel and taking a smaller door on the left. They followed him through a large room lined with ovens, hobs and sinks where a middle-aged woman in a white tunic and striped apron was engaged in cutting tomatoes in half and arranging them on a large tray. She looked up when they entered and then dropped her eyes to her work again. Another woman wearing the same uniform bustled in and collected a tray of bacon from one of the ovens.

They followed her back out to a long narrow room with three large serving hatches along one side. A younger woman stood loading slices of bread into a toasting machine and stacking the cooked toast on a rack in front of one of the hatches. A murmur of conversation could be heard through their closed shutters.

'OK Kerry, we'd better get the show on the road!' The older woman put the tray of bacon down by one of the hatches and then leaned forward to open it.

'What time do you call this?' demanded a young, male voice as the woman moved on to open the next hatch. 'We've been waiting here since eight!'

'It's a disgrace,' came a second voice. 'Get a move on! I've got a lecture at nine!'

'I'm sorry,' the woman with the bacon apologised. 'We're short-staffed this morning.'

'Well, it isn't good enough!' came the first voice. Now that the hatch was fully open, Andy could see that it belonged to a plump young man with an untidy mop of blond hair. 'We've paid for breakfast and it's up to you to see it's served on time.'

'Excuse me.' Andy walked calmly across the room and held up his warrant card at the hatch. 'I'm DI Lepage. I'm here to investigate the killing of a young man in the street outside here sometime last night. Some of the staff here found his body this morning. I'm afraid that they will be too busy answering my questions to serve you breakfast just now. So, I suggest that you try to be a bit more understanding and let these ladies get on with their jobs without any more harassment – OK?'

The blond youth fell silent, but his mutinous expression told Andy that he was neither convinced by the argument nor repentant of his behaviour. He picked up a tray and a plate and began helping himself to toast. His friend with the nine o'clock lecture, followed suit. The woman who had brought the bacon gave Andy a grateful smile before hurrying to serve bacon, eggs and sausages to the young men. 'I'm sorry, there aren't any tomatoes cooked yet, but we do have beans, if you'd like those instead?'

'Over here.' Ben led Andy and Alice to a corner of the room shielded from view by a tall refrigerator. Andy recognised PC Stella Gilbert, a young police officer of Afro-Caribbean descent, sitting with two older women, both of whom were clutching mugs of tea. Stella got up when she saw them approaching.

'This is Mrs Doreen Chalmers,' she told them, indicating a bony woman with grey hair in tight curls, who sat very upright in her chair. 'And this is Mrs Valerie Plumpton.'

Andy turned his gaze towards a slightly younger woman with a round face, out of which large brown eyes stared with an air of incomprehension. She probably could still hardly believe what she had seen back out there in the street.

'Good morning,' Andy greeted them. 'I'm DI Lepage and this is DC Ray. I know this must all have been a great shock for you, but do you think you could answer a few questions please?'

'Certainly,' Mrs Chalmers replied, speaking for both of them, while her friend at first remained staring ahead and then nodded perfunctorily as if the question had taken some time to sink in.

'I've taken down their addresses and telephone numbers,' Stella told him, holding out her notebook. Alice took it from her and photographed the page on her phone before handing it back. Looking over her shoulder, Andy read that Mrs Chalmers lived in Botley and Mrs Plumpton in North Hinksey, two villages that had become suburbs of Oxford as the city expanded to the west.

'Thank you.' Andy smiled at the young officer. This was probably the first time that she had been involved in what might well turn out to be a murder enquiry. 'That will save us a bit of time.'

He turned back to Mrs Chalmers. 'Perhaps you could tell me what you did this morning, starting from when you set out for work. What time was that, do you remember?'

'Ten to seven,' Mrs Chalmers answered promptly. 'I always leave at the same time. I walked to the Elms Parade shops and got there just before seven. Val was already waiting at the bus stop.'

'We go in together on the bus every day,' Mrs Plumpton added, suddenly eager to contribute. 'Usually I walk – it's not far – but today Jim dropped me off in the car. He was going to Coventry to visit his brother, and it's hardly out of his way at all, so he gave me a lift. He's very good like that.'

'I don't suppose the officer needs to know all about that,' Mrs Chalmers cut in. 'We got the number 4 bus into the city centre,' she resumed. 'It's supposed to go at four minutes past, but it was late, as usual.'

'But we always allow for that,' Mrs Plumpton broke in, 'so we were still in good time for work when we got to Goose Lane. We get off the bus at the Westgate Centre and walk through the back way – along that little alley between Lichfield and St Luke's – and down Goose Lane to the kitchen entrance. It only takes about five minutes.'

'It had just turned half past seven when we got to Goose Lane,' Mrs Chalmers said stiffly. She seemed to resent her friend's loquacity. 'The clock over the chapel struck the half hour just as we turned the corner.'

'We start work at quarter to eight, so we were in plenty of time,' her colleague explained. 'We don't cook the breakfast; we just serve it and then clear away afterwards. Madge and Pauline do the cooked breakfast, and Tina warms the plates and puts out the cutlery. They finish earlier than us, so it all works out fair.'

'We didn't notice anything unusual at first,' Mrs Chalmers took up the narrative again, 'but then we saw something lying next to the bin.'

'We thought at first it was just rubbish piled up. You do sometimes get that. The bin gets full and then the students just pile things up any old how. But not usually as much as that. And then I saw the shoes!' Mrs Plumpton paused dramatically and looked Andy in the face for the first time.

'The shoes?' he enquired, realising that he was expected to express some sort of surprise at the apparently innocuous revelation.

'The man's shoes caught the light from the street lamp,' Mrs Chalmers told him. 'And then we realised that it was a person and not a heap of old clothes or bin sacks of rubbish.'

'We thought at first it must be someone sleeping rough,' Mrs Plumpton went on. 'There *is* a man who often sleeps in the lane, but he goes on the other side, in a sort of hole in the wall of Lichfield College. But the shoes didn't look right. They were too shiny, as if they'd just been polished. And then we saw that he didn't have a blanket or anything. He wasn't even wearing a coat! We didn't know what to do then. We didn't like to go up to him in case he was violent. You never know, do you? So, Doreen phoned the porters' lodge and Vince came out and had a look. And he said the man was dead and he was going to call the police.' Her voice rose in pitch as she re-lived the events of the previous hour. 'When I looked at him again, I could see he was dead. He looked awful! And there was a pool of blood on the floor underneath him.'

'I don't suppose either of you recognised the man?' Andy asked.

'No.' They shook their heads in unison.

'I did think for a moment it could be Dr Adomakoe,' Mrs Chalmers volunteered, 'but Val reminded me that he's got grey hair, so it couldn't be him.'

'And he is …?' Alice asked, looking up from the notebook where she had been taking down key points of the interview.

'One of the dons,' Mrs Chalmers told her. 'He lives in college, so we see him quite often at breakfast. Always very polite – unlike a lot of the students.'

'I suppose it's awful of us thinking it might have been him,' Mrs Plumpton added, glancing across at Stella and then back at Andy, 'just because of his colour. It was just that we couldn't think why someone who wasn't to do with the college would be out there at night, and he couldn't have been there earlier yesterday or someone would've seen him, wouldn't they?'

'Well, thank you both. You've been very helpful. I'm afraid that we may need to get in touch with you again and ask more questions, but that's all for now.' Andy nodded and smiled towards Stella and then signalled to Alice to follow him back outside.

When they got there, the lane was busy with people in crime scene overalls. A van was pulled up on to the pavement just beyond the line of police tape, its doors standing open. Andy recognised Ruby Beech, a senior Scenes of Crime Officer, and guessed that she had been allocated the job of Crime Scene Manager for the incident.

'Hi Ruby!' he called out. 'What can you tell me?'

'Not a lot at the moment; we've only just got here,' she smiled back. 'Mike Carson's giving the body a once-over at the moment, so we're keeping out of his way and checking the surrounding area for blood spatter and footwear marks. Nothing particularly interesting so far.'

'OK. Keep me posted. I'll go and have a word with Mike.' Andy turned to Alice. 'Can you go and find the porter who made the emergency call – Vince, didn't they say his name was? – and get his version of what happened this morning. Oh! And ask him if he moved the body at all while he was checking that he was dead.'

Alice walked back into the college in search of the porter while Andy walked round the litter bin to where the burly Irish pathologist was bending down, peering into the lifeless eyes of the young black man. For the first time, he noticed the long, elegant legs encased in black trousers protruding beyond the bin and terminating in shiny black shoes. Mrs Plumpton was right; these shoes were not those of a tramp or even a common-or-garden drug-dealer. If this was a member of a drugs gang, he must be quite high up in the hierarchy. The sort of man who pays others to do his dirty work. So how had he come to be lying dead, here in a back street of Oxford?

Mike looked up. 'Hello, Andy! Congratulations on your promotion. I gather you're in charge of investigating this?'

'That's right. Do you have anything you can tell me yet?'

'Not a lot,' the pathologist shrugged. 'It looks almost certain that he was slashed with a knife and bled to death.'

'Slashed, rather than stabbed?' queried Andy.

'I would say so.' Mike put out a gloved hand and prised apart the edges of a slit in the fabric of the man's trousers, near the top of his inner thigh. The material appeared stiff, presumably caked with dried blood. 'There's just a single wound, which seems to have severed the left femoral artery, which is quite close to the surface here.'

'And that was enough to kill him?'

'Oh yes! We're talking about the main artery supplying blood to the leg. Blood loss would be quick and extensive – as you can see!' Mike gestured towards the stained paving stones. 'He'd most likely have fallen unconscious within seconds and death would have been anything from five minutes to a few hours.'

'So, he was almost certainly killed here? Where all the blood is?'

'That's the most likely scenario certainly,' Mike replied with his usual reluctance to make absolute pronouncements. 'He certainly couldn't have got himself far after it happened. Someone else could've moved him, but he must've got to his current position within minutes of the injury and it'd most likely have left a trail of blood – but that's the SOCOs territory, not mine.'

'Any sign of the knife?'

'No, and he doesn't have one on him either. And, before you ask, no, I can't tell you what sort of blade it was yet. I may know more after the post mortem, but …'

'Are there any other injuries? Could he have been in a fight?'

'Nothing obvious, but there could be something under his clothing. I'll be able to tell you more after the post mortem. A couple of torn fingernails, which could be defence wounds, but that's not definitive. I'll get a proper look at them when I've got him back to the mortuary.'

'And how likely is it that a slash with a knife would kill someone? I mean: what's the chance of cutting through a major artery like that?'

'Depends where you're aiming at.' Mike straightened up and signalled to his assistant to prepare the body to be loaded into the waiting ambulance. 'Low down like that, maybe not very likely. The femoral artery is deeper lower down in the leg. This guy was really unlucky that the knife got him in the femoral triangle, where the artery is fairly superficial and before it divides into separate branches. Basically, at every beat, his heart was pumping the entire blood supply to his leg out on to the ground.'

'Gruesome,' Andy murmured. 'OK, so when can you do the post mortem?'

'I can probably squeeze it in this afternoon, if you like. Do you want to be there?'

'Someone needs to be.' Andy thought for a moment. 'Yes, I'll come myself. What time?'

They agreed the arrangements and Mike left. Andy stood watching as the body was lifted on to a trolley.

'Excuse me, sir!' It was PC Gavin Hughes, a burly police officer of the old school, who had joined the force straight from school and never looked for promotion. 'I'd like to show you something – before the SOCOs find it.'

'Oh?'

'I'm sure it's nothing to do with this ... I just don't want ... you'll probably think I'm being stupid ....' Gavin trailed off in confusion. Then he seemed to make a conscious effort to pull himself together and continued, 'well the best thing is for me to show you.'

He led the way along the other side of the road, keeping close to the high wall that enclosed the Fellows' Garden of Lichfield College. They passed an open window in the ground floor of the college and a vent through which smells of frying bacon made Andy feel hungry. He had skimped on breakfast in his eagerness to get to the crime scene. A little further on there was a niche in the wall, about six feet long and four feet high. Gavin stopped and pointed down at a small pile of cigarette ends in one corner.

'My guess is that if the SOCOs test these for DNA, they'll find they belonged to a homeless man called Doug Finney,' he told Andy. 'This is his usual sleeping place. I came to find him as soon as we got here, to check he was OK.'

Andy remembered that Gavin had a long history of working with homeless people and was one of the very few police officers whom they trusted.

'But he wasn't here?'

'No. He probably got scared off when all the fuss started this morning. What I'm worried about is, if they do get a DNA match for these, someone might assume he was involved. There's no way he'd go round knifing anyone. He hasn't got the bottle for it apart from anything else. He'd run a mile from any trouble.'

'OK. I get the picture.' Andy smiled reassuringly towards Gavin, for whom he had considerable respect. He had no desire to become anything more than just a "bobby on the beat", and realistically it was unlikely that he would ever have been successful if he had aspired to join CID, but he knew all about violent death from the inside. His son, Kenny, had been killed only two years ago. In fact, they must be coming up to the anniversary now.

'I'll have to get someone to bag these up,' he went on, 'but I'll bear in mind what you said about him being a very unlikely murderer.'

'Thanks.'

'However,' Andy continued, 'if he *was* here last night, he could be a witness. Would you be able to find him for me?'

'Maybe,' Gavin replied uncertainly. 'I can have a go, but he won't be keen to talk to you.'

'Well, do your best – and maybe, could you put some feelers out in the wider homeless community? They're out on the streets at all times and nobody takes much notice of them. You never know: they may have seen something that would help us.'

3. TEAM BRIEFING

'So here we have our victim.' Andy looked round the room as he began the evening briefing. A dozen or so faces gazed back at the photograph displayed on a screen at the front of the room, eager to hear what he had learned at the post mortem – or perhaps just eager for the meeting to be over so that they could go home. 'As yet unnamed, he is a black male in his late twenties or early thirties. It has been confirmed that he bled to death from a single knife wound to his left thigh, which completely severed the femoral artery. Death would have occurred within minutes – an hour at the maximum.'

Andy looked down at his notes, feeling very conscious of the eyes watching him, waiting to see how he would fair in charge of a murder case for the first time.

'Death occurred sometime yesterday afternoon or evening. Dr Carson says it almost certainly took place before 9pm, and it could be several hours earlier than that if the cold weather delayed the onset of rigor mortis.'

'Funny no one saw him last night then,' commented Detective Sergeant Iestyn Williams, a recent transfer from South Wales Police. 'You'd think there'd have been people coming and going until the early hours, students being what they are.'

Andy looked up, suppressing the smile of amusement which always threatened when he heard the sergeant's sing-song voice. Did anyone really speak like that unless they were putting it on for comic effect? That's a good point, sergeant,' he said at last. 'So, tomorrow, you can get out there and see if you can find anyone who did see him, but didn't report it.'

'It's not very well-lit in that part of the street,' Alice put in, 'and he was partly hidden by a litter bin.'

'Exactly,' Andy agreed. 'And the women who found him this morning initially thought he was just a rough-sleeper dossing down in the street. So, there could've been plenty of people who saw him and didn't think anything of it. And now, to get back to our victim, he had torn fingernails and some bruising on face and hands, which may suggest that he was involved in some sort of fight shortly before he died.'

'I thought you said this morning that there were no injuries apart from the knife wound,' Williams interrupted.

'That's right,' Andy agreed patiently, 'but on closer inspection, the pathologist found bruising that he hadn't seen in his initial examination because the victim's dark skin masked it. He's taken samples from beneath the fingernails, which may provide us with DNA from his attacker.'

He consulted his notes again. 'The stomach was almost empty, which implies that he hadn't eaten for some time. Probably his last meal had been taken five hours or more before he died.'

'Probably his lunch then?' suggested Williams. 'If he was killed that evening.'

'Yes,' agreed Andy curtly, continuing without further comment. 'There were no signs of drug-taking or intoxication, but we can't be sure about that until the toxicology report comes back. The femoral nerve was damaged as well as the artery, which means that it's very unlikely that the victim could have walked or even crawled after he'd been wounded. So, the attack almost certainly took place in Goose Lane within a foot or two of where he was found.'

Andy clicked a button and the victim's photograph was replaced by a view of the crime scene.

'We still have nothing with which to establish his identity,' he went on. 'No credit cards, driving licence, ID card or anything. We have post-mortem fingerprints, which have been sent off for checking against the database, but unless he has a criminal record that's not likely to help us much until we have some idea where we ought to be looking for him. We may have to resort to a public appeal, but I'm reluctant to do that until we've explored other avenues, because of the possible impact on his family if the first they know of his death is seeing him on the news.'

Andy put down his notes and looked round the room. 'That's all I can tell you from the post-mortem. Now DC Pitchfork has some news for us from the drug squad.' He sat down and a rather nervous-looking Joshua Pitchfork got up from his inconspicuous seat near the back of the room and walked to the front.

'Based on our assumption that this is most likely related to rivalry between different drug gangs, I asked them about likely suspects for this sort of killing,' he began. 'They didn't recognise the victim, but they said there have been rumours of a new gang operating in Oxford. The word is that they bring in drugs via West Africa. They thought our guy might be the boss of the outfit and one of the established gangs didn't like him muscling in on their territory.'

'So, our victim may be from West Africa?' queried Williams.

'Or at least has contacts there,' Pitchfork nodded. 'They came up with a possible suspect. His name's Leon Black, but he likes to be known as the panther.'

'Black panther,' chortled Sergeant Williams from the back of the room. 'Nice one!'

'He heads up a gang of drug-dealers and pimps operating in central Oxford, mainly targeting the student market,' Pitchfork continued. 'He's had a few convictions for possession, but so far he's managed to keep out of major trouble by delegating all the risky jobs to his minions. The drugs guys reckon he could be behind the killing, but there's no way he'll have done it himself. He's been suspected of doing away with a few of his rivals, but he's always had watertight alibis.'

'Thank you, Josh,' Andy said, momentarily forgetting his plan to be more formal with his team as a way of establishing his new authority. He turned to face the room again. 'I think that's all. I've arranged for someone from the drug squad to come along tomorrow to give us a run-down on the student drug supply scene, and Uniform are going to get together some officers to help us interview people at the two colleges that back on to Goose Lane, in case they saw any suspicious activity there yesterday afternoon or evening. The other thing we need to do is to monitor any missing person reports. It surely won't be long before someone wonders what's happened to him and goes to the police. But, that's all for us today. You'd better all get off home. Back here bright an early tomorrow!'

Andy dropped Alice off at her home in Iffley just as Monica arrived back. He watched her getting out of her car, looking very smart in her inspector's uniform. Did she resent him having got his more senior post in CID, which she would have been equally qualified to apply for? Did she find it galling that her perfect job had fallen into his lap almost entirely because he had lacked the drive to seek out promotion? He probably wouldn't even have taken the inspector's exam if Jonah hadn't pushed him into it. Jonah! Nobody could ever have accused him of indolence. Even after being paralysed from the shoulders down his energy was frightening – and contagious! Nobody dared to slack while he was in charge of the team. Would they continue to go the extra mile in every investigation, now that Andy had taken over? Only time would tell.

He turned on to the ring road, heading east and then north. Overtaking a lorry shortly before the turning to his home in Headington Quarry, he found himself in the right-hand lane as he approached the junction with Kiln Lane. A sudden impulse to call in on his old boss, who lived in the part of Headington that lay outside the ring road, prompted him to turn right at the lights and he was soon pulling up outside the large house where the now ex-DCI Jonah Porter lived. He walked up the ramp to the front door and rang the bell.

As he waited for a reply, he felt a pang of misgiving. What would they make of his calling unannounced? What if he were interrupting their evening meal? What was he hoping to achieve through sharing the case with Jonah? Was he looking for confirmation that he was doing the right things? Or advice on what to do next? It was all pretty routine so far, so why was he worried? There wasn't even much for him to share at this stage – just the post mortem findings and a vague idea that the killing was likely to be related to the drug gangs that preyed on the student population.

'Andy! How nice to see you!' The door opened and Jonah's friend and personal assistant, Bernie, looked out. She was also the owner of the house, having inherited it from her first husband, Detective Superintendent Richard Paige, late of Thames Valley police. 'Are you coming in or what?'

'Thanks.' Andy knew the exiled Liverpudlian well enough to realise that this typically Scouse greeting was an invitation rather than a question. 'I was hoping to have a word with Jonah – about a new case I'm working on.'

'I'm sure he'll be delighted. Go on into the living room and I'll let him know you're here.' Bernie stepped back to make space for Andy to enter, whispering as he passed her, 'He's still not really reconciled to this retirement business. You'll make his day giving him a crime to get his teeth into. I hope it's something interesting.'

'It looks like murder, but probably not all that interesting – just another knife crime, I'm afraid'

'Not for the victim – or the victim's family. Nothing's ever "just another crime" for them.' Peter, Bernie's second husband, was standing in the shadows of the hall. He had come out of the kitchen when the doorbell rang to see who the visitor was. He, too, was a former police officer.

'Yes, of course.' Andy felt his cheeks burning as he remembered that Peter had lost his first wife in a frenzied knife attack by a gang of youths. 'I didn't mean … I just don't suppose there's much here that Jonah will find interesting.'

'Well, why don't you tell me all about it and we'll see, won't we?' Andy swung round to see that they had been joined by Jonah himself, gliding silently out from his study in his electric wheelchair. 'Go and sit down and tell me all about it.'

Peter returned to the kitchen with the excuse that he was in the middle of preparing their evening meal. Bernie led the way into the lounge with Jonah close on her heels and Andy scurrying after them. He knew that his old boss would be impatient to hear his news.

'It's most likely just a turf war between drugs gangs,' he began apologetically. 'It's looking as if the hardest part is going to be working out who our victim is. None of his associates are likely to be keen on talking to the police.'

'Well, why don't you just tell us what you know so far and we'll take it from there?' suggested Jonah, looking at him intently.

Andy described the crime scene and ran through the post-mortem findings, finishing by holding up a photograph of the body lying by the litter bin and a close-up of the victim's face for Jonah to see.

'We're going to go door-to-door in both colleges tomorrow, in case anyone saw anything and didn't think to report it,' he finished, 'but I don't see how that's going to do much more than fix the time of death. As I said, the biggest problem at the moment is finding out who he is. And if he's a drug-dealer, nobody's likely to admit to knowing him, even if they do.'

'Hang on! Aren't you jumping the gun rather with this fixation on drug gangs?' demanded Jonah sharply. 'What evidence do you have that this killing is connected with them at all?'

'Only that drugs are at the bottom of about ninety percent of the knifings that we come across,' Andy defended himself. 'Youngish, black guy, knifed to death in the street, the first thing you think of is drug gangs, isn't it?'

'How do you explain his clothes?'

'Not wearing a coat, d'you mean?'

'Well yes, that – and the quality of them. Those shoes, for example. Wouldn't trainers be more typical of a member of a drug gang?'

'We thought he might be the boss of the outfit – probably fancies himself as a bit of a cool dresser. The drug squad say there's a new gang working the student scene, but they don't know who's heading it up.'

'I'd say he hasn't come far,' observed Bernie, staring intently at the photographs. 'It's not just the absence of a coat. Those shoes aren't made for walking and he's got his shirt buttoned up right to the top, as if he should be wearing a tie. Most people leave the top button undone otherwise.'

'That's a good point,' Jonah agreed. 'I hadn't noticed that.'

'Shiny shoes, smart trousers and white shirt, probably late afternoon or early evening. Those all make me think he was in the middle of dressing for dinner,' Bernie went on.

'You mean he was from one of the colleges?' asked Andy. 'He's a bit too old to be a student.'

'He could be a postgraduate student,' Bernie pointed out, 'or a don or a visiting academic.' She had once been a fellow of an

Oxford College herself, and knew that their membership was very diverse.

'But why would he go out into the lane in the middle of changing his clothes?'

'Any number of reasons,' Jonah replied promptly. 'Maybe something out there attracted his attention; or maybe someone called him and asked him to come out to meet them.'

'Or his attacker could have come to his room, and he ran out into the lane to escape,' suggested Bernie.

'You're right,' Andy sighed. 'Both of you. I should have taken the lack of a coat more seriously. And I should've noticed the buttoned-up shirt and realised what it meant. I got tunnel vision after we started thinking of it as just an ordinary gang-related knife-crime – especially with the drug squad seeming to be almost expecting something like this to happen. Oh well! I've already got officers lined up to go round both colleges tomorrow morning. I just need to brief them that the victim may well be a member of one of them.'

'Yes,' Bernie agreed. 'You don't want some plod asking one of the fellows if they've seen this suspicious character lurking around the lane, and having it turn out that he's their prestigious guest on a visit from Harvard!'

Peter's head appeared round the door. 'I've got the macaroni cheese keeping warm in the oven, so we can eat whenever you're ready.'

Bernie turned to Andy, 'you'd be welcome to stay. I'm sure there's plenty.'

'No thanks.' Andy looked down at his watch in consternation, realising that his mother would have been expecting him home. 'I ought to go. I rang Mum when I left the station to let her know I was on my way. She'll have our dinner ready and be wondering what's happened to me. Thanks for … well thanks.'

Bernie went with him to the front door. 'Good luck with the case. I'm sure you'll be fine.'

'Thanks.' Andy slipped out.

Just before the door closed behind him, he heard Jonah calling down the hall, 'Be sure and keep us posted!'

4. A QUESTION OF IDENTITY

Detective Sergeant Jack Myers had been working in Oxford for more than a decade, but he still exuded an air of superiority, having trained with the Metropolitan Police, which he considered to be a cut above any provincial force. Andy had never met him before, but he was aware of his reputation for retaining the belief that most Thames Valley officers were country bumpkins with no idea of what went on in today's urban jungle. An ambitious young man, he had applied for the transfer after repeatedly failing to obtain promotion within the Met. He was now looking for some big success that would attract the attention of his superiors and smooth his way towards inspector rank and beyond. Solving a murder case might just fit the bill!

He looked round the room from his perch on one of the desks in the front row, sizing up Andy's team. At the other end of the row, an eager-eyed woman with blond hair tied back in a ponytail seemed to be watching his every move. He smiled at her and she smiled back. It looked like he was in there! She was obviously gagging for it and the men that surrounded her were no competition at all. That DC Pitchfork, for example, the one who'd been sent to pick the brains of the drug squad. A girl as tasty as her could hardly be expected to go for that ungainly lump, with his big feet and untidy brown hair! He was sitting at the back of the room in conversation with another officer, dark-haired with deep-set brown eyes. Every so often his voice rose enough for

Myers to identify a comical sing-song Welsh accent. No competition there either! And as for the boss of the outfit! Myers could hardly keep himself from laughing as he watched DI Lepage studying his notes, getting ready to begin the morning briefing. A token black officer if ever there was one! Chosen to head up this enquiry to fend off any accusations of institutional racism, and promoted to DI for the same reason, while experienced officers like Myers got pushed to the back of the queue just because they didn't tick any of the right diversity boxes!

Andy got up from his seat behind a table at the front of the room and clapped his hands for silence.

'I think everyone's here now,' he began.

His words were immediately contradicted by the arrival of DC Hitchin, a young officer, recently transferred to CID from a community policing role in Banbury. He hurried to find a seat, muttering, 'Sorry I'm late. The traffic was bad on the motorway.'

'OK, Toby, you're here now.' Andy waited while Hitchin settled himself behind his desk and then looked round the room again. 'I'd like to start by introducing Detective Sergeant Myers from the drug squad. He and his colleagues have been monitoring the supply of illicit drugs in Oxford and he has some information which may be relevant to our mystery murder victim. So, over to you Sergeant Myers.'

He sat down next to Alice and watched as Myers walked forward nonchalantly to take up a position standing in front of the table and then leaning back against it. To Andy it seemed as if he was signalling that their little knife crime was insignificant compared with the important work that he was used to, certainly not worth hurrying himself about.

'I've had a look at the stuff you've collected on this "mystery man" as Andy here calls him,' he began casually, 'and I think we may be able to solve your mystery for you. We've been keeping tabs on the student drug scene and we've noticed that there have been a few changes recently. Since the beginning of term, there has been an increase in supply of both cocaine and cannabis. *And* there's been an increase in the number of violent incidents associated with the drugs scene. We're pretty sure there's a new supplier out there – a disrupter who's upsetting the balance of power – but we don't yet know who he is. We're calling him Mr X. We don't know much about him, but we've got evidence he may be bringing in drugs via West Africa, so that would fit quite nicely with your dead man.'

He paused and looked round the room with a self-satisfied expression on his face, as if expecting applause.

'The main player in this game is Leon Black.' Myers pressed a small clicker concealed in his hand and a face appeared on the screen at the front of the room: a black man with hair shaved at the sides and trimmed into a smooth dome on top. It looked like a simple style, but Andy knew that the perfect shape must have been done by an expert hair stylist. Not for Leon Black a quick once over with the electric clippers by his mother!

'Known as the panther,' Myers went on, 'Black heads up a gang of drug-dealers and pimps operating in central Oxford and particularly targeting the student market. A couple of years back, we had a lot of trouble with two rival gangs fighting over territory. The other gang was headed up by this guy.'

Myers pressed the clicker again and a new face appeared. This man was white with a shaved head and both face and arms covered with tattoos. His eyes stared blankly out from the screen.

'This is Lee Hammond,' Myers told them. 'He's served time for possession with intent to supply and for GBH. As I said, his gang used to be very active among the students, but he had a showdown with Black's outfit and Black came out on top.'

He clicked the button again and a photograph of square, plastic-wrapped packages appeared on the screen.

'Things had been pretty quiet since then,' he continued, 'until a couple of months back when we got this influx of stuff coming in from some other source. Black won't like the competition, so it's no surprise to us that it looks like he may be trying to eliminate it by removing his rival. Your guy could be Mr X himself or one of his lieutenants. Black won't have confronted him himself; he'll just have ordered the execution.'

'Excuse me!' Williams raised his hand. 'Didn't the pathologist say that the attacker probably didn't intend to kill him? It was just a slash to the leg, which wouldn't normally have been serious.'

'That's a good point,' Andy agreed, feeling guiltily pleased at this flaw in Myers' reasoning. 'Whoever killed him, it definitely doesn't look like an execution.'

'Probably intended as a warning then.' After a brief moment of uncertainty, Myers had an answer ready. 'This guy is most likely a freelancer who thinks it'll be easy targeting freshers. Black won't like him muscling in on his turf, but he probably reckons that, if he's on his own, it won't take much to frighten him off. He probably can't believe his luck that it turned out to be fatal.'

Williams opened his mouth to argue, but closed it again at a look from Andy. Myers turned back to the screen and pressed the clicker to display a rucksack, its false bottom cut open to reveal bags of white powder.

'Detailed analysis of some samples,' he continued, 'makes us think it's coming in from West Africa. It matches a haul that the border force seized at Heathrow off a plane from Accra. We think that may be where your dead male comes in.'

Alice raised her hand. Myers smiled towards her and nodded to her to speak. 'Yes, love. Did you have a question?'

'I just thought it was worth mentioning that the report on the victim's fingerprints has come back. They don't match anything on the database.'

'That's because he hasn't been caught yet,' Myers explained condescendingly. 'He's the new kid on the block, maybe fresh in from Africa. He's just been unlucky that Black got to him before we did.'

'What about the missing jacket?' asked Alice innocently. 'Why would Black's hit-man take that?'

'What makes you think he was wearing one?' Myers asked, treating Alice to another patronising smile.

'It was a cold night,' she replied promptly. 'Why would anyone be out in the street in their shirt-sleeves? And if he was pushing drugs, where were they? Not in his pockets and there's been no bag recovered from the scene either.'

'Of course, we can't be sure that this *is* Mr X,' Myers admitted, hastily back-tracking. 'He could be a punter who didn't pay up or one of Black's own gang who didn't toe the line and needed teaching a lesson, or the rival gang I was telling you about could've knifed him in revenge, or-'

'Or this may have nothing at all to do with the drug scene,' cut in Andy. 'I'm afraid that it's starting to look as if we may have been wasting your time with that hypothesis. We're still waiting on the toxicology report, but the post mortem indicated that he's never been a drug-user. There were no needle marks or damage to his nose. He appeared to be in very good health.'

'Not all suppliers are users,' argued Myers.

'But if he wasn't one of Black's customers –a student living in one of the colleges, say – and he didn't have any drugs to sell, why was he there, with no coat on, on a cold November night?' persisted Alice.

'She's right, you know,' called out Williams. 'This drug connection just doesn't stack up.'

'Come off it!' protested Myers, the colour rising to his cheeks. 'You know as well as I do what a high proportion of violent street crime is drugs-related. And this has all the hall-marks: young black male, knifed to death in the street, no witnesses prepared to report it. It's a textbook example of gang-related black-on-black violence. Just another routine knife crime.'

This briefing was not going at all according to his plans and expectations. The bumpkins did not seem to possess an appropriate appreciation of his superior experience and expertise. Well, if that's how they felt …

'Thank you, Sergeant Myers. Your input has been very useful.' Andy got up from his seat and held out his hand for the clicker. 'I'm sure you're very busy, so we won't detain you any longer.'

He turned back to address his team. 'Now, we're all up to speed on the possible drugs connection, we'd better get down to some hard graft. Sergeant Williams has drawn up a plan for the door-to-door across the two colleges. He's got you each paired up with a uniformed officer. Each pair has been allocated a section of the buildings.'

He clicked on to display a close-up picture of the victim's head and shoulders.

'This is an enhanced photograph of our man. The techy guys have tried to make it closer to how he probably looked when he was alive. Jennifer has run off enough for you all to take some to show to people. Collect them from her on your way out. There's a strong chance that he may be known to someone at one of the colleges. If he has a room there, it would explain how he came to be outdoors with no coat on. So be sensitive, in case you come across anyone who may get a shock when they see the photo. OK? Any questions?'

Andy watched as the officers climbed out of the van that had brought them to the end of Goose Lane, sorted themselves into their pairs and headed round the corner to the main entrances of their allocated colleges. Once they had all dispersed, he walked down the lane to where the police cordon still prevented access to the back entrances of both places of learning. Ruby saw him and came over.

'Found anything interesting?' he asked.

'Well, there are these,' Ruby replied, holding up a sheaf of plastic evidence bags, each containing a piece of sheet music. 'We found them blowing around in the gutter. The chances are they're nothing to do with the incident, but we've bagged them all just in case.'

Andy studied the scores. 'Organ music,' he murmured. 'That's a bit niche.'

'Maybe less so in Oxford than most places,' Ruby observed. 'Every college has a chapel with an organ and an organ scholar or two. Still, this stuff isn't cheap. You wouldn't expect to find it just dropped in the street.'

'So maybe their owner got caught up in whatever altercation ended up with our victim breathing his last collapsed against a litter bin,' suggested Andy. 'Get these fingerprinted and check the prints against his. If he *is* an organist, that should narrow down our search quite a bit.'

'Indeed,' agreed Ruby. 'I've sent off those cigarette ends for DNA testing and some others that we picked up just outside the door into Holy Cross. The chances are those are just from staff or students hanging around there because they're not allowed to smoke in the buildings, but you never know …. We've got fingerprints from the litter bin and the door too, but so many people must touch those all the time that I'm not very hopeful that they'll be any use.'

'How much longer before we can release the crime scene?'

'We'll probably be done by the end of the day. I'll let you know.'

'Sir!'

Andy turned to see PC Stella Gilbert approaching.

'DS Ray asked me to fetch you, sir,' she said, as soon as she was close enough to speak to him without raising her voice. 'We've found someone who can identify the victim.'

'That was quick! Who is it?' Andy followed Stella back along the road at a fast pace. At the corner, she turned right, heading for the main entrance to Lichfield College.

'The head porter at Lichfield, sir. We called in at the Porters' Lodge to explain what we were doing, and he recognised the picture. He says it's a student from Nigeria.'

'Good work! Lead me to him!'

They found head porter, Bernard Malpas, in conversation with Alice outside the entrance to the lodge. Alice began to introduce them, but Malpas interrupted. 'I know you, don't I? You were with that woman detective a year or two back, looking into that man who died in the Fellows' Garden[1].'

'That's right,' Andy confirmed. 'As I remember it, you helped to identify that murder victim too. Now, tell me about this man: do you have a name for him?'

'I can do better than that,' the porter told him. 'I was just showing your colleague here – this is his entry in our emergency contacts folder.' He held out an A4 sheet. 'It's got his name, course, tutor, term-time address, home address, next-of-kin ...'

'Everything we need, in other words to trace his family and the people who may know him here in Oxford,' Andy nodded. 'Thank you. That's just what we need. Can I have this? Or a photocopy, if not?'

'Yes, you can keep that. I can always get another copy printed out, if we need one – although, he's not likely to be having any more emergencies now, is he?'

---

[1] See "A Secret Gardener?" ISBN: 978-1-911083-62-7

Andy read the name, sounding it out slowly to himself, 'Jibrilu Danjuma.' And his home address was in Nigeria. He was in the first year of a postgraduate degree in mathematics, supervised by a Dr Tom Carrington. That name was familiar. Where had he come across it before? He folded the paper and put it in his pocket before looking up at the porter again.

'Would you show us to his room, please?'

Malpas led them across the main quadrangle, skirting round the rectangular lawn with its stone sundial, and through an archway into what he announced to them was Overton Quad. Turning to the right, they walked along a line of cloisters and entered the building through a heavy oak door, which opened into a rather dark passageway.

Malpas ushered them through double doors on their right into the Hall. 'It's rather an awkward room to get to,' he explained in answer to Andy's questioning look. Originally, this staircase was servants' rooms,' he continued as he led the way through the large dining room to a small door at the far end on the right. 'But none of the domestic staff live in these days, so they've been converted for students. There are two study bedrooms and a shared bathroom on each floor.'

'And they can only be accessed through here?' queried Andy.

'That's right. The Hall goes right up to the top of the building and on the other side it's the Fellows' Garden, so this staircase isn't joined on to any of the rest of the college.' He opened the door and groped inside for a light switch. 'Mind your feet,' he warned. 'There's a couple of steps down here. The ground floor rooms are at a lower level than the Hall.'

Andy and Alice followed him through into a cramped vestibule. A narrow staircase wound upwards on their right, while to the left and straight ahead there were doors, presumably leading to the study bedrooms that Malpas has described.

'That's Mr Danjuma's room,' he told them, gesturing to the left. 'I'll let you in.'

He took a bunch of keys out of his pocket, selected one and put it into the lock.

'That's a master-key, I take it?' asked Andy. 'How many other people have those?'

'We keep two of these in the lodge and there's another in the Master's office. This key opens all the student rooms. There's a separate master-key for the offices, seminar rooms and so on. The scouts are each issued with a sub-master for each of the staircases that they're responsible for. Students are each given a key to their own room when they arrive, and we keep a spare in the lodge to lend them if they mislay it.'

'So, in total, there are … six keys in circulation that would open this door,' Andy said, counting rapidly in his head. 'Three master keys – two in the lodge and one in the office – a sub-master that the scout for this staircase keeps, one belonging to Mr Danjuma and a spare in the lodge?'

'That's right, sir,' Malpas confirmed, pushing open the door and flooding the vestibule with light from a window at the far side of the room. A chilly breeze made Andy shiver. The window was standing wide open allowing the cold November air to flow in.

'That's not right!' Malpas exclaimed, striding across the room. Andy put out a hand just in time to stop him touching the windowsill as he leaned out to pull the window shut.

'Don't touch anything,' he instructed. 'Remember, this is a crime scene.'

'I'm sorry, sir.' Malpas stepped back. 'I wasn't thinking. It's just … we have a strict rule that ground floor windows must never be left open without putting the gates across.' He pointed to either side of the window. Andy pulled on a pair of latex gloves and examined the "gates", which turned out to be collapsible metal frameworks like old-fashioned lift doors. He pulled them across in front of the window and saw that they could be locked together to prevent intruders from entering while the window was open. Then he pushed them open again and peered out through the window.

It opened directly on to the street, only about two feet above the level of the pavement. Opposite, Andy could see Callum McLaughlin standing guard outside the back entrance to Holy Cross College. Beyond him, he had a clear view through the door into the passage behind and even a glimpse of the sunlight in the quadrangle at the far end.

'Hi, Ruby!' he called out. The crime scene manager looked round from where she had been studying an object that one of her team had drawn to her attention further down the road. She spotted his face at the window and hurried over to see what he wanted.

'Have you examined this window for prints?' he asked. 'It turns out that this is the room where our victim lived.'

'No, not yet. We've been working down the other side of the road first. I'll get someone on to it right away. I gather you know who he is now?'

'Yes. He's an overseas student from Nigeria, doing a DPhil. His name's Jibrilu Danjuma. If you find any more pieces of paper floating about, keep a look out for that name on them.'

'Will do.'

Andy withdrew his head and stood gazing round the room. Alice had already found a laptop and slipped it into an evidence bag. Now she was searching through the drawers of the desk, which stood against the wall, to the right to the window.

'The top one's locked,' she told Andy. 'I wonder where the key is.'

'He didn't have any on him,' Andy recalled, 'so either they were stolen by the killer – along with his jacket – or they'll be in here somewhere.'

'The jacket that matches the trousers he was wearing is over there.' Alice pointed to the wardrobe door, which was slightly open, allowing a coat hanger to be hooked over the top of it. On the hanger was a dark-coloured jacket. 'It looks like your theory that he was in the middle of dressing for dinner checks out.'

'It does, doesn't it?' murmured Andy, going over and feeling in the pockets of the jacket. He retrieved a mobile phone, which Alice immediately bagged and labelled, a silk handkerchief, a wallet, containing three ten-pound notes and some credit cards, and a bunch of keys.

A small amount of experimentation identified Mr Danjuma's room key, the latch key to the wicket gate that enabled students and staff to enter the college after the porters had locked up at night, the key to the gates at the windows, and finally the key that opened the desk draw. Inside Andy found a Nigerian passport in the name of Jibrilu Muhammadu Danjuma, some official papers from the Home Office relating to his student visa, and a small cash box with a combination lock. Alice put each of these items into evidence bags, labelling them in her neat handwriting.

Andy turned his attention to the top of the desk. In the centre lay a pad of lined paper, with incomprehensible mathematical formulae written on the top sheet. There was a pen laid down next to it, as if the writer had been planning to resume his work shortly. Two photographs stood near the wall. Andy picked them up in turn and studied them.

The first was a full-length picture of a young couple. In their twenties? Possibly only in their teens. Andy always found it more difficult to judge the ages of black people. She was wearing a full-length white dress with orange trimmings which matched the orange turban that covered her hair. He had on a co-ordinated white-and-orange hat – a bit more extensive than a skull-cap, but similarly close-fitting – and a long flowing white robe. They were both smiling broadly. A wedding photograph, perhaps. Could they be the victim's parents?

The other photograph was a portrait of an older man. Closer inspection convinced Andy that it was the same man as in the first picture, confirming in his mind that it was Mr Danjuma senior. His hair was grey at the temples and his face had lines at the corners of eyes and mouth. His expression was serious. His clothes, what could be seen of them, were dark and drab.

Andy added the photographs to the store of personal effects, which would be examined, photographed, in some cases fingerprinted and ultimately, returned to the victim's family. He looked towards Alice.

'OK. I think we've got enough to be going on with. Take these back to the station and get the IT guys checking out the laptop and phone.'

Then, turning to the porter, 'Lock this room and don't let anyone else in it. I'll send a uniformed officer to stand guard until the forensics team can go over it properly.'

'Right you are, sir,' Malpas nodded. 'I'll get you the spare room key, if you like, so that your forensics people can get in when they're ready. And, would you mind asking them to close the window and lock the gates when they've finished?'

'Yes, of course. And they'll hand back the key at the porter's lodge when they're through, too.'

As they walked back through the main quadrangle, Alice commented, 'It's all rather weird, isn't it? Why would he go out leaving the window wide open like that? He must have been in a hurry and thought he'd be back right away.'

'Or maybe he went out through the window,' suggested Andy with a smile. 'That was what occurred to me when I saw it like that. I think he saw something – or somebody – in the road outside and he climbed out through the window to deal with it.'

'But why?'

'It's a long way round through the Hall and out to the lane,' Andy replied. 'The only doors on that side of the college are from the Fellows' Garden – which is out of bounds to students – from the kitchens – also not for students – and from the main college gardens on the other side of the Hall.'

'So, he was in too much of a hurry?'

'Or he didn't want anyone to know he'd left the building. It was just before dinner time, remember? So, he'd be bound to be seen going out through the Hall. There'd be staff in and out of there laying the tables. Now, you go on back. I've got a few calls to make.'

'Hello?' Dr Thomas Carrington's face had a puzzled expression as he looked round from his desk to see who his visitor was.

Andy held up his warrant card. 'I'm DI Lepage. I'm investigating the death of a young man who was killed in Goose Lane sometime yesterday evening. I'm sorry to have to tell you that we've now identified him and he is one of your students.'

'One of my …?' the don's mouth dropped open as he assimilated this information. 'Which one? I mean, who is it?'

'Mr Jibrilu Danjuma,' Andy told him. 'I gather he recently began a postgraduate degree with you as his supervisor.'

'Yes, that's right. And you're sure that it's him?'

'Your head porter, Mr Malpas, has identified him from this picture.' Andy handed Dr Carrington a copy of the post-mortem photograph.

He looked down at it and nodded. 'Yes. That's Jibrilu. What happened? Was it a mugging?'

'Not as far as we can tell. His valuables appear to still all be in his room. But we're keeping an open mind regarding the motive for the attack. Presumably you aren't aware of anyone who might wish him harm?'

'No. But then, I can't say that I know him very well. He only arrived in Oxford a couple of months ago. And that's another thing, how could he have made any enemies in such a short time? I can't help thinking that it must have been a random attack or a case of mistaken identity.'

'Yes,' Andy agreed, 'those are certainly possibilities. Now, we need someone who knew him to do a formal identification of the body. Would you be willing to do that?'

'Yes, of course. What exactly does that involve?'

'I'll arrange for one of our uniformed officers to liaise between you and the mortuary to arrange a time and accompany you there. We'd like to do it today, so that I can inform his family. Will that be OK with you?'

'Yes, I'll be working in my room here all day. Just let me know what time you want me.'

Andy left the tutor's room and made his way back out down the winding staircase to the quadrangle. He got out his mobile phone to ring the mortuary, but was interrupted by the arrival of PC Melanie Stanton and her drug-detection dog, PD Wesley.

'Hi Andy!' she called out to him. 'I got your message. Wesley is raring to go. Where is it you want us?'

Andy led the way to Jibrilu's room. Stella Gilbert was standing outside looking rather self-conscious. She smiled at the sight of Mel and Wesley.

'The SOCOs say they've finished,' she informed Andy. 'They said to tell you there was no sign of drugs and nothing out of the ordinary in any other respect either.'

'Yes,' Andy nodded. 'That was how it seemed to me too. But who knows? Wesley's nose may pick up something that isn't visible to the human eye.'

Stella opened the door and let dog and dog-handler inside.

'Lock up when Mel's finished,' Andy told her. 'And then I think we can let you go back to your normal duties. I don't think there'll be anything more that this room can tells us.'

He went back outside and made his call to the mortuary. He was about to start making his way back to his office to review what they knew about the case so far, when his phone rang. It was Gavin.

'I've managed to find Doug Finney,' he reported. 'We're in the covered market. I've told him we'll buy him lunch at the café there. Can you join us?'

'Yes, I'll be right over.' Andy slipped his phone into his pocket and set off at a brisk walk. This was a piece of luck! Just so long as he didn't scare the elusive Doug into silence by pushing him too hard with questions. These homeless people were often very wary of talking to the police.

Doug Finney looked considerably older than his forty-six years. His eyes were bloodshot and his hair was grimy. He wore a black greatcoat, several sizes too big for his skinny frame, beneath which poked out worn trainers with trailing laces. He was sitting at a table in the café with a plate of beans and sausages in front of him. A grubby pair of knitted gloves lay next to it, the wool beginning to unravel around holes in the fingertips. Gavin, sitting opposite him, got up as Andy approached. Smelling the food, Andy felt suddenly hungry. He had left the packed lunch that his mother had prepared for him in his office.

Gavin introduced him to Doug, who looked back anxiously and then turned his attention back to his plate. Andy pulled out a chair and sat down, wondering how best to begin. Gavin pushed a plate towards him.

'I got you a bacon sandwich. I hope that's OK.'

'Great! Thanks. How much do I owe you?'

Gavin waved aside Andy's proffered banknote and addressed Doug.

'You tell the inspector here what you just told me about the night before last.'

'Doug?' Andy prompted gently after a few seconds of silence.

'I was going to my usual place for the night.' Doug stopped to put a piece of fried bread loaded with beans into his mouth.

'In the cubby-hole in the wall in Goose Lane?' Andy suggested.

'Mmm!' Doug nodded. He swallowed and then went on, 'and I fell over this man lying on the ground, over the other side, in the corner between the bin and the wall. I thought he was drunk – or asleep! I never knew he was dead!' He looked up with scared eyes. 'Maybe he wasn't then. I dunno. He was still warm anyhow. I put my hand on his arm – only accidental, like – getting myself back up and it felt warm through his sleeve. It did seem odd, that – only a thin shirt on a cold night like that, but I never … you don't think I killed him, do you? I swear, I never!'

'No Doug,' Andy assured him. 'I'm sure you didn't kill him. But what you've told me is very important, because it means it can't have been long after it happened that you found him. What time was it?'

Doug shrugged as he cut through a sausage and inserted a piece into his mouth. 'Haven't got a watch, have I?' he mumbled.

Andy thought for a moment. 'There's a clock in the wall of the chapel at Holy Cross College,' he said at last. 'It strikes every quarter of an hour. Did you hear it chime at all?'

'Nope!' Doug shook his head. 'There's always bells going off in Oxford. I don't take no notice of them.'

'Well then … what was it made you think it was time to bed down for the night?'

'One of your lot moved me on from my spot on the Broad,' Doug muttered resentfully. 'I wasn't doing nothing – just sitting there, minding my own business! Anyhow, it was dark and the shops was all shut up for the night, so I reckoned I might as well.' He speared his last piece of sausage with his fork and pushed it round his plate, wiping up the dregs of the sauce from the baked beans. He put it in his mouth and looked up hopefully towards Gavin.

'I'll get us all a doughnut for afters while you think about what time it was you went to Goose Lane that night.' Gavin got up and walked across to the counter.

Andy looked hopefully towards Doug.

'I dunno – honest!'

'OK.' Andy tried unsuccessfully to think of something that Doug might have noticed that would pinpoint the time more accurately. 'OK,' he repeated at last, 'can you remember seeing anyone else in the lane that evening? Were there any people around when you got there?'

Doug shook his head and stared at the table to avoid eye-contact.

'Is there anything else – anything at all – that you remember about that night?' Andy asked, in a desperate last attempt to extract more information from what seemed to be his only witness.

After a long pause, Doug appeared to dredge up a memory from deep within his mind. 'They was cooking dinner,' he muttered. Then louder. 'It must've been round about dinner time in the college. Roast lamb it was. I could smell it cooking.'

'That's great!' Andy told him enthusiastically. 'And could you tell which college it was? Which side of the road did the smell come from?'

'It was the one on the left. There's a grid in the wall. It was coming from there. Them's the kitchens behind there. There's a bloke works there called Nico. He sometimes brings me out stuff – food they'd chuck away otherwise. So, I always take a sniff, like, to smell what's cooking.'

'And did Nico come out to see you the night before last?' Andy asked, trying to keep the excitement out of his voice. This could be someone who could corroborate Doug's story.

'Yeah. He did. Not 'til a while after that, mind you. I'd almost dozed off when he come and gave me some left-overs – scraps of meat off the joint, potatoes that nobody wanted. Like I said, stuff they'd have to throw out.'

'Well, thank you, Doug.' Andy got to his feet just as Gavin returned with three doughnuts and three mugs of tea. 'I'm afraid I've got to go now. You've been a great help.' He took out a twenty-pound note and put it down on the table. 'You'll have to have my doughnut, I'm afraid, and then, when you're finished here, Constable Hughes will take you to buy some new gloves to keep your hands warm now the cold weather's setting in.'

Andy looked towards Gavin, who nodded back before pocketing the note and resuming his seat opposite Doug. Andy hurried out of the covered market and headed back to Lichfield College, anxious to get there while they were still serving lunch. Of course, Nico might only work the evening shift, but at least there should be someone there who would be able to tell him when and where he might be found.

He was in luck. Nico turned out to be a Kosovan refugee who had worked his way up to second-in-command in the catering department at Lichfield College. He had seen Doug sleeping on the street and had felt sorry for him. He knew what it was like to have nothing, and did what he could for him by giving him food that would otherwise go to waste. He confirmed that Doug had been there on Monday night. He had taken out a plate of leftovers to him after they had finished clearing up after dinner. It must have been about half past eight. Formal Hall was at seven, so there would have been smells of cooking any time from about six until half past seven.

A QUESTION OF IDENTITY

Andy smiled to himself as he walked briskly back to his office. He had the time of the incident narrowed down nicely now. Mike had said death had occurred no earlier than four in the afternoon and probably more like five or six or any time up to nine. Doug must have stumbled across Mr Danjuma's body at about seven – at any rate no later than half past. And that all fitted in very nicely with the theory that he had been dressing for dinner when something – or someone – attracted his attention in the street and prompted him to climb out of the window to deal with it – or them.

Sitting at his desk in the room that had once belonged to DCI Jonah Porter and which he still found it hard to think of as his own, Andy reached for the telephone. He must inform the victim's family, but first he would contact the Nigerian police, in case he was known to them, and to ask for their help in finding out if the student could have been involved in smuggling drugs. He could have seen that as an easy way of supplementing whatever grant or scholarship he had to support his studies, or drug barons in Nigeria could have put pressure on him to act as their "mule".

To his relief, the Nigerian police officer that he was eventually put through to in Jibrilu Danjuma's home city was eager to help. He appeared to be rather in awe of the British police and determined to demonstrate that his own force was just as efficient and effective as any that the old colonial power could muster. He promised to investigate the student's background and to visit his father in person to break the news. He would get on to it right away. Andy could expect a preliminary report later that day and a full report by the end of the week. He must not worry about a thing at the Nigerian end of this business. The Nigeria Police were quite capable of finding out all that he needed to know.

At the end of the lengthy telephone conversation, Andy put down the phone and got up to make himself a cup of coffee. At least he had been spared the more difficult call to Professor

Yakubu Danjuma, the victim's father. He had been dreading the task of breaking the news of his son's untimely death, which was always a difficult thing to do, even without the added problems of a cultural divide and a potential language barrier. Admittedly, a professor would be likely to speak good English, but it might well be his second or third language, his native tongue being some weird African tribal dialect full of strange and unfamiliar sounds. Andy often struggled with foreign accents, and it would have been dreadful to have misinterpreted anything that the bereaved parent said.

He sat back down at his desk and picked up the phone again. He did not have long to wait before it was answered.

'Andy! How's the case coming along? Have you identified your mystery man yet?' Jonah greeted him cheerfully, evidently delighted to receive the call.

'Yes, we have. That's sort of why I'm ringing you. It's a student at Lichfield College. I think Bernie knows his tutor – Dr Thomas Carrington? Isn't he a friend of hers?'

'An ex-colleague certainly,' Jonah agreed. 'I don't think she sees much of him these days – not since she retired from the university. But I'm sure she'll be pleased to be told about it.'

'I thought I'd got it right. I suddenly remembered where I'd met him before. He was at that meeting when their bursar was killed[2]. And then I remembered that he and Bernie knew each other. He's agreed to identify the body. I'll be off to pick him up and take him to the mortuary in a few minutes.'

'And what else do you know about the victim?' Jonah asked quickly, clearly anxious that Andy might end the call without filling him in on all the developments in the case. 'You said he was a student, but where was he from? Had he been in Oxford for long?'

---

[2] You can read about this in *Awayday*, ISBN: 978-1-911083-06-1

'He's from Nigeria. He only arrived in the country in September. He'd just begun a DPhil with Dr Carrington. The Nigerian police say that his name, coupled with the region he was from, suggests that he will have been a Muslim from the Hausa tribe. Dr Carrington told me that he seemed to have settled in OK and he wasn't aware of any disputes with other students. So, we're not any further on in terms of finding out who killed him or why.'

'Well, at least now you know who he is, you've got a better chance of working out why someone might want him dead,' Jonah observed encouragingly. 'It's early days yet. You're doing fine.'

'Thank you, sir – I mean Jonah. It just seems … anyway, I'd better go. I don't want to keep Dr Carrington waiting.'

After having been the unintentional cause of spoiling his mother's spaghetti Bolognese the previous evening, Andy took care to leave for home promptly after the evening briefing with his team. A delicious odour of cooking assailed his nostrils as he entered the house. He could hear his mother singing as she joined in with an old ABBA song from her youth. She stopped abruptly and turned the CD player off when Andy entered the kitchen.

'The dinner's just on ready,' she smiled. 'Sit down and I'll dish up.'

Andy sat down in his usual place at the table and took a sip from the glass of water that his mother had put there ready for him. 'Is there anything I can do to help?' he asked, already knowing that the answer would be negative. Mum prided herself that she could run the house like clockwork singlehandedly as well as holding down a full-time job in the university library. To accept help would, in her eyes, amount to an admission of inadequacy.

'No. Everything's all ready. Just relax and enjoy your food. You've had a long day.'

Not as long as yours, Andy thought, remembering that she had been up at six, loading the washing machine so that it would be finished before she had to go out to work.

She drained potatoes and carrots into the sink and spooned them on to two plates, which she set down on the table.

'How are you getting on with your first murder?' she asked. 'Do you know who it is yet?'

'Yes,' Andy said, as she turned away again and bent down to open the oven. 'He was a postgraduate student from Nigeria. He'd only been here a couple of months.'

His mother put on oven gloves and took out a steak-an-kidney pie, which she had made that morning while the washing was on and left in the fridge to bake after work.

'From Nigeria?' she echoed, pushing the oven door closed with her elbow and then turning back to face Andy.

'Yes. He had a funny name: Jibrilu Danjuma. The Ni-'

Andy broke off as his mother gave a little gasp and set the pie down on the table with a bump.

'Are you OK?'

'Yes. I'm fine. The pie was just a bit hotter than I thought,' she said quickly. She picked up a knife and spoon and began cutting into the pie and transferring portions to the plates, keeping her eyes lowered so that Andy could not see her face clearly.

'As I was saying,' he went on, carefully ignoring his mother's distraction, which she was clearly keen for him not to see, 'the Nigerian police say that he's most likely a Muslim from the Hausa tribe, judging by his name. His father's name's Yakubu. He's a professor at a Nigerian university. I haven't spoken to him yet. The Nigerian police have informed him about what happened, so I suppose I'd better ring him tomorrow, after he's had a chance to take it all in.'

'Yakubu Danjuma,' his mother murmured as she placed Andy's plate in front of him. She took off the oven gloves and sat down. 'I suppose it only sounds like a strange name to us because it's unfamiliar. I expect there are lots of people called Yakubu Danjuma in Nigeria.'

'Yes,' Andy agreed, unsure what this was all about. 'I expect you're right. The police certainly didn't seem to think it was out of the ordinary anyway.'

His mother sat eating her meal in silence.

'How was your day?' Andy ventured when the lengthy pause became uncomfortable.

'The same as usual,' she answered absently.

After more silence, Andy tried again. 'What we still can't figure out is why anyone would want to harm him. He hasn't been here for long enough to make any enemies.'

'No, I suppose not.'

'There's this Sergeant Myers from the drug squad who thinks he was probably smuggling cocaine into the country, but I'm not so sure. There was nothing in his room to suggest that he was involved in drugs. We've even had a sniffer dog in there and ... nothing! Clean as a whistle – which must be quite unusual for a student room, I should think!'

'*I* didn't take drugs when *I* was a student.' At last Mum seemed to be listening again. 'And I don't suppose you did either!'

'No, I didn't,' Andy grinned, 'but I did know a few people who did. Only cannabis, though, not the hard stuff. Oh well! I expect things will get a bit clearer once I've had a chance to speak to his dad. Maybe he'll have some ideas about who could've had it in for him.'

5. OUT OF AFRICA …

Andy arrived early at work the next day, hoping to get a chance to review the case by himself before the rest of the team arrived with questions and ideas. He groaned inwardly when his phone began ringing as he stepped through the door into his office. Was this a new lead to be followed up or a new case to be added to their workload? Either way, his time of reflection over a cup of coffee was not going to happen after all!

'Am I speaking to Detective Inspector Andrew Lepage?' The voice was deep and thick and had the same accent as the Nigerian police sergeant from yesterday. Did they have news for him on Jibrilu Danjuma's background?

'Yes,' he answered. 'How can I help you?'

'My name is Professor Yakubu Danjuma. I understand that you are leading the investigation into the death of my son.'

'Jibrilu Danjuma? Yes. That's right. I'm very sorry for your loss, and I'd like to assure you that we are doing everything that we can to find the person who killed him and bring them to justice.' Andy felt inadequately prepared for this conversation, which he had not anticipated would come so soon.

'I need your help. I have been trying to get a visa to come to Britain to bury my son, but the application process is so slow. They say three weeks or it might be six weeks or even twelve weeks. I do not know what to do. Can you intervene and tell the British High Commission that they must grant me a visa quickly?'

'I don't know,' Andy floundered. 'Have you tried talking to the police in Nigeria? They might be able to help better than I can.'

'They say it is not for them to tell a foreign government how to run their immigration service. I need help from Britain. Will you speak to them? My son's body should not remain above ground. It should be buried with the proper rites and ceremonies and I should be there to oversee it.'

'Well, I'll see what I can do,' Andy promised cautiously. 'I'm afraid it may be some time before the coroner releases the body for burial in any case. But I will look into whether there's anything we can do to get your visa application pushed up the priority list.'

'Thank you. I hope that you can do something. I remember when Jibrilu applied for his student visa, it took so long, and we had to make so many journeys to Abuja to the application centre.'

Andy suddenly remembered what the police sergeant had said about the professor's name suggesting that he was a Muslim. 'And, if you're worried about how your son's body is being looked after, maybe I could ask someone in Oxford to go to the mortuary and say the right words over it or whatever. There's a mosque in Oxford. Someone from there might be able to help.'

'That is very kind of you.' The voice changed. Andy could sense that the professor's emotions had transitioned from anger and frustration to something softer and more tender. 'Yes, I think that would help. If someone from our faith could just go and see him, so that I know …. Could you arrange that?'

'I can certainly try. I'll talk to one of my colleagues who goes to the mosque,' Andy promised. 'I expect that he'll know the right person to talk to about it.'

'Thank you. And you will try to help about the visa, won't you?'

'I'll do my best. Now, I know this is a difficult time for you, but it would help our investigation if you could answer a few questions about your son. Are you OK for me to do that now?'

'Of course. Anything, if you think it will help to find whoever did this.'

'Good.' Andy paused for a moment to gather his thoughts. Then it occurred to him that an international call from Nigeria to the UK might be expensive for the bereaved father. 'On second thoughts, could I ring you back in about ten minutes – so I can get the file and give you the latest update?'

'Now Professor Danjuma,' Andy resumed a few minutes later, seated at his desk with a pen and a pad of paper in front of him, 'can you tell me when you last spoke to your son?'

'Five days ago. He telephoned me on Saturday evening. He telephones every Saturday.'

'And how did he seem?'

'Just as usual.'

'He didn't seem upset or anxious about anything?'

'No.'

'What did you talk about?'

'He told me about the reading that he was doing for his DPhil, and I told him about some changes that were going on at the university where I work. He asked after his two aunties and his cousins and I told him they were all well.'

'What about his mother? Is she not around anymore?'

'All of my family apart from Jibrilu were killed in a house fire in 1992. Jibrilu was just a baby then. His mother threw him out of a first-floor window and he survived.'

'Oh! I'm so sorry.' Andy hardly knew what to say. 'You and your son must have become very close,' he suggested after a long pause. 'It must have been difficult for him being so far away – and in such a different culture too.'

'I was a student at Oxford university myself, so I was able to prepare him for what he would find. I also took a DPhil. I came to Oxford shortly after marrying Jibrilu's mother. Of course, a lot has changed during the intervening years, but there are many things that are still the same. I think he was enjoying seeing the places that I had been to and knowing that he was living in the same college and working in the same library and so on.'

'Had he made many friends in Oxford?'

'He said that he got on well with the student in the room next door to his. He was surprised that there were two women on their staircase – on the floor above. In my day, men and women were housed on separate staircases. And there were very few women. The first women were admitted to Lichfield college the year that I went there.'

'So that would be … late seventies, early eighties?'

'1979. I was in Oxford from 1979 to 1983.'

'I see. Yes, I should think quite a lot of things have changed since then. Now, to get back to your son: did he ever tell you about anyone bullying him or harassing him in any way?'

'No. He talked as if he was getting on well with everyone. He said his tutor was very nice and the other mathematics students had been very helpful about showing him where everything was. That's something else that is different now. I studied at the old Mathematical Institute on St Giles. They've built a brand-new mathematics building now, on the site of the Radcliffe Infirmary. But, of course, you'll know all this.'

'Yes. My mother works in the Radcliffe Science Library. She was invited to a tour of the new building when it opened. She said it was very impressive.'

'Really? Does your family come from Oxford then?'

'Yes,' Andy was too taken aback by the personal question to think of a way of fending it off without answering. 'My mother and her sisters grew up in Headington. My mother and I still live there.'

'Now that's interesting, inspector.' Andy was even less prepared for what came next. 'I was struck by your surname when the police gave it to me. I knew girl called Amanda Lepage when I was studying in Oxford. I wondered if she could be a relation of yours?'

Andy felt his heart speeding up and he had to muster all his self-control to keep his voice steady. 'No. I don't think so.'

'That's a pity. But I suppose Lepage is probably a common name in England?'

'I – I don't know. Not as common as Smith or Jones, but … Anyway, I think that's all I need to ask you for now. I won't forget to see what I can do about your visa. And once again, Professor Danjuma, I am very sorry for your loss.'

Andy ended the call, surprised to see his hand shaking as he replaced the telephone receiver. Would the professor think that his abrupt termination of their conversation was rude? He hoped not, but he had really felt unable to carry on with this probing into his family history. Lepage was not a common name, and its combination with "Amanda" could not be a coincidence.

He did not have time to dwell on the matter, however, because his thoughts were immediately interrupted by a knock on the door heralding Alice bearing news.

'You remember all that sheet music that was blowing around in Goose Lane?' she asked, holding up a brown leather music case encased in plastic. 'Well, the SOCOs have found this bag with some more of it in it. Some of it is stamped with "Holy Cross College Chapel". I was thinking of going there and having a look around. Someone there may recognise the case.'

'Good idea,' Andy agreed, getting to his feet. 'I'll come with you. I'd forgotten about the music. I was talking to the victim's father just now. I ought to have asked him if he played the organ.'

'Not very likely, I wouldn't have thought! How many organs do you think there are in Nigeria?'

'I know, but if the music isn't his, who does it belong to? Was someone else also attacked that night? Or did the music belong to whoever knifed him?'

'I suppose he could've dropped the case when he reached for his knife,' Alice suggested, as they walked briskly down the road towards the crime scene. 'Or maybe he just witnessed the attack and dropped it running away so as not to get involved.'

'Yes, you're right. The case needn't belong to the victim *or* the killer. It's more likely the owner was a witness who got scared and wanted to get out quick.'

They soon reached Goose Lane and squeezed under the police tape to reach the back door of Holy Cross College.

'There's someone in there,' Alice commented as they entered the tunnel that led through to the rear quadrangle – the one that the Principal had told them was called Al Qahtani Quad. 'I can hear the organ playing.'

'Well let's hope whoever's playing it is the same person as dropped the music in Goose Lane on Monday night,' Andy replied. He stopped by a small door on the right of the corridor. The sound's coming from here. Do you think this door goes into the chapel? I was expecting something a bit more grand.'

'Maybe it's the back entrance,' Alice suggested.

Andy took hold of the black metal ring that formed the door handle and turned it. He could hear, and feel, a latch lifting on the other side. He pushed the heavy oak door and it swung open. He found himself hemmed in by oak panelling on either side. The organ music was much louder now. Looking up, he could see the pipes high above him on the left. Ahead was the main body of the chapel with its long wooden pews arranged sideways, like choir stalls. Coloured light from stained glass windows high up in the walls made jewelled patterns on their varnished surfaces.

Walking forward, he found a narrow wooden staircase on the left. He ascended it and was soon level with the bench on which sat a young man in sweatshirt and jeans playing the organ. He stopped abruptly at the sound of the two police officers approaching across the bare wooden floor of the organ loft.

'Can I help you?' he asked, twisting his body round to speak to the strangers and frowning in puzzlement.

'Perhaps.' Andy held up his warrant card. 'I'm Detective Inspector Andy Lepage and this is DC Alice Ray. We're investigating the death of a man in Goose Lane on Monday evening.'

'Oh yes!' the young man's frown disappeared and he looked interested, perhaps excited. 'I heard about that. Do you know who he is yet?'

'Yes.' Andy replied. There could be no harm in admitting this. The victim's family had been informed and the name would, no doubt, be in all the papers and on all the news websites before the end of the day. 'He was a student at Lichfield College.'

'Oh! Who was it? I've got a few friends at Lichfield. It could be someone I know.'

'Perhaps you could tell us your name first,' Alice suggested, getting out her notebook and a pen.

'I'm Aidan Moorcliffe. I'm the organ scholar here.'

'Good. In that case you may be able to help us.' Andy held up the music case. 'We came here because we found this in the street near to his body. It has music in it stamped with "Holy Cross College Chapel". Whoever dropped it, presumably plays the organ here. We wondered if it could have belonged to the dead man. His name's Jibrilu Danjuma. He's a postgraduate student from Nigeria.'

Alice held up some of the sheet music, each piece in its own transparent plastic evidence bag. The young man took it from her and examined the pages. 'Yes,' he murmured. 'This is music from our collection.'

He swivelled round on his seat and swung his legs over the bench to face the back of the chapel. Andy saw that the wooden barrier, which prevented the organist from falling down on to the red and black tiled floor below, was lined with shelves full of sheet music. Aidan gestured with his hand. 'We keep it all here. I suppose anyone could come in and take it, but I can't think why they would want to.'

'And you haven't come across Jibrilu Danjuma?' Andy pressed him. 'He doesn't play the organ here at all?'

'Not that I know of. I did only start here this term though, so I suppose …'

'He was new this term too,' Alice told him. She held up one of the photographs of the victim. 'This is what he looked like. Have you ever seen him – hanging round the chapel, maybe?'

The student took the picture and stared down at it. Then he handed it back, shaking his head as he did so. 'No. I've definitely never seen him in chapel. I'm sure I'd remember if I had. We don't have many – I mean there aren't many overseas students at Holy Cross.'

'And you don't recognise this case?' Andy asked.

'No. Well, it's a pretty standard kind of music case. Loads of people have them. I've got one.' Aidan reached down and picked up a seemingly identical brown leather case from the floor next to the organ bench. He held it up for the police officers to see.

'Well, it looks as if one of those people was out in Goose Lane on the night that a man was killed there,' Andy told him seriously. 'So, they may have witnessed the attack. We need to speak to them – even if only to eliminate them from our enquiries. Can you suggest anyone else – apart from you – who could have dropped this case and a whole lot of music from this chapel last Monday night?'

Aidan thought for a few moments. His face had gone white and he fiddled nervously with the metal rod which held the music case closed. 'I think you need to talk to Dr Claughton. He's my tutor, and he's in charge of the organ music. He'll be able to tell you who had these.' He pointed at the sheets of music, which Alice had taken back. 'And he'll know if this Danjuma guy ever played the organ here.'

Their search for Dr Piers Claughton, music tutor and organist, was fruitless. There was no answer when they knocked on the door of his college room, and the porter who helpfully agreed to telephone his home failed to elicit a response either. He had not left a mobile number at the lodge, so there seemed to be nothing else that they could do to trace him.

'You'd better have another go tomorrow,' Andy told Alice. 'I know it's a bit of a long shot, but we need to know who dropped that music case. Sheet music like that is expensive stuff. You don't just go flinging it around the streets for fun. Now, I think our next job needs to be to-'

He broke off and started feeling in his pocket for his phone, which had begun ringing. It was Joshua Pitchfork.

'We could do with you back here, sir. Uniform have remembered seeing a black youth running away from the Goose Lane area on Monday evening, round about the time our man was killed. I've got one of them here now. I thought you'd want to speak to him yourself.'

'Thanks, Josh. I'll be right back.' Andy turned to Alice. 'I need to go back to the station. Can I leave you to talk to each of the students on Jibrilu's staircase? Find out everything they know about him and in particular if they've heard of him getting on the wrong side of anyone.'

'I'll get on to it right away.' Alice smiled broadly, pleased to be entrusted with a significant piece of solo investigation. She was not ambitious like her partner, but it was nice to feel that her ability had been recognised.

When Andy entered the open plan office, he saw Joshua Pitchfork sitting at his desk, drinking coffee with a fair-haired man in uniform, whom he recognised as Sergeant Neil Duffield. He had met him a few times before, but did not consider that he knew him well. Joshua immediately leapt to his feet.

'This is Sergeant Duffield. He stopped and searched a youth who was behaving suspiciously on Monday evening, and he's now wondering if it could have anything to do with our case.'

Andy pulled over a chair from a vacant desk and sat down a few feet from Duffield, who had not bothered to get up. 'Tell me about it.'

'I spent the afternoon patrolling the streets, providing a reassuring police presence to encourage the tourists and shoppers back into the town centre after COVID. I was just passing the time of day with one of the PCSOs when this black youth comes careering out of a side street like a bat out of hell and collides with her. We questioned him and searched him, but he didn't have anything on him, so we let him go.'

'What time was this?'

'About twenty to seven in the evening.'

'Presumably either you or the PCSO will have made a note of the precise time in your pocket book? Perhaps you could let me see the notes you made of the incident.'

'We didn't bother.' The sergeant looked boldly into Andy's eyes as if daring him to reprimand this omission. 'We were expecting to find either drugs or a knife on him. When there wasn't anything, we didn't think it was worth recording it.'

'And if he subsequently brings a complaint of police harassment?' asked Andy coldly, holding Duffield's gaze for a few seconds before moving on to his next question. 'Did you, by any chance, think it was worth asking him for his name?'

'Yes. It was a weird one – a girl's name … Gabriel! That's it – like the angel in those Christmas plays that nursery schools put on.'

'And his last name?'

'Even weirder – one of those unpronounceable African names. I can't remember.'

'So, no chance that you'd be able to suggest where I might find him?' Andy asked sarcastically. 'No home address? No indication of where he was coming from or where he was going?'

'I saw him go across the High to wait at one of the stops for buses heading out of town across Magdalen Bridge. He *said* he was going home to his mum, so, if he was telling the truth, I guess he lives out that way somewhere. Look – I didn't have to tell you about this,' he went on, suddenly on the defensive. 'I don't suppose it's got anything to do with your knifing. I just thought, seeing as it was the same day and, as far as I knew, the same time, you might be interested.'

'Oh yes, I'm certainly interested. What was the name of the PCSO that you were with? I'd better talk to her. Maybe she'll remember more about it – like the lad's surname or which bus he took home.'

About half an hour later, Andy was sitting in a coffee shop drinking an Americano while PCSO Tanya Tidworth scooped the froth off the top of her latte with a long spoon.

'I think he said it was Sibunda,' she told him when he asked about the youth's last name, 'but I may not be remembering it right. It was a name I'd never heard before and Neil said to forget about it, after he found he wasn't carrying a weapon or drugs.' She looked apologetically across the table at Andy. 'I wasn't sure about searching him, to be honest; he looked more frightened than threatening to me. But I'm still quite new. I imagine Neil knows the signs better than I do.'

'Can you describe this youth? Sergeant Duffield didn't seem able to get beyond, *he was black*.'

'Well, I wouldn't have called him a youth exactly,' Tanya began slowly. 'More of a boy, really. That was another reason I was uneasy about searching him. He was wearing a long black coat, but I had a feeling that he had school uniform on underneath it. But I'm probably wrong.'

'So, how old would you say he was?' Andy asked eagerly.

'Fifteen, sixteen, maybe. He was quite tall – taller than me, but then the same goes for both of my own boys and Alfie's only twelve.'

'And you thought he looked scared? Could he have been running away from something that had frightened him?'

'Yes. Yes, that's exactly how it seemed to me. But, as Neil said afterwards, a lot of youngsters carry knives on the streets because they're scared of being attacked and think that'll help them defend themselves.'

'But this boy wasn't carrying a knife, was he?'

'No.' Tanya stirred her coffee nervously, looking increasingly uncomfortable.

'Sergeant Duffield told me that the boy went and waited at a bus top on the High. Did you happen to see which bus he caught?'

'Yes.' Tanya's face brightened up a little. 'I waited around to see that he got on it OK. I was a bit afraid … Well, like I said, I thought he was younger than … And if it had been one of my boys … Anyway, I saw him get on a number 8.'

'Good.' Andy sat back in his seat and gave Tanya a reassuring smile. 'I know that bus. It goes up Headington Hill and out to Barton. And he told you he was going home?'

'Yes. He said his mum would be worried if he missed the bus. That was something else that made me think he must be younger.'

'Right.' Andy hesitated. 'And can you tell me anything else about his appearance? His hair, for example, was it short or long?'

'Oh short. Trimmed all over to the shape of his head – like yours.'

'Anything else?'

'No, not really. I'm sorry. I know it's an awful thing to say, but I do find it hard to describe black people. It's not that they all look the same exactly, it's just that ... well normally, I'd be looking at the colour of their hair and eyes and ...'

'They all have curly black hair and brown eyes,' Andy finished for her. 'Don't look so mortified. I'll let you into a secret: I'm just the same. I grew up in a white family and I sometimes find it hard to tell black people apart too.'

'Were you adopted then?'

'No. It's just, my mum's white and I never knew my dad. He disappeared off back to Africa before I was born.'

'Oh. My boys' dad did a runner too. He found them cute while they were small, but once George was talking – and constantly asking questions – he started staying out of the house, hanging round with his mates as much as he could and in the end he just up and left. We're better off without him.'

'I think that's probably how my mum feels too,' Andy nodded.

'Alfie keeps asking about his dad, though,' Tanya went on. 'I worry he'll want to find him when he gets older and I don't honestly want him to. They're just *my* boys now and I'm not sure I want to share them with Chris. Is that awful of me?'

'Not at all. I've never wanted to find my dad. And even if I did, I wouldn't in case it upset my mum.'

Tanya nodded and smiled. 'But getting back to the boy – Gabriel Sibundu or whatever he was called – there was one thing I can tell you about his appearance. He was a lot darker-skinned than you. I didn't think about it until you said your mum was white, but that explains it. This Gabriel was much darker. I don't know if that helps at all?'

'Well, it's a start. And knowing he lives out Headington way is a big help too. Thanks Tanya. This has been useful.'

Andy left the coffee shop and wandered through the back streets in the direction of Lichfield College. While he was in the area, he might as well catch up with Alice, who would be there interviewing Jibrilu's fellow-students.

As he entered at the porters' lodge, he met Tom Carrington coming the other way.

'Inspector! I've been meaning to ring you. I had a thought about who might be able to fill you in on Jibrilu's background. Have you spoken to Bev Greenhalgh? She's the tutor who looks after all the overseas students at the college. She always makes a point of getting to know them during their first few weeks. She's very keen on making sure they settle in OK. She'd probably be able to tell you who his friends are and if he's had any aggro from anyone.'

'Thanks. I'll speak to her. Can you tell me where I'll find her?'

Dr Beverley Greenhalgh, Fellow in Plant Sciences and Overseas Students Tutor, was a no-nonsense northerner from a former mill town high up in the Pennines. She was forthright in her speech and firm in her convictions, which included a belief that very few of the male half of the human race could be fully trusted. She looked Andy up and down as he entered her study.

'You were here with that disabled officer when Tony Bridgefield was killed. You were his sergeant.'

'That's right: DCI Porter. He's retired now.' Andy held up his warrant card, 'My name is DI Lepage and I'm leading the investigation into the death of one of your overseas students – Jibrilu Danjuma. What can you tell me about him?'

'He was a postgraduate student from Nigeria. He was studying for a DPhil. He had a lectureship lined up at a university there, conditional on him getting a doctorate. His father also worked at that university, which I daresay wasn't totally unconnected with the job offer.'

'And you were responsible for seeing that he settled in alright?'

'I suppose you could express it like that.'

'And did he? Did he seem happy here?'

'As far as I could tell. He didn't complain about anything and his tutor seemed satisfied with his work.'

'Do you have many overseas students at the college?'

'Not as many now as we usually do. Our undergraduate numbers have been particularly badly hit by COVID. And Brexit hasn't helped with European students. But our postgraduate intake has held up. In fact, we have more new DPhil students from overseas than usual this year, because of the ones who had to postpone their travel in 2020.'

'Are there any others from Nigeria?'

Dr Greenhalgh paused and pursed her lips as if she were thinking. 'Just one,' she answered reluctantly. 'They didn't know each other before they came,' she added quickly. 'So, you needn't think that she bore him a grudge or anything like that. They were from completely different parts of the country and different tribes. He was Hausa and she was … I forget. Anyway, I made the mistake of introducing them to one another, thinking they would be able to support one another, but … Well, let's just say they both had a lot of baggage to bring to that relationship.'

'What sort of baggage?'

'Oh, just inter-tribal resentment and …,' Dr Greenhalgh began. Then, seeing from his face that Andy knew that she was hiding something, she sighed. 'OK. I admit it. It was a major miscalculation on my part. It turned out that Jibrilu is – was – a practising Muslim, while Esther's family are Christians. An aunt of hers was killed by Boko Haram militants in an attack on their church. So, she wasn't exactly well-disposed towards Nigerian

Muslims. But, she's the gentlest, kindest person you can imagine. There's no question of her having stabbed the poor lad!'

'You may be right, but I'd still better speak to her. What's her full name and where would I find her?'

'Esther Orugun. She's one of my own students. Her project is all to do with finding new strains of food crops to yield better harvests in sub-Saharan Africa. Her room in on the same staircase as Jibrilu. We put all the new overseas postgraduates there, thinking that they'd help each other to settle in. She's on the first floor with another woman – Marie-Claire Charbonneau. We never put women on the ground floor, especially in those rooms which have windows opening on to the street.'

The don's sudden loquaciousness made Andy suspect that she was giving him lots of extraneous facts in order to divert him from something that she did not want him to know – but what?

'One of my colleagues may already have interviewed her, in that case,' he told her. 'We're speaking to all the students on that staircase, in case they saw anything that evening. Just for the record, where were you on Monday afternoon and evening?'

'I was working here, in my room, in the afternoon and then I went to the SCR for afternoon tea and came back here until it was time for dinner. I dined on High Table. The Master had a guest from DEFRA[3] whom he was hoping might help us with a funding bid for a research project I'm planning jointly with Dr Martin Riess – he's in Earth Sciences here.'

'Are you sure you aren't aware of any trouble among the overseas students – or *any* of the students, come to that? No fallings-out over boy and girl friends? No trouble between the overseas students and the British ones?'

---

[3] The Department for Environment, Food and Rural Affairs

'No!' Dr Greenhalgh broke off suddenly and looked sheepish. 'Well … yes, there were a few incidents. It was just silly teasing – all just a joke, I'm sure – but Jibrilu does – did – have a tendency to take offence where none was intended. Some of the students used to enjoy winding him up with so-called *innocent* remarks that he managed to interpret as insults. That's what I meant when I said Esther wouldn't have ever done anything violent. She was quite different. She just shrugged it all off with a "boys will be boys" sort of attitude.'

'And can you give me the names of any of these students – the ones who liked to wind Jibrilu up?'

'No. I never actually witnessed it. So, I suppose it may not even be true. It's just something I heard on the grapevine. Look! If you really want to learn about Jibrilu, you ought to talk to his friends at the Islamic Society. Go to their prayer room in the Robert Hooke building tomorrow afternoon and you'll probably find them all there.'

'I spoke to Yakubu Danjuma on the phone today,' Andy said casually as he helped his mother to wash the dishes that evening. 'He's the father of the Nigerian student whose death we're investigating. He was hoping I could help him to get a visa to come over here to bury him.'

'That's not your job, surely?'

'No, but I suppose he thought the police might have some influence. I've passed it on up the food chain. Anna says she's put it to the Chief Super that we need to interview him and it'll be cheaper to let him come here than to send an officer to Nigeria. I don't think Alison was taken in by the threat to send me to Nigeria, but she agreed to speak to the DCC. I don't know how long it'll take to get anywhere near Immigration or whoever it is that deals with visas from Commonwealth Countries.'

'Oh well!' his mother shrugged. 'I don't suppose it makes that much difference how long it takes. They'll be keeping the body in cold storage anyway, won't they?'

'Well, apparently it's his tradition to bury people within a day or two of their dying, so he's upset that he can't be here. He's a Muslim, so I spoke to Arshad Khan about it. He's a DCI who specialises in cases involving ethnic minority victims. To be honest, I'm quite surprised he wasn't given this case. I suppose it's because everyone thought it was just a routine knife incident.'

'And isn't it?'

'No. At least *I* don't think so. He's not a local youth who's got himself involved in a gang. And there's no evidence that he was mixed up in drugs – nothing in his room and nothing in his bloodstream either. The toxicology report came back this afternoon and he was clean as a whistle – no drugs, not even alcohol! Anyway, as I was saying, DCI Khan's arranging with someone from the mosque to take care of the body once it's released. Apparently, they have like a funeral parlour there where they do ritual washing and stuff to prepare the bodies for burial. They'll take care of everything including the funeral, if his father can't get here in time.'

Mrs Lepage silently tipped out the washing up bowl and held it in her hand as she waited for the water to drain away.

'He remembers you,' Andy said, suddenly plucking up the courage to mention the thing that had been on his mind ever since that morning call from Professor Danjuma.

'That's clever of him.' Amanda Lepage replaced the bowl in the sink, but remained staring down into it. 'Seeing as we've never met.'

'He asked if you were any relation to me.' Andy saw his mother's neck and shoulders stiffen. She still did not turn round.

'What did you tell him?'

'I said not that I was aware of.'

'Good.' Still without looking towards her son, she filled the coffee machine with water and then went over to a wall cupboard to fetch the beans. For a minute or two the noise of the coffee grinder prevented further speech.

'Well?' Andy demanded, as soon as the noise stopped. 'Aren't you going to tell me about it?'

'About what?' his mother tipped the finely ground coffee into the machine and switched it on.

'About your relationship with Yakubu Danjuma.'

'There was no relationship. I told you – we've never met. He must be getting me mixed up with someone else.'

'Oh, come off it, Mum!' Andy's frustration suddenly boiled over. 'Stop pretending! You recognised his name last night. I could tell. And he remembers you. He was in Oxford doing a DPhil the same time as you were at the university. Oh, come on! How many Amanda Lepages can there have been in Oxford in the early eighties?

'Alright,' his mother growled in a low voice, still refusing to meet his eye. 'Alright, I knew him. If you must know, I cleaned his room. It was just a holiday job, while I was still at school – helping the scouts at Lichfield. That's all it was. There was no *relationship*! I just cleaned his room and he asked me what my name was, and I told him. That's all.'

'OK.' Andy was very far from being convinced by his mother's protestations, but he decided not to press her any further. He dried the last fork and hung up the tea towel. 'I'll take my coffee up to my room. I've got a stack of emails I need to deal with.'

6. SEX, DRUGS AND ... RACISM

Andy studied the face that had appeared on the screen in front of him. This was the first time that he had seen the father of the dead man – well, apart from a tiny photograph on the webpage of his university department. Professor Yakubu Danjuma looked older than he had expected. His dark chocolate-coloured skin was creased in folds around his mouth and sagged under his eyes, and his hair was almost completely white. His eyes appeared bloodshot, but perhaps that was due to grief rather than age.

'Good afternoon, Professor Danjuma. Thank you for agreeing to this video call.'

'Thank you for keeping me informed, inspector. What can I do for you?'

'First, let me just tell you what we've arranged regarding your son's body. The coroner will open the inquest on Monday, but that's just a formality and it'll be adjourned almost immediately. All the necessary tests have been done, so I expect they'll also release him for burial then too. Once that happens, you can choose either to have him kept in cold storage at the mortuary or to go ahead with the funeral. The local mosque has a team of people who could do that for you and you could watch it all on a video link.'

'I see. I suppose there's no news on speeding up my visa application?'

'No. I'm sorry. Our Deputy Chief Constable is going to speak to the Home Office to see if there's any sort of emergency visa that they could give you, but …'

'Yes, I know. We have bureaucracy here in Nigeria too. I suppose, for Jibrilu's sake, I must allow him to be buried without my presence. I would not like to think of him being kept in a mortuary freezer for many weeks. Can you give me the names of the brothers who will prepare his body?'

'I can't, but you'll be getting a call from Detective Chief Inspector Khan, who'll be able to explain everything to you. He attends the mosque himself. I'm sure he'll be able to arrange for you to speak to them.'

'Thank you. I appreciate this.'

'DCI Khan says that, since COVID, they've had a lot of people joining in funerals remotely,' Andy went on, sensing that, despite his words, Jibrilu's father was still disappointed that he would not be able to say a final goodbye to his son in person. 'That's one good thing that's come out of the pandemic. A lot of Muslims have family in other parts of the world and, now they've got the technology, they don't have to travel to be there. Anyway, DCI Khan will be in touch either today or over the weekend.'

'Thank you.'

'I was wondering if you've had time to think about anything your son might have said that indicated he'd fallen out with anyone in Oxford?'

'No, not at all. As I said before, he seemed perfectly happy there. He was excited about following in his father's footsteps. I told you that I studied at Lichfield College myself, when I was young, didn't I? He told me so much about Oxford – how things had changed since my day – and how some things were still just the same! He sent me some pictures of the new mosque. I was astounded. We had nothing like that when I was in Oxford.'

'I'm afraid I've never seen it,' Andy confessed. 'I'd hardly realised we had one in Oxford.'

'You must go and pay it a visit! Jibrilu's pictures are quite stunning. We were both looking forward to me going to Oxford to visit him next summer, so that I could see it for myself. And I was hoping to renew my acquaintance with a few old friends. My old tutor, for example.'

'Yes,' Andy said, feeling that some sort of response was required but not knowing what to say.

'And now, my visit will be in such different circumstances,' the professor went on, apparently happy to continue his monologue. 'But, although it will be a much sadder occasion, I hope that my old friends will still be there and I will seek them out while I am in England. Amanda Lepage, for example. I would very much like to see her again. Are you sure she is not one of your relatives? Perhaps you could ask your mother if she knows?'

'I suppose I could ask,' Andy replied uncertainly. He knew! Professor Danjuma knew! Or at least he suspected. What would he think when he found out that a police officer, whom he should have been able to trust, had lied to him? He suddenly became aware that the other man was speaking again.

'Or I could always try the library where she works. It's very strange, you know, I looked on the website and there's a librarian there called Amanda Lepage. It's quite a coincidence, isn't it? I'm surprised you mother hasn't mentioned her to you. What *is* your mother's first name, if you don't mind me asking?'

'I do actually,' Andy blurted out. Then, adopting a very formal tone, 'your son's death has some of the hallmarks of a drug-related killing, and we've had an increase in illicit cocaine being sold in Oxford recently, which we believe came from West Africa. Have you ever had any sus-'

'Never!' the enraged father roared back. 'Are you suggesting that he was a drug smuggler? That is total nonsense! My Jibrilu would never have anything to do with such things.'

'I'm sorry, sir, but I had to ask.'

'And I am answering you. He never took drugs of any kind, and he would never give them to anyone else.'

'And you're not aware of anyone approaching him and asking him to take any sort of package with him to the UK? Sometimes young people can be duped into becoming drug mules without even knowing.'

'He was young, but he was not a boy. He was twenty-nine years old. At that age, I had two wives and a daughter! Jibrilu was old enough to know how to recognise someone who was trying to deceive him. No. I tell you again, he would never have had anything to do with that vile trade!'

'Thank you, Dr Danjuma. That's very clear. Now, I'm sure you're very busy and I have other things that I need to follow up in this case, so we'd better end here. Thank you again. I'll be in touch as soon as I have any more news.'

Andy ended the videocall without waiting for a reply. He sat for several minutes staring at his blank computer screen. Why had he lied to the professor? He was bound to discover eventually that Andy had known exactly who Amanda Lepage was the moment he mentioned her name. In fact, it was clear that he already knew and was trying to get him to admit it. What would Mum think when she found out? Why had he been so stupid as to mention where she worked?'

A reminder popped up in the corner of the screen. It was time for him to leave if he were to catch the students from the Islamic Society at the end of their Friday prayers. He clicked the mouse to cancel the reminder and then locked the screen before getting up to go. He would have to have another conversation with his mother that evening, but meanwhile, there was a killer to catch!

SEX, DRUGS AND … RACISM

When Andy arrived at the Robert Hooke Building, after battling through a strong wind that sent damp leaves swirling around his feet, the prayers were still going on. He stood nervously outside the door of the prayer room listening to the rhythmic chanting. Then, noticing that the door was slightly ajar, he crept forward and peered through. Rows of men were standing barefoot or in socks all facing the same way, spaced apart and wearing face-masks. Then, in unison, they all knelt down and leaned forward to touch the floor with their foreheads. He stepped back and stood waiting uncomfortably for the prayers to end. Was he allowed in here? Should he take off his shoes? No, surely it was OK provided he didn't go inside the prayer room.

Eventually the chanting stopped. A few moments later, the door opened and men began emerging. Andy stepped forward nervously, holding up his warrant card.

'Excuse me, I'm DI Andy Lepage from Thames Valley CID, I was wondering is any of you could help me?'

Several of the students walked past without speaking to him or making eye contact. They pulled on their shoes and hurried out of the building.

'I'm investigating the death of Jibrilu Danjuma. Did any of you know him at all?'

At first it seemed that all the young men who were coming out of the prayer room were studiously ignoring him, pretending to be in a hurry to put on their shoes and go off to lectures or tutorials or whatever else they had planned for that Friday afternoon. Just as Andy was about to give up and return to the police station, a small group approached him.

'You're trying to find out who killed Jibrilu?' a young man of South Asian appearance asked in a broad Yorkshire accent.

'Yes, that's right. Do you know if he'd fallen out with anyone at all?'

'No, I don't think so.'

'There was that guy on his staircase,' another of the group suggested, his voice betraying his Black Country origins. 'Jibrilu had words with him about bringing girls back to his room at all hours. I told Jib to lighten up. He didn't understand how things are here, did he Abdullah?'

'Yes,' agreed a third man, his grin showing teeth that seemed very white against his dark lips, 'he was shocked at the amount of female skin on show in college, wasn't he Mohammed?'

'His dad had been at Lichfield years ago, when it was a men-only college,' agreed the first man, smiling broadly, 'I don't think he realised there would be women there too now!'

'And do you know the name of the man he quarrelled with?' Andy asked.

'No.' Mohammed shook his head. 'What about you, Hassan? You said you knew him.'

'You bet I knew him!' his friend nodded. 'He was my tutorial partner.'

'And his name?' Andy asked mildly.

'Piers Addison,' Hassan answered promptly. 'We're both in our final year, doing PPE[4]. Piers is a white South African, which is why he was put on the staircase with Jibrilu. For whatever reason, the college seems to think it's a good idea to stick all the overseas students together.'

'But you're not so sure about mixing white South Africans and black Nigerians?' suggested Andy.

---

[4] Politics, Philosophy and Economics, also known as "Modern Greats", is a popular subject for would-be members of Parliament.

'Well, maybe some white South Africans are OK,' Hassan smiled back, 'but Piers! He father owns a gold mine or a diamond mine or something like that, and the way he talks, you'd think they owned all the workers too – black workers, of course! I don't think he could get his head round the idea of someone like Jibrilu criticising his behaviour.'

'No,' Abdullah broke in. 'It would've been like one of their servants answering back.'

'He was a racist?'

'He was a white South African – what do you think?' answered Mohammed scornfully.

'And he wasn't impressed by Jibrilu lecturing him on morality!' chuckled Hassan.

'Was he ever violent?'

'Not that I know of.' Hassan's grin vanished and his voice became suddenly serious. 'Are you asking me if he could've killed Jibrilu?'

'Maybe by mistake,' Andy said hastily. 'Did he ever carry a knife?'

'Is that how he was killed?' blurted out Mohammed.

'He did sustain a knife wound shortly before he died,' Andy confirmed, still looking towards Hassan. 'You knew this Piers. Did you ever see him carrying a knife?'

'Not carrying one,' Hassan said slowly, 'but he does own one. He has it hanging up in his room. He calls it his hunting knife. He has a whole collection of tall stories about how he used it to defend himself from being attacked by lions and how he butchered an antelope with it in the bush. Complete fiction, all of them, but they seem to impress the girls.'

'That and the way he flashes his money around,' Abdullah agreed.

'OK. Thanks. We'll be talking to all the students on Jibrilu's staircase as a matter of course, but it's useful to know that he didn't get on with this Piers. Now, is there anyone else that he'd crossed swords with since he arrived in Oxford?'

The three friends shook their heads in unison.

'I didn't really know him that well,' Mohammed told him. 'I only ever saw him at Friday prayers.'

'He kept himself to himself,' Hassan agreed. 'I sometimes bumped into him at breakfast – and here on a Friday, like Mohammed said – but mostly he stayed in his room or worked in the library.'

'We wouldn't know if he fell out with anyone else,' Abdullah agreed.

'OK. Well, thanks again.'

Returning to the open-plan office to catch up with his team, Andy found Jack Myers waiting to speak to him.

'Leon Black and Lee Hammond both have alibis for the time of the killing,' he told him at once. 'But that could well mean that they *were* involved in it. Their sort don't do the dirty work themselves – not now they've got plenty of other thugs under their thumbs to do it for them – and if they did give orders for your man to be taught a lesson they'd make sure they had a cast iron alibi so we couldn't pin it on them.'

Or it could be that they genuinely didn't have anything to do with it,' Andy pointed out. 'We still don't have anything that suggests Jibrilu Danjuma was involved in drug trafficking.'

'Except that he's recently arrived from Nigeria and so have large quantities of cocaine and cannabis,' Myers countered.

'And, of course, he's a young black man who's been knifed to death in the street, so this must be just another of those gang-related killings that happen to black youths all the time,' Andy replied with heavy irony.

'I'm sorry, no offence intended.' There was no hint of contrition in the officer's voice. He evidently thought that Andy was a black officer with a chip on his shoulder, probably only promoted to inspector rank to improve the racial balance of the police service. 'I know we're not supposed to say it, but we both know that nine times out of ten, it *is* drugs and gangs that are at the bottom of street killings – especially when it involves knives and young black men. Anyway, that's all I've got for you so far. I'll carry on looking into both gangs and get back to you if we come up with anything.'

'Thanks,' Andy murmured absently, waving his hand to indicate that Myers was dismissed and turning to address his own team of officers. A quick glance round the room told him immediately that DS Williams was bursting with eagerness to share his discoveries.

'OK, Iestyn, let's kick off with you. Have you made any progress in finding possible suspects?'

Williams got up and walked out to the front of the room. 'I've been looking into the racist aspect of the crime,' he announced, glancing down at his notebook. 'I've found a couple of offenders with the right sort of profile. First up there's Kyle Bancroft, age twenty-four, unemployed, lives in New Hinksey with his mum, recently released after serving a six-month custodial for sending threatening tweets to two MPs.'

'Black MPs?' asked Andy.

'No,' Williams admitted. 'But he did call one of them a race traitor and threatened to kill her. His social media profile shows that he's a great admirer of Thomas Mair – you know, the guy who killed Jo Cox.'

'So, who were these two MPS?' Andy asked patiently. 'What makes you think that someone who threatened them might have attacked an unknown black man in the street?'

'Layla Moran and Anneliese Dodds,' Williams said, sounding slightly reluctant to give the names. 'As I said, he accused Ms Dodds of being a race traitor, which goes to show that he's racist.'

'And Layla Moran?'

'He said she was a pervert.' The sergeant's tone had now mutated from reluctant to sulky.

'Well, I wouldn't rule him out as a possible suspect,' Andy said, trying to give Williams the benefit of the doubt, 'but I can't help thinking that he doesn't have the psychological profile that we're looking for. He may be racist, but his targets seem to be women in positions of authority, rather than young black men at the university.'

'You should see some of his social media posts,' Williams argued. 'He doesn't just target women, and recently he's said some very vicious things about overseas students and ethnic minorities taking university places away from white kids. He's been reading posts from people who say that white working-class boys are the most disadvantaged at school, but universities are bending over backwards to admit more black students. He seems to think he'd have been able to go to Oxford University if he'd been black. Nothing to do with spending time in a young offenders' institute and then failing all his exams!'

'OK, we'll keep him on the radar,' Andy conceded. 'Jennifer! Can I leave you to trawl through his social media posts and see what you can find?'

'I've already done that,' Iestyn cut in eagerly. 'That's where I found my other likely lad. It's a Facebook friend that Bancroft does a lot of chatting with. Now he really is an extreme racist!'

'OK.' Andy turned to Jennifer Moorhouse again. 'Did you get that? Have a look at the social media accounts of both of those guys and their online associates and let me know if you find anything that might link them to Jibrilu Danjuma or either of the colleges that back on to Goose Lane.'

He looked round the room again and spotted Alice, sitting with her notebook lying on the desk in front of her. He caught her eye.

'How did you get on with tackling the students on Jibrilu's staircase?' he asked. 'Did you get a picture of what he was like?'

'I'm not sure, sir.' Alice picked up her notebook and flicked through it. 'There are five other students living on that staircase, all from overseas. Two of them were out when I went round and I haven't had time to go back to have another go yet.'

'OK. Tell us about the ones you did speak to.'

'The ground floor room next to the victim's is occupied by a German student called Volker Schmidt. He's near the end of a DPhil in chemistry, supervised by a Professor Graham Weldon. He said he didn't really know the victim because he'd only been there a few weeks.'

'Was he there last Monday evening?'

'I asked him about that. He said he was in his room working on his thesis all afternoon and evening. He didn't go to dinner in Hall; he got a pizza delivered.'

'To his room?' Williams queried.

'No. He had to fetch it from the porters' lodge. He said that was at about seven-thirty. He didn't notice anything unusual. The victim's door was closed and there was nobody hanging around outside. He didn't hear anything from the room either, but there's a bathroom between the two rooms, so he said he wouldn't, even if there had been something going on in there.'

'Does his room have a window on to Goose Lane?' Andy asked.

'No. His room faces on to the Fellows' Garden, and he had the window closed, so it's not surprising that he didn't see or hear any disturbance there may have been out in the Lane.'

'OK. Go on.'

'On the first floor, there are two female students: Esther Orugun and Marie-Claire Charbonneau. Esther was out. Marie-Claire said that she was working in the lab. Apparently, her project has a lot of practical work involved. Marie-Claire's room is directly above the victim's and has a window that overlooks Goose Lane. I asked her about last Monday evening and she couldn't remember anything special happening. She said there's often noise out in the lane at night, so she wouldn't notice if there was a disturbance. She went to dinner in Hall, as usual. She didn't notice anything unusual when she passed the victims room.'

Alice turned over the page of her notebook and looked up at Andy. He nodded to her to continue.

'On the second floor, we have Piers Addison and Muhammad Ghaffar,' she resumed. 'Piers has the room above Esther's and Muhammad's is above Marie-Claire. There was no reply when I knocked on Piers's door. Muhammad said he was probably sleeping off the drinks he had the night before. He's in the college rugby squad and they'd been celebrating their success in a match against Pembroke College. I was planning to go back later in the day, but ...'

'Not to worry,' Andy assured her. 'It's probably just as well, as it turns out. I want to interview Piers Addison myself. His name cropped up in conversation with a few of Jibrilu Danjuma's friends as someone he didn't see eye-to-eye with. We can go to see him together. Now, go on: what about the other student?'

'Muhammad Ghaffar is from Pakistan. He's in the second year of a postgraduate degree in Earth Sciences. Or at least, he should be. He was due to start in 2020, but he couldn't travel because of COVID, so he was supervised remotely for about eighteen months and only came to Oxford at the start of this term. His supervisor is ...,' Alice said, looking down at her notes, '... Dr Martin Rice.'

'Riess,' Andy corrected her. 'It's a German name. It's spelled *R-I-E-S-S* and pronounced *Rees*. I've met him. But sorry, I interrupted. Go on.'

'Muhammad was working late in the labs on Monday evening,' Alice continued. 'He didn't get back to college until after eleven at night. He remembered seeing light coming from under the victim's door as he passed it on the way upstairs. He was surprised because Jibrilu was usually an early-to-bed-early-to-rise sort of person.'

'That's interesting,' commented Andy. 'Was the light still on when the porter let us in on Wednesday morning?'

'I don't remember,' Alice admitted. 'It was daylight then, so I didn't notice.'

'Neither did I. I wonder if any of the forensics people who went over the room did? Or, come to that, anyone who was in Goose Lane between Monday night and Wednesday morning might have noticed the light on. Iestyn! Could you look into that for me? If the light was left on all that time, it's surprising no one has commented on it yet; and if it wasn't, someone must've been in and switched it off.'

'Right you are, boss. I'm on to it!' Williams grinned back, evidently pleased with this assignment, which would give him an opportunity to hob-nob with the crime scene investigators and perhaps glean some information before it was officially passed on to the police team.

'Muhammad said he'd spoken to the victim a few times, but he didn't really know him very well. Apparently, Dr Greenhalgh tried to push him into mentoring him, because they were both Muslims and Muhammad was further on in his course. I think he rather resented that, particularly since he hadn't been in Oxford for any longer than Jibrilu and he had a lot of lab work to catch up on, so he didn't want any distractions.'

Andy smiled to himself, recalling conversations with the Botany tutor several years earlier, when he and Jonah were investigating the untimely demise of the college bursar. It seemed that her well-meaning attempts at helping overseas students to overcome culture-shock and fit into Oxford life still had a habit of back-firing.

'And did he have any suggestions as to who might have wanted to harm Jibrilu?'

'No.' Alice shook her head. 'He thought it was much more likely to be some sort of random attack.'

'I see.' Andy thought for a moment or two. 'And did any of the students comment on relations between Jibrilu and Esther Orugun? She's the one person that we know of who had a genuine reason to be antagonistic towards Nigerian Muslims.'

'No.' Alice shook her head again. 'I didn't ask them outright, though, so I suppose it might be worth talking to them again.'

'OK.' Andy looked up at the clock on the wall. 'I think we'd better call it a day. 'Alice, we'll go together tomorrow morning and try to speak to Esther Orugun and Piers Addison. Everyone else, carry on with what I've asked you to do. And remember, we're still keeping an open mind about this case. It could be a random racially-motivated attack or it could be drug-related or it could be a more personal vendetta against the victim. So, be careful not to jump to conclusions or say anything that might imply that we know one way or another – is that clear?'

Back home that evening, Andy ate his mother's quiche Lorraine in silence, brooding on his lack of success that day. Officers from his team had diligently questioned dozens, if not hundreds, of students and staff at the two colleges without finding any eye-witnesses to the assault on Jibrilu or any convincing explanation for why it had happened.

The investigation wasn't getting anywhere! Both Myers and Williams seemed intent on pursuing lines of enquiry that, in

Andy's opinion, were based on false premises. He was becoming more and more convinced that this was a long way from being a routine knife crime, and that there was a good chance that the perpetrator was not a known offender. Should he assert his authority and insist that they concentrated their efforts on finding out more about the victim? But he was far from sure that he wanted to know everything there was to know about Jibrilu's family. In particular, he was worried about what might eventually be brought to light concerning the victim's father, Yakubu. He must persuade his mother to open up about her relationship with him all those years ago. What if ...?

'How's your murder case coming on?' The question caught him unawares and he mumbled back something vague about there being lots of different lines of enquiry.

'I spoke to Professor Danjuma again this morning,' he added.

'He's a professor now, is he?'

'Yes, and I rather get the impression that he was hoping that his son would follow in his footsteps. He told me he'd been looking forward to visiting him and going round to all his old Oxford haunts together. Now it's too late, and he can't even get a visa to come over to see his body.'

'I suppose he'll have other family he wants to bring with him,' his mother suggested.

'No. He doesn't have any. He told me they were all killed in a house fire when Jibrilu was a baby. He survived – Jibrilu that is – because someone threw him out of an upstairs window, but both of Professor Danjuma's wives and all of his children were killed.'

'Oh!' The news seemed to take her by surprise and knock her off her stride. 'That must have been ... How come Yakubu wasn't killed too?'

'He was away from home. He came back and found the house burnt to the ground and only the baby left, out of all of his family. That must be why he's so very upset at not being able to come right away to give him the last rites or whatever it is that Muslims do when someone dies.'

'Oh!' she said again. 'It must be very distressing for him.'

'So, that makes it even more important for me to find out who did it.' Andy sensed that his mother's defences were coming down and this might be the time to try to press her for more information. 'You can't remember anything from when you knew him – Professor Danjuma, I mean – that could …? It occurred to me that, it wasn't impossible that it was revenge for an old grudge against him.'

'That doesn't sound very likely to me!' Amanda Lepage retorted, getting up and collecting the plates together. 'It was forty-odd years ago. Who would bear grudge for that long? And, in answer to your question, no I don't remember anything. I told you: I hardly knew the man. I cleaned his room. We talked occasionally. That was the end of it.'

She carried the plates over to the sink and returned to the table with two bowls and a jug of custard.

'It's apple pie for pudding,' she told him. 'I used some of the apples that your friends gave us. You will remember to thank them for me, won't you?'

7. CONFLICT OF INTEREST?

Andy slept badly that night. He lay awake listening as Storm Arwen rattled the back gate and drove rain against his bedroom window. Although his mother had steadfastly refused to answer any of his questions and continued to maintain that Yakubu Danjuma had been no more than a passing acquaintance, he was tormented with the possibility that, not only was Yakubu's relationship with his mother of considerably greater importance than she was willing to admit, he might very well have a much more personal interest in Andy himself.

His mother had only ever confided to him the bare minimum of information about who his father had been. Of course, it had been necessary from an early age to provide him with some sort of explanation as to why his own appearance was so radically different from every other member of his extended family. She had told him that his father was from Africa and she had somehow managed to imply, without actually saying so, that he was no longer alive. The young Andrew had accepted his orphaned status without question, until a time came when he worked out that it was odd that he and his mother shared the same last name with her own parents, his grandparents. Didn't children and their mother usually have their father's name?

That prompted his mother's admission that she had never been married to Andy's father and that, rather than dying, he had deserted them and returned to his home in Nigeria.

'He never told me that he already had a wife,' she explained. 'In fact, he had two wives and a baby, which he only told me about when he was explaining why he had to go back to Africa. I never told him about you. We're better off without him.'

And that had been that. Amanda never volunteered any more information about Andy's father and Andy did not like to ask. Not that he was all that interested. He accepted her version of events unreservedly. If she said they were better off without this man who had left her to care for him alone, then he had no desire ever to meet him or know more about him.

It was his grandmother, who gradually filled in a few of the gaps. When Amanda took up a degree course with the Open University, while still attempting to juggle a full-time job and childcare, "Nana" played an increasingly large role in young Andy's life, collecting him from school each afternoon and often entertaining him at the weekend as well. From her, he learned that his mother had fallen pregnant when she was a student in her first year of a degree that she never managed to finish. That was why she was spending so much time studying now. Her boyfriend had been a student too, but much, much older than her. He had swept her off her feet with declarations of love and promises of a life together, and then gone home to his two wives without a care in the world.

Neither Mum nor Nana had ever mentioned his name. But how many Nigerian students could there have been who completed their studies in 1983? And Yakubu Danjuma had asked after his mother by name. And Mum hadn't denied knowing him; she was just trying to play down the extent of their relationship.

Andy rolled out of bed and made his bleary-eyed way to the bathroom. It was a cold-shower day, he decided. He needed something to wake him up and get his mind moving properly. The water was truly freezing and he could not bear to stay under it for long, but he did emerge feeling a little more wide-awake. He quickly towelled himself dry and pulled on his clothes. Should he tell anyone in the police that he suspected that Yakubu Danjuma was his own father? If he did, he would most likely be taken off the case, because it would be a conflict of interest. Except that he was still not sure …

As he came downstairs, tugging the sleeves of his pullover so that they aligned neatly with the cuffs of his shirt, he made up his mind to confront his mother and ask her straight out whether Yakubu was his father. It was the only thing to do. He must know for sure. And then, if she confirmed his suspicions, he would have to go to Anna Davenport and ask her to take him off the case.

By the time he reached the hall, he had changed his mind. That was too confrontational. He would in effect be calling her a liar. No, he would simply ask her to tell him his father's name. She would be bound to realise why he was asking, but at least it wasn't quite such a blatant accusation.

Then he opened the kitchen door and saw her standing there at the table, pouring out a mug of coffee for each of them. She was dressed in the smart clothes that she wore to go to the good job that she had worked so hard to gain the qualifications for, so that she could support him to stay on at school and do his A' levels and then go to university himself. She had devoted her life to him, with no help apart from the childcare that Nana and Gramps had provided. He couldn't remember her ever going for an evening out with her friends – what friends? – never mind having a boyfriend. Why should she submit to having her life disrupted by the sudden reappearance of the man who had forced motherhood on her at age nineteen and then vanished from the scene?

She looked up and smiled. 'I made porridge. I thought you could do with something to keep the cold out while you're out and about.'

'Thanks.' Andy sat down and pulled his mug of coffee towards him.

Amanda tipped porridge from a pan into two bowls and then filled the pan with water, leaving it in the sink to soak. She brought the bowls over to the table and sat down opposite her son. 'I'll be late in this evening,' she told him. 'We've got this leaving do for one of the other subject librarians. Do you think you could pick yourself up a takeaway on your way home?'

'Of course. Or I could even cook for us, if I'm in in time. When are you expecting to be back?'

'I'm not sure. It depends whether I get dragged out to the pub afterwards. I wouldn't go normally, but Brian was very decent to me when I first came – he was my mentor, if you like. I wouldn't want him to think I didn't want to wish him well in his retirement. So, if you could just get something for yourself and I'll decide what I want when I get back. I may not be very hungry. They're promising us drinks and nibbles.'

'OK.' Andy sprinkled demerara sugar over his porridge. 'I was thinking overnight about Yakubu Danjuma.'

'What about him?' Amanda snapped back.

'Oh, nothing much.' Andy picked up his spoon and started eating his porridge. 'I was just thinking how odd it must be for him to be coming back here after all these years. He said he was hoping to look up some old acquaintances – his college tutor and that sort of thing.'

His mother ate her porridge in silence.

'He did talk about looking you up at the library. He found your name on the website.'

'I can't think why he would want to.' Amanda sipped her coffee. 'Anyway, I don't expect he'll have time for all that. He'll be busy sorting out his son's funeral and everything, won't he?'

'Not if that all happens before he gets here. It's his tradition for it to be as soon as possible, and he's still waiting for his visa.'

'In that case, it's hardly worth him coming at all, is it?'

'He wants to see where his son was killed.' Andy paused and ate another spoonful of porridge. 'And he'll want to see me – to hear how the investigation is coming on. He'll be looking to me to give him answers to why his son was killed. And … I think he wants to meet me because …'

'Because what?'

'Because you're my mother.'

'Have you told him that? I thought you said you told him you didn't know any Amanda Lepage?'

'I did, but … I don't think he believes me. Not after finding your name on the library website, with me having let slip that was where you worked.'

'Well, I can't sit here all day gossiping about some old man from Nigeria who's lost his son.' Amanda got to her feet and picked up her coffee mug. I'll take this into the lounge. I need to check my emails before I go out.'

Various administrative tasks overtook Andy when he got to work and it was not until after lunch that he and Alice arrived at Lichfield College to seek out the two remaining residents of the Hall Staircase. There was no reply when they knocked on the door of Esther Orugun's room. Her next-door-neighbour was out too. Alice shrugged her shoulders and began the ascent to the next floor.

The door of Addison's room was ajar and they could hear voices inside. Alice knocked briskly on the wood with her knuckles. The voices fell silent. After a few seconds, there were footsteps and then the door was pulled fully open by a young man in expensively casual trousers and sweater. He stood there with a glass in one hand and the other on the edge of the door. He smiled at Alice as he looked her up and down.

'And what brings you here?' he asked in a self-satisfied purr.

'Detective constable Alice Ray,' she replied smartly, holding up her warrant card. 'And this is Detective Inspector Lepage.'

Andy stepped forward and presented his own identification. 'Piers Addison?'

'Yes. Why do you want to know?'

'We're investigating the death of one of your neighbours, Mr Jibrilu Danjuma. We need to ask you some questions. May we come in?'

'Be my guest.' Piers stepped aside, waving them through the doorway with an elaborate arm gesture. 'And let me introduce you to my friends: Victor Lansdown.' He pointed to another fashionably-attired young man lounging on a well-worn sofa. 'And Hugo Dewar.'

The third member of the group was a surprise. As his friend named him, he rose from his armchair to reveal that he was clad in full highland dress: kilt, sporran, tartan tie and tweed jacket. It seemed incongruous when the young man greeted them in the accent of an English Public School rather than the broad Scots that his costume had led Andy to expect.

'Good afternoon, officer. And how may we be of service?'

'Are you all members of Lichfield College?' Andy asked.

'No,' Piers told him. 'Hugo and Victor are both at Holy Cross.'

'All living in college?' Andy looked round at each of them in turn. They all nodded.

'Do you ever use the back entrance – the one that opens on to Goose Lane?'

'Sometimes,' Hugo answered. 'Our rooms are in Al Qahtani quad, so it's quicker than going past the porters' lodge.'

'Did either of you happen to be in Goose Lane at all on Monday afternoon or evening?'

'Monday? Let me think.' Hugo sat back down in the armchair and picked up a glass from a small table in the middle of the room. A bottle of single malt whisky stood next to it. Andy got the impression that he was deliberately taking his time to annoy him. 'I had an essay to write for my Tuesday tutorial. I took lunch in Hall and then worked in my room for a bit and then – yes! I went out to look something up in the Bod. I got back about six and went back to my room.'

'Through the Goose Lane entrance?' Alice asked, looking up from her notebook.

'Yes – no! I came back through the main entrance so I could check my pigeonhole on the way.'

'So, you wouldn't have seen if there was any sort of disturbance going on in Goose Lane?' Andy asked.

'No. Sorry!' The young man grinned up at him and took a sip of his whisky.

'What about you?' Andy looked towards Victor.

'I went home for the weekend,' the student replied, leaning back on the sofa, and stretching out long legs in front of him. 'It was my mother's birthday on Sunday and Pa summoned us all back for a family weekend together. Rather a bore, having to be polite to ancient aunts and uncles and trying to remember the names of all one's nephews and nieces and all that. But that's family, isn't it? I bet *you* have some fun times when you all get together! Playing reggae music and drinking rum! That's more my kind of party, if I'm honest but-'

'What time on Monday did you get back to Oxford?' Andy cut in curtly, trying not to laugh at the thought of his mother and aunts dancing to reggae music.

'That's just it,' the young man smiled back. 'I didn't. I slept late on Monday morning and by the time I was up I'd already missed my morning lecture, so it didn't seem worth making the effort to get back. I got the early train on Tuesday. By the time I got to college, your lot were already there taping off the Goose Lane entrance and sending everyone round to the front.'

'I see.'

'So, I'm afraid I can't throw any light on who killed old Jib,' Victor went on, 'but at least you know it couldn't have been me. Good old mater and her birthday party have their uses after all!' He gave a little laugh and, putting his hands behind his head, leaned even further back on the sofa.

'You knew Jibrilu then?' Andy asked sharply.

'Not exactly *knew*, but I passed him on the stairs a few times and, of course, I heard all about him from Piers.' Victor smiled complacently up at Andy from his semi-prone position.

'What exactly did Piers tell you about him?' Andy was liking this young man less and less with every supercilious sentence that he uttered.

'Oh! Just what a monumental bore he was! And what a prig! Always criticising us for making a noise on the staircase. He went bananas when we had a party in Piers's room – didn't he Piers?'

'Yes,' Piers agreed. 'And he used to lecture me about having girls in my room. He said my behaviour was immoral. Talk about double-standards! I've seen him gawping at female students, trying to see up their skirts and down their tops. I reckon he was just jealous none of them fancied him!'

'It's about time the university stopped taking these international students from third world countries,' Hugo pontificated. 'They don't fit in here and they drain talent from their own countries. The idea is that they're going to go back and be doctors and teachers and political leaders helping their own people, but how many of them actually do go back in the end? How many of them ever have any intention of going back? They're just looking for a better life over here.'

'Jibrilu's father was an international student who went back,' Andy said quietly. Then, turning back to Victor, he asked more forcefully, 'just for the record, I'd like your home address and telephone number, in case we need confirmation of your whereabouts on Monday.'

'Are you accusing me of lying?' the young man demanded angrily.

'No, sir. It's just a matter of routine, to save time later if …'

'Well, I think it's a ruddy cheek!' Hugo protested. 'We're not criminals. Why are you treating him like one?'

'I told you: it's a matter of routine. We're asking all the students – and the staff – in both colleges, where they were and whether they saw anything. It's a very serious matter. A man has been killed.'

Alice held out her notebook towards Victor, who took it and scribbled a few lines before handing it back. She nodded to Andy to indicate that he had supplied the requested information. He nodded back and then turned to address Piers.

'Mr Addison, were you in your room on Monday afternoon or evening?'

'Yes, I believe I was. I went to the gym after lunch – got to keep the old body in trim for the ladies!' He treated Alice to a smile which she studiously ignored. 'On the way back, I stopped off to pick up some supplies: I was right out of whisky *and* brandy. You know how it is when you have friends round at the weekend. Well, no you probably don't,' he added with a smirk that indicated his doubt that Andy had any friends or at least not the sort who would consume quantities of the best Napoleon brandy. 'And by the time I got back it was almost time to dress for dinner. I was booked in for Formal Hall. The food is so much better than the buffet they serve at six, and you don't get so many of the "widening participation" students. I know we ought to make allowances for them, but it's an awful bore.'

'Some of them are quite aggressive,' Hugo added. 'Going on about privilege and lack of opportunity, as if they hadn't been given places on summer schools and reduced A' level requirements and all sort of advantages to justify letting them come here ahead of people from good schools.'

'They don't fit in,' Hugo agreed. 'The ones who come from grammar schools are OK, but some of the others can't even speak English properly! I heard one of them asking for "one of them sandwiches" at lunch the other day!'

'Sssh Hugo! I expect the inspector here went to a comprehensive.' Piers smiled towards Andy. 'I must apologise for my friend. He can be so insensitive at times.'

'You were telling me about Monday night,' Andy said evenly. He had, indeed attended a comprehensive secondary school from which he had gone on to achieve a first class honours degree in criminology. 'Your window looks out on to Goose Lane. Did you happen to glance out at all while you were dressing for dinner?'

'Not that I recall. I will have had the curtains drawn by then. I always close them when it gets dark. It helps to keep the draughts out.'

'And you didn't hear any disturbance going on out there?'

'I don't think s- oh! Yes, I suppose it probably was Monday night. Or it could've been Sunday … or … no, I think it was definitely Monday between six and seven.'

'Something happened?'

'It was probably nothing, but there was some shouting. I thought it was coming from inside, but it could've been out in the lane. I thought it was Jib sounding off about something, the way he often did: telling some girl her blouse was too tight or her skirt was too short or complaining that someone was talking too loudly on the stairs and disturbing his work.'

'He always thought he knew better than anyone else,' Hugo put in. 'Ruddy cheek! Coming over here and lecturing us on how to behave.'

'Too right!' Victor agreed. 'I've lived in Nigeria. My father's an oil executive and he spends a lot of time out there. Everyone's on the fiddle and the only way to get anything done over there is to bribe every official you come across. And even then, if the bribe isn't as much as the other side …! I wonder how much he had to put up to get his state-funded scholarship to come here.'

'You were telling us about some noise that you heard on Monday evening,' Andy reminded Piers. 'I gather there were raised voices. Did you hear anything that was said?'

'No. Like I said, I thought it was just Jibrilu shouting at someone for doing something he disapproved of. He may have said, "stop that!" or something like that, or that may just be my imagination.'

'I see. Thank you.' Andy looked round at the three students. 'Now, can any of you think of any reason why someone might want to hurt Mr Danjuma or to kill him?'

They shook their heads in unison.

'I hardly knew this guy,' Hugo declared.

'Me neither,' chimed in Victor.

'I wouldn't have been sorry if he'd moved out of college or on to a different staircase,' Piers admitted, 'but I'm not daft enough to want him dead. And I can't think why anyone else would either. He was a pain in the you-know-what, but not worth killing over.'

In accordance with his mother's instructions, Andy bought a curry on the way home and sat eating it in the lounge while watching the television news. He was glad that "his" murder had not been sensational enough to reach the national media. The Oxford Mail and local radio stations were quite enough for him to contend with. What if they were to get to hear that the victim was his half-brother? His half-brother! He hadn't thought about Jibrilu like that before – not even when he was contemplating the likelihood that Yakubu Danjuma was his father.

He must decide what to do about declaring this potential conflict of interest. Was it time that he revealed his suspicions to his superiors? But what if his mother's story *was* true and, unlikely though it seemed, Yakubu was just a chance acquaintance? It wasn't impossible that there were two postgraduate students from Nigeria that year and that she had met them both. Perhaps Yakubu had introduced her to his real father. That would explain the apparent coincidence. And Mum might be reluctant to renew their acquaintance in case Yakubu told him and he came over to find the son he did not know that he had.

What was absolutely crystal clear was that Mum did not want Andy's father to know about his existence. Was she afraid that he would try in some way to steal her son away from her? It was a ridiculous idea, but …

He needed some advice, but who was there who would understand his predicament? All those reality TV shows in which people sought out their birth families seemed to end in joyful reunions with long-lost parents and siblings. Was it really always like that? Surely there must be instances where it turned out that the mother whose baby had been taken into care really was the violent drug addict that social services had considered to be an unfit parent? And siblings who resented a new adult brother or sister being welcomed into their family? And spouses who felt betrayed to discover that their partner had children that they had never spoken about?

Peter! Andy suddenly remembered. His old boss, DI Peter Johns, had actually had a similar experience[5]. How could he have forgotten about that? What exactly was it that had happened to him? He'd been brought up in a children's home, back in the days when they still had those big homes for orphans and children whose parents couldn't support them. And then years later, when he was middle-aged and recently re-married following the death of

---

[5] See Peter's own account in his short story, *Mixed Feelings*, incorporated into his collected memoirs, *My Life of Crime* ISBN: 978-1-911083-20-7

his first wife, his mother had suddenly turned up from nowhere. Andy was still a PC back then, but he remembered the desk sergeant remarking about a strange woman having turned up asking for her brother, DI Johns, and Peter at first denying that he had a sister.

Yes, Peter was about the only person who would understand where he was coming from. And he had been married to a black woman and had two mixed-race children, so he would even have an inkling of what it was like to be treated differently from everyone else in your family. He reached for his phone and scrolled through his contacts, only remembering to turn off the TV set when the ringing tone was drowned out by music as the news bulletin ended.

'Andy?' Peter's voice sounded anxious, but perhaps it was just surprise at getting a call from his old colleague so long after his retirement.

'Hi Peter. Do you have time to talk?'

'Sure. Go ahead. I'll just go somewhere a bit quieter. I've got the grandkids over.' There were some odd bangs and crackles and then, indistinctly, 'Be a good boy Ricky and stay with Aunty Bernie while I go in the kitchen for a bit. I won't be long. You carry on building your castle and I'll have look at it later.'

Andy could hear a shrill voice protesting and then soft footsteps followed by a door closing.

'Sorry about that,' Peter apologised. 'Ricky is still having trouble accepting that grownups sometimes have things to do other than entertaining him and listening to his stories. Now, what was it you wanted to talk about?'

'Well, I need some advice,' Andy began.

'Yes?' Peter prompted as Andy's voice tailed off.

'It's like this,' Andy started again. 'It's … you know this murder case I'm leading on?'

'Yes?'

'The victim is a postgraduate student from Nigeria …'

'Yes, Jonah told me.'

'And …,' Andy continued to hesitate. It was difficult to know how to explain his problem without implying that his mother had lied to him or at least been economic with the truth. 'Well, I told you my Dad was Nigerian, didn't I? He was a postgrad too, just like the guy who was killed in Goose Lane. I was wondering … Well, I was thinking maybe it's a conflict of interest. I mean, I'm not sure yet, but if he *is* … well it does seem a bit of a-'

'How was your day?' Andy looked up to see Amanda standing in the doorway with her coat half off, smiling towards him.

'Sorry, Peter, I've got to go. Hi Mum. How was the leaving do?'

Peter stood staring at the phone, wondering what the call had been all about. He knew that Andy's father had left the scene long before he was born and that, having felt resentment towards this unknown parent for many years, he had come to accept that there was no point wasting energy on being angry with someone whom he would never meet. Why had investigating the death of a student who just happened to have come from the same country as his estranged father had such a powerful effect on him? And what did he mean by a conflict of interest?

He put the phone away and went back to the lounge. As he closed the door behind him, Bernie looked up from the floor, where she was sitting cross-legged, helping Peter's five-year-old grandson to build a castle from Lego bricks.

'What did Andy want?'

'I don't know. He said something about a conflict of interest and about his father being from Nigeria, and then he rang off suddenly. I didn't get it at all.'

'Did he tell you anything about the case?' Jonah asked eagerly, spinning his wheelchair round to face Peter and making little

Abigail, who was sitting on his lap listening to a story, giggle with delight.

'No. Or at least, only that the victim was Nigerian, but we knew that already. I really didn't get it all – except that he seemed worried about something. And if it's to do with his work, why ring me? I've been retired for so long. Jonah's a lot more in-touch than I am these days.'

'Why not invite him to tea this weekend?' suggested Bernie. 'It's ages since he's been. It'd be nice to catch up with him and if he's got something on his mind, it'll give him an opportunity to tell you what it is.'

'Good idea,' agreed Jonah eagerly. 'And if he's worried about this murder case he's investigating, I'll be happy to give him the benefit of my experience.'

'I bet you will!' Bernie grinned. 'OK. I'll give him a ring later and invite him to come round on Sunday afternoon. He can help us eat up our glut of apples and pumpkins!'

8. DAY OF REST

As Peter, Bernie and Jonah entered St Cyprian's church on Sunday morning, they were greeted by strains of Bach coming from the tiny pipe organ. This was a surprise. It was unusual to have live music at this first mass of the day, which catered for a small congregation, mainly comprising elderly folk who continued to observe the old-school rule of fasting from midnight until they received the sacrament.

'Who's the lad at the organ?' whispered Jonah to Bernie, as they took their places near the front, where a pew had been shortened to make space at the end for Jonah's wheelchair.

'I don't know,' Bernie whispered back. She stared towards the organ console where a dark-skinned boy in his early teens sat playing with an expression of deep concentration on his face. Then her eyes moved to the far end of the front pew, where two more strangers were sitting. 'I think those are probably his parents,' she added, with a slight jerk of her head in their direction.

Jonah gazed across at the couple: a tall man in a dark suit and a woman in a coat buttoned to her chin, her hair concealed within a brightly-coloured turban-like headdress that towered above her making her appear even taller than her husband. He studied them for a few seconds before turning his head towards Peter, who was standing a few feet away gazing up with rapt attention at a statue of the Virgin Mary. He crossed himself clumsily, gave a brief head bow and came across to join his wife.

'Any idea who the organist is?' Jonah asked him, as he squeezed past to take his seat next to Bernie.

'I think I've seen them at the eleven o'clock Mass,' he murmured back. 'I have a feeling Father Damien said she works at the university, but I may be wrong about that.'

'The boy certainly knows how to play,' Bernie observed. 'It makes a nice change from Father Damien's collection of CDs!'

'He certainly does!' Jonah agreed. 'That piece isn't an easy one, either.'

The tune ended with a final flourish and there was silence for a few moments while the boy replaced the sheet music with a well-worn book that was lying on the bench beside him. They waited as he carefully positioned his hands on the manual and began to play the haunting tune *O come, o come, Emmanuel*.

A few minutes later, Father Damien appeared from the vestry and took his place at the front of the church. The boy at the organ looked up and fumbled his way to a slightly jerky cadence. As the organ fell silent, he looked anxiously towards his mother who gave him a reassuring nod. Damien smiled in his direction and waited to give him time to slip off the organ bench and join his parents on the front pew, before greeting the congregation by proclaiming, 'In the name of the Father, and of the Son and of the Holy Spirit!'

When the time came to distribute the bread, the boy and his parents came forward first. As soon as he had received the wafer on his tongue the boy hurried back to the organ and began adjusting the stops. His mother, following at a more dignified pace, took up a position at the front of the empty choir stalls, adjacent to the organ. As the boy began to play, she sang, softly at first then rising in a gentle crescendo,

Let all mortal flesh keep silence,
and with fear and trembling stand;
ponder nothing earthly-minded,
for with blessing in his hand

Christ our God to earth descendeth,
our full homage to demand.'

At the end of the service, Father Damien introduced them to the young musician.

'I don't think you've met Gabriel Sibanda before,' he said as the worshippers gathered in the open air to say their goodbyes. Vaccination had made the threat of COVID-19 seem less important, but it was still considered prudent not to congregate indoors. 'He usually comes to the later service, but I persuaded him to play this morning, and he asked to do a trial run at the early service as a sort of dress rehearsal. Poor Veronica had a fall yesterday and broke her wrist, so she won't be able to play for a few months. We're very lucky to have such an accomplished organist able to step into the breach.'

'Poor Veronica,' Peter exclaimed. 'How did it happen?'

'She slipped on fallen leaves in her garden. It was lucky it was only her wrist that was broken and she managed to get herself up and back to the house. At her age, it could easily have been a lot worse. She rang me the moment she got back from the hospital, very concerned about letting us down.'

'It's good that you've got some young blood coming along to take on her mantle,' Jonah said. 'I'm very impressed,' he added, looking up at Gabriel, who gave an embarrassed smile in return. 'Those Bach fugues are real virtuoso stuff. You certainly don't believe in playing things safe!'

'I'm afraid I have to take responsibility for that,' the boy's mother smiled, evidently very pleased at Jonah's remarks. 'I put him up to it. Bach is a passion of mine. I can't help thinking that his music is what organs were invented for.'

'This is Dr Precious Sibanda,' Damien added. 'She's a tutor at Holy Cross College. And Gabriel's father, Moses, is a journalist.' He turned to address the Sibanda family, 'and these are my old friends Bernie, Peter and Jonah. They all keep me on my toes by criticising my homilies and asking difficult questions!'

'Enquiring minds!' Precious smiled round at them. 'That's what I try to cultivate in my students.'

'We're very proud of Gabriel,' his father added. 'He's been learning the piano since he was four, but he only branched out into the organ when we moved to Oxford two years ago.'

'The Music tutor at Holy Cross is an organist,' Precious chipped in, 'and he very kindly agreed to teach Gabriel. The college has got an excellent organ,' she added, looking down at Jonah. 'If you like Bach, you should come to one of his recitals. I can give you a copy of the chapel Term Card, if you like, which has them all on it.'

'That's very kind of you,' Jonah smiled back, 'and speaking of Holy Cross College, what do you make of the incident in Goose Lane last week? Were you there on Monday evening?'

'No. I was working in the science area all afternoon and went straight home from there. I only heard about it the next day.'

'Gabriel was there,' her husband interjected. 'He had an organ lesson after school.'

'Really?' Jonah looked towards the boy with renewed interest.

'Yes, and he left his music case behind, didn't you Gabriel?' his father went on, his tone expressing both amusement and annoyance, 'I don't know! You'd forget your own head if it wasn't screwed on!'

'Did you really?' Jonah studied the boy's face carefully. Gabriel caught his eye briefly and then turned away in confusion. 'Are you sure you didn't drop it? The police found a music case in Goose Lane – kicked into a corner under a pile of leaves. And there was some sheet music scattered around too.'

'Gabriel?' his mother asked, her tone a mixture of anxiety and sternness.

'I – I – I –,' the boy stammered, looking round at the faces that surrounded him all waiting for his answer. 'I didn't drop it. They took it from me. I tried to stop them!'

'Who?' his father demanded. 'What are you talking about? Who took your case?'

'Just some people. They were standing outside the chapel when I was going home. I asked them to let me past, but they wouldn't. So, I said I'd go round the other way, but then they grabbed my case and they wouldn't give it back. They said I must have stolen it.'

'What!' Moses exploded. 'They accused you of stealing your own property? Who were these people?'

'I don't know! I'd never seen them before.'

'Well then, what did they look like?' his father demanded. 'Why didn't you tell us about this before?'

'I don't know,' Gabriel insisted miserably. 'I don't remember. I just wanted to get away.'

'But this is robbery,' Moses insisted. 'The police must be informed.'

'And the college – if they were students,' Precious added. 'Your father's right – you should have told us about it.'

'They said they were going to hand it in at the porters' lodge,' Gabriel pleaded. 'They said it couldn't be mine and I must have stolen it.'

'What business did they have accusing you like that? Who are these people?' his father's voice rose in indignation.

'I don't know!' Gabriel was looking increasingly uncomfortable. 'I told you. I'd never seen them before.'

'Your parents are right,' Jonah said calmly in the short pause that followed as they all drew breath. 'The police need to be told about this. I can do that for you, if you like. It just so happens that we're meeting the Senior Investigating Officer this afternoon.'

'What do you mean – Senior Investigating Officer?' asked Moses.

'The inspector in charge of investigating the death of the young man in Goose Lane last week. He's a friend of ours.'

'Jonah used to be a police officer himself,' Father Damien explained, 'and so did Peter.'

'Are you suggesting that these people who took Gabriel's music case went on to kill that young man?' Precious asked in a shocked voice.

'Not necessarily.' Jonah, by contrast seemed to be enjoying himself. 'However, it would be a bit of a coincidence if the two incidents are totally unrelated. How likely is it that a black youngster is harassed and has his property stolen and then a few minutes later another young black man is killed only a few yards away, and there's no connection between the two assaults?'

'So, these people might have killed my Gabriel?' The boy's mother stared at Jonah wide-eyed with horror.

'He did the right thing, running away,' Jonah told her. 'But it's a pity he didn't report the whole thing to the police as soon as he reached a place of safety. He'll need to be interviewed a-'

'But not here and now,' Father Damien interjected. 'This isn't the time or the place.'

'Absolutely, Father,' Peter agreed firmly, giving Jonah a warning look. 'You'll have to forgive our friend,' he added, smiling apologetically towards the Sibandas, 'he keeps forgetting that he's retired now.'

'I'll speak to DI Lepage this afternoon,' Jonah promised, unabashed, 'and with your permission, I'll give him your contact details so that he can call and take a statement from Gabriel.'

'Don't be nervous,' Peter added, seeing the consternation on the boy's face. 'I'm sure you'll like Andy Lepage. He's very kind. And he won't be cross with you for not going to the police right away. Victims often don't report crimes until some time afterwards.'

'Victims? Crimes?' Precious picked up on the words and stared at Peter. 'You're saying my son is the victim of a crime?'

'Of course, he is!' her husband cut in. 'Robbery and intimidation – isn't that right?' He looked towards Peter for confirmation.

'Yes,' Peter nodded, 'possibly racially-aggravated. Serious offences, but luckily Gabriel got away safely.'

'Unlike Jibrilu Danjuma,' Bernie added grimly.

'Which is why we need you to tell us all you can remember about the people who took your music case,' Jonah put in quickly.

'*When* DI Lepage gets in touch,' Peter added firmly. 'And now, we really have to go. It was nice meeting you. And you played the organ brilliantly.'

Andy was, indeed, interested to hear the story of Gabriel's encounter at the Goose Lane entrance to Holy Cross College. 'Did he say what time it was?' he asked eagerly as he sat at the big kitchen table watching Peter ladle out helpings of his home-made spicy pumpkin soup.

'No,' Jonah answered regretfully. 'Peter spirited us away before I could ask for any details. His father just said "after school" so I suppose he could have got to the college any time from about four o'clock onwards.'

'The incident happened after his organ lesson,' Bernie put in, 'so that would probably mean after five, if you assume the lesson would have been at least an hour.'

'This term card that Precious Sibanda emailed to me says that there's a short service in the chapel at seven,' Jonah added, 'so the lesson must have finished before then.'

'And that must have been about the time that Doug Finney stumbled over the dead man in the lane,' Andy said excitedly. 'Your Gabriel must have been there just before he was killed.'

'And so were those bullies who stole his music case,' Jonah pointed out. 'You need to find them. It they're not the killers, they must be the closest you've got to eye witnesses.'

'And if they're innocent, why haven't they come forward?' asked Bernie. 'Gabriel said they were hanging around *inside* the college, which means they're most likely either students or staff.'

'I've met a couple of Holy Cross students that I wouldn't be surprised to hear had behaved the way you described,' Andy murmured through a mouthful of crusty bread, 'and they're best mates with a guy on Jibrilu Danjuma's staircase. Anyway, thanks for the tip-off. I'll ring the Sibandas tomorrow and arrange to go round and speak to Gabriel. I wonder why he didn't tell his parents about the incident.'

'Afraid they'd make a fuss,' Peter answered confidently. 'My kids were the same. It wasn't until years afterwards that I discovered Eddie had been bullied at school. He kept quiet because he knew I'd go storming up there with accusations of racism, when he just wanted to keep a low profile and avoid trouble.'

'I suppose so,' Andy sounded unconvinced. 'I mean, you're right about things that happen at school. I never told my mum the half of what went on there when I was a kid. But this was different. It was a criminal offence – robbery and assault! Why didn't he … hang on a minute!' Andy stopped speaking and gazed towards the ceiling in thought. 'What was it that Sergeant Duffield said about catching a black youth running away from the direction of the crime scene?'

'What?' Jonah shouted out. 'You didn't tell me about that?'

'I didn't think it was relevant. I thought it was just Duffield trying to get in on the action – to make himself important. I'm afraid I more or less ignored it. But it all fits. In fact, I'm sure of it now. He even had the name right – Gabriel. He made fun of it. He thought it was a girl's name!'

'So, what exactly did he tell you?' demanded Jonah impatiently.

'He said that he and a PCSO ran into Gabriel in the High. He was running full-pelt and Duffield thought he looked suspicious.'

'Knowing Duffield, I think you can be pretty sure all that means is that he was young, male and black,' Peter observed darkly.

'So, he searched him.'

'Searched him?' Bernie exclaimed indignantly. 'He was a thirteen-year-old boy for goodness' sake! What did he want to search him for?'

'He described him to me as older than that,' Andy told her. 'Whether he really believed it or just thought it wouldn't sound good to be searching a minor – especially since he didn't follow the proper procedures.'

'Oh?' Peter pounced on this information.

'He didn't make any record of it, for a start. When he didn't find anything, he just pretended it hadn't happened. I suppose he didn't want the bother of dealing with the paperwork.'

'Sounds like Duffield alright,' Peter muttered.

'So, I talked to the PCSO,' Andy resumed, 'in case she could give me more details – the exact time, the boy's full name, that sort of thing. It was obvious that she was uneasy about the whole business, but Duffield's a sergeant and very experienced, and she's quite a newbie I think. So, she didn't like to make a fuss. I really took my eye off the ball with that one,' he added regretfully. 'And with the music tutor too! If I hadn't let that slip, he'd have told me about Gabriel's organ lesson and I'd have got the whole story by now!'

'Don't beat yourself up about it,' urged Peter. 'You can't do everything.'

'I could have got someone else to do it,' Andy pointed out. 'Iestyn Williams would've got hold of the tutor's home mobile number somehow or found someone who knew where he was or just kept on coming back to his room until he showed up. He's like a dog with a bone when you give him something like that to do.'

'Well, you know now,' Peter said encouragingly. 'And there's no reason to assume it'd have made any difference if you'd heard Gabriel's story earlier. You've got two good leads to follow up and you're still less than a week into the investigation. You're doing fine.'

Bernie gathered the soup bowls and stacked them next to the sink, while Peter fetched a sponge flan from the larder. He had made it that morning using pears from the garden. He served portions to everyone and Bernie passed round jugs of custard and cream. Once everyone was settled with their dessert in front of them, Peter looked at Andy.

'Now, when are you going to tell us what it was you were phoning about yesterday?' he asked.

Andy sighed and put down his spoon.

'Like I said, I'm afraid I may have a conflict of interest, and I don't know whether I ought to tell anyone about it. But, if I'm wrong then I'll just be making a fuss about nothing, and Mum'll get upset that I'm off the case because of her, but she won't tell me one way or the other, which makes me think ...'

'But what exactly *is* this conflict of interest?' Peter asked as soon as there was a gap in Andy's rambling speech. 'You never actually said.'

'Didn't I? I thought I explained it all over the phone.' Andy paused and took a deep breath. 'I think Yakubu Danjuma is my father.'

There was a long silence while this unexpected announcement sank in.

'And I'm pretty sure he thinks so too,' Andy went on, 'but Mum insists they were just casual acquaintances, and she shuts me up every time I mention him.'

'I don't understand,' Bernie said. 'I thought this Yakubu Danjuma was in Nigeria. How did he ever even come to meet your mum?'

'He was a student here in Oxford back in the eighties,' Andy explained. 'A postgrad at Lichfield College, just like Jibrilu. He was following in his father's footsteps. I always knew that my biological father had been a student – a mature student with wives and kids back home, as it turned out – but Mum never told me his name or anything else about him.'

'So, what makes you think he was this Yakubu Danjuma?' asked Jonah. 'There could have been dozens of Nigerian doctoral students up at Oxford in the eighties.'

'That's what Mum keeps telling me, but she won't say what his name really was and she admits to knowing Yakubu. She just insists that all she ever did was to clean his room.'

'Clean his room?' echoed Bernie in puzzlement.

'She had a part time job while she was in the sixth form,' Andy explained. 'Assistant scout at Lichfield College. She claims that she met him then and that's how he knew her name. But why would he remember it after so long, if there wasn't more to it than that? On the other hand, my Nan told me Mum was a student when it happened; so maybe there was someone else who came along later – after she'd started at college. But the dates all fit: Yakubu Danjuma graduated in November 1983 and I was born in 1984.'

'Personally, I think you've already got a conflict of interest, regardless of whether or not this Yakubu is your father,' Bernie said forthrightly. 'Think about it: what does a conflict of interest mean? It's all about your judgement in the case being skewed because of your own personal involvement. It doesn't matter whether he *is* your father. So long as you think he could be, you're going to be subconsciously influenced by the fact that he *might* be.'

'And, even if you aren't actually influenced, a jury might be led to believe that you had been,' Peter chimed in. 'You can't afford to give the defence team any excuse to claim that the police investigation wasn't squeaky clean. My advice would be to tell Anna about it right away. And, to be honest, in her place, I'd take you off the case. You don't want to find the murderer and then have the prosecution case fall apart on a technicality!'

'Chance'd be a fine thing!' Andy muttered. 'I don't seem to be making any headway at all as far as finding the killer is concerned.'

'Then maybe it's time to hand it over to someone else,' Peter urged. 'A new pair of eyes may see something you've missed.'

'Hold on there, Peter!' Jonah objected. 'There's no need to rush into things. I don't see the problem,' he added, turning to Andy. 'You've made good progress as far as I can see. Five days ago, you didn't even know who the victim was. Now you've got half a dozen possible suspects and a new line of enquiry all ready to follow up tomorrow. It'd be a pity to let yourself be taken off the case just on the off-chance that you're personally involved. Why don't you go back to your mum and explain to her that you need to know your father's name?'

'Because I don't want to accuse her of lying to me!' Andy blurted out. 'Don't you see? She keeps saying that she hardly knew Yakubu. If I go telling her that I think he's my father, that's as good as calling her a liar!'

Andy heard the door click closed behind him as he set off for home that evening. He walked briskly, swinging his arms to keep warm. The air was chilly, but still not as cold as you might have expected for the tail end of November. Climate Change, he supposed.

He passed St Cyprian's church. It was in darkness, but there was a sliver of light coming out between the closed curtains of a window in the presbytery next door. Father Damien must be in. It was a big house for just one man living alone. Or did he have a live-in housekeeper, the way catholic priests were often depicted in television dramas? An older woman – a widow, perhaps – who would be above suspicion. But even so, there must be four bedrooms there – enough for a large family.

Not far now to the by-pass, and then only a short distance beyond to his own home. He paused at a side road to allow a car to turn out. Its headlights lit up the name. It was the road where the Sibanda family lived. He got out the piece of paper where Bernie had written down the details for him. Yes, he had remembered correctly. He hesitated for a few moments and then turned into the cul-de-sac of new houses, built on the gardens of older properties whose owners had cashed-in on the high price of building land in the Oxford area.

He counted the houses as he walked, more slowly now so as not to miss the one he was looking for. Number one was bright with fairy lights on the walls and an illuminated sleigh and reindeer on the front lawn. Next door, the blinds in the front room of number three were drawn back so that passers-by could see a Christmas tree in the window, bright with silver lights that twinkled, simulating the flickering of candle flames. But number five lay in darkness. It looked as if the Sibandas must be out.

As Andy walked up to the front door, a security light went on, bathing him in harsh white light. He pressed the bell and stood back to wait for a response that he was confident would not come. Sure enough, there was no reply. He turned round and headed back towards the main road and home. He would ring them first thing tomorrow and arrange an appointment.

9. CRIMINAL RECORD

"First thing tomorrow" was delayed until nearly nine o'clock by a deluge of emails that arrived overnight demanding Andy's attention. Sitting at his desk listening to the unanswered ringing tone, he reflected that, in all probability, the Sibandas had all left for work or school by now and it would be pointless attempting to contact them on their home landline until the evening.

He replaced the receiver and was startled when the phone immediately started ringing. It was Ruby with news on the forensic examination of the crime scene.

'We found a fingerprint on the litter bin,' she told him. 'It was just by where the victim's head was resting, so we thought it was worth running it through the database, just in case.'

'And?'

'We've got a match. A juvenile offender from a long while back – robbery and threatening behaviour. Nothing more recent, but that only means he got better at not being caught.'

'And the name?'

'Leroy Gilbert. Have you come across him?'

'No, I don't think so. I'll have a read of his record and then pay him a call. Thanks.'

'You're welcome!' Ruby replied cheerfully, as she rang off.

Andy turned to his computer and searched the database for Leroy Gilbert. Why did that name ring a bell? Had he perhaps apprehended him when he was a young PC patrolling the streets at night? He should have asked Ruby how long ago "a long while back" actually was. Did she mean ten years – or twenty? Ah! Here he was! Andy studied the photographs on his screen. They showed the head and shoulders of a black teenager, first from the front and then in profile from either side. They were dated 2005. No, Andy had only just begun his police training that year. He could not have been involved in detaining the youth.

He read on. The notes beneath the images stated that the offender was 16 years old and he had been arrested for participating in an attack on another teenager and stealing his mobile phone. He was subsequently found guilty in the magistrates' court, alongside three other lads. It looked as if he belonged to a gang operating in the Cowley Road area of the city.

Andy scrolled down to read more about the teenager. His last known address was also in the Cowley Road area. But that was sixteen years ago. It might not be easy to track him down after so long. And why was the name so familiar?

The door was opened by an elderly Afro-Caribbean woman with grey hair tied back in an austere bun. She looked out at them with enquiring eyes that became anxious when Andy and Alice held up their warrant cards.

'We're looking for Leroy Gilbert,' Andy told her. 'Does he still live here?'

'No.' Anxiety turned to bewilderment. 'He moved out years ago. What's all this about?' Her accent still held traces of her Jamaican origins not quite obliterated by more than sixty years in Oxford.

'We need to talk to him,' Andy explained, speaking as gently as he could. 'We think he may be able to help us with a case we're investigating.'

'What do you mean? What sort of case? Leroy hasn't been in trouble since he was a child.'

'And he isn't in trouble now,' Andy assured her earnestly. 'We just need to talk to him. Can you tell us where we can find him?'

'He's got a flat in the Windrush Tower,' the old woman told him. 'But he'll be at work now, I expect. Don't go round there. You'll frighten his kids.'

'We'll be very careful,' Alice put in. She was becoming impatient at the delay. The old woman looked innocent enough, but was all this a ploy to give the miscreant time to get away? They only had her word for it that he wasn't inside waiting for them to go away – or, by now, making his escape over the back wall into the alley that ran along behind the terraced houses. 'Just give us his address and we'll be out of your hair.'

'I don't know...,' the woman hesitated.

'Andy! Alice! What's going on? What are you doing here?' Both police officers swung round at the sound of a new, younger voice. It was PC Stella Gilbert, in her uniform, hurrying up the short path to reach them. 'Gran! What's all this about?'

'They've been asking after Leroy,' Celeste Gilbert answered her granddaughter. 'They want to speak to him about something.'

Stella turned to Andy and fixed him with a stare. 'What's happened? What do you want with Leroy?'

'We just want to talk to him, that's all,' Andy began.

'The SOCOs found his fingerprints at the scene where that Nigerian student was knifed,' Alice explained. 'We want to ask him what he was doing there.'

'He didn't have anything to do with that!' Stella's voice rose in indignation. 'He never carries a knife – never!'

'That's not what his record says,' Alice told her calmly.

'That was years ago! He'd never get involved in anything like that now. He's got Olivia and the girls to think about.'

'That's right,' Celeste agreed. 'Leroy got in with the wrong crowd when he was young and they led him astray, but he hasn't been in trouble once since he met Olivia.'

'If he was there last Monday afternoon, he may have seen something that would help us find out who did it,' Andy told them, trying to be conciliatory. 'Something that he didn't think anything of at the time, but which could be important. We only want to talk to him. Where can we find him?'

'OK,' Stella said grudgingly, 'I'll ring him – but only if you let me come with you to interview him.'

'Fair enough,' Andy nodded. 'Now, please?'

Stella took out her phone and scrolled through her contacts. After a brief conversation she ended the call and looked up at Andy.

'He's working now, but he's got a break for lunch at twelve thirty. I've arranged for us to meet him in Blackbird Leys Park. Could you pick me up here at twenty past? I need to get changed and have a bath and something to eat. It was a long night.'

'Yes. Of course. You go on in. We'll come back at twelve twenty.' Andy turned to speak to the older woman. 'And don't worry. We're not in the business of raking up the past. If your Leroy hasn't done anything illegal, he won't be getting any hassle from us.'

He turned and led the way back to the car.

'What do you think, sir?' Alice asked as soon as they were inside with the doors closed, safe from being overheard. 'Those two seem convinced this Leroy's a reformed character, but are they looking at him through rose-tinted spectacles? If he was in a gang, they could be putting pressure on him. It's not that easy to escape once you're in.'

'I don't know,' Andy sighed, staring out of the window at a house opposite. 'I'd like to think they're right about him. It's just such a coincidence, finding his fingerprint there! See that house over there?' he added, pointing across the road to another terrace of houses. 'The one with the loft extension? Peter Johns used to live there. Did you know Peter? Or was he before your time?'

'DI Peter Johns? Bernie's husband? No, I never met him, but Monica told me about him. She said he was a good boss to work for.'

'He was,' Andy agreed. 'Not so charismatic as DCI Porter, but not so demanding either. I sometimes wonder how Jonah got away with it. I think it was only because everyone knew that he was even harder on himself than on everyone else! But with Peter, you knew so long as you did your best, he'd back you to the hilt. The only times I ever remember him raising his voice was calling out racism. I remember now why *Leroy Gilbert* was such a familiar name. Peter told me he testified against the men who killed his first wife.'

'Killed?' Alice gasped. 'What happened?'

'It was in her own kitchen.' Andy pointed back across the road at the very ordinary-looking Victorian house, with its old-fashioned quarry tiled path leading to a smart new front door. The old sash windows had been replaced with modern double-glazing too and the walls were newly-pointed with fresh, clean mortar. 'Over there. They broke in through the back, and when she came in, they went berserk and stabbed her to death.'

'How dreadful! And did DI Johns find her there?'

'No. Bernie did.'

'Bernie?'

'They were friends. They'd arranged to go shopping together. Bernie called to collect her and …'

'How awful for her!' Alice sat in silence, while Andy started up the car and moved off. 'So where does Leroy Gilbert come in?' she asked at last.

'The gang that killed Angie Johns were mates of his. They were some of that "wrong crowd" that his gran talked about. He was with them when they broke in, but they left him outside on guard.

He didn't say anything for years, but in the end, he came clean and gave the names to the police and then he was a witness at their trial.'

'Where are they now?' asked Alice. 'Could they have put pressure on Leroy to go back to his old ways?'

'I don't know. I suppose it's possible. I don't know the details of their sentences, and it must be a good few years back, so maybe they'll be out of prison by now. And who knows what he'd do if someone threatened his kids?'

They reached a T-junction and Andy stopped the car to wait for the traffic to pass. Instinctively, Alice looked to the right, watching for a gap in the stream of cars heading towards the centre of Oxford. The road was clear now, but Andy still waited. His eyes were now directed to the left. When it was clear in both directions, he released the handbrake and pulled out, turning to the right.

'Where are we going?' Alice asked.

'Headington. I want to see Peter and ask his advice. He'll know how to handle Leroy.'

'It looks as if they're all in,' Andy said, as they walked up the drive to the front door of Bernie's house, pointing towards the specially-adapted people-carrier with the space in the back for Jonah to sit in his wheelchair and the smaller electric car that Peter and Bernie used as a run-about for shopping and other journeys without their friend. He walked up the ramp and pressed the bell-push firmly, hearing an answering buzz from inside. There was also a continuous hum going on, which Andy could not identify.

The door opened and Bernie looked out. The humming sound was louder now. 'Hello Andy! To what do we owe the pleasure?'

'I was hoping to speak to Peter,' Andy told her. 'Is he around?'

'He's just upstairs. Go on in and sit down in the living room, and I'll fetch him. He's only hoovering the bedrooms.'

Ah! That was the noise. Andy recognised it now. He led the way inside and turned to the left.

'Hang your coats up and then go on in,' Bernie said, pointing to a row of hooks attached to the wall, as she started up the stairs. 'I'll tell Peter you're here and then make us all a brew.'

They obediently took off their coats and put them on two of the hooks.

'It's that way,' Andy told Alice, pointing to an open door to the left of the stairs. Alice took a step towards it then stopped at the sound of a voice behind her.

'Hello, 'ello, 'ello! And what brings you two here?' It was Jonah, emerging on silent wheels from his own quarters at the front of the house. 'Have there been developments that I ought to know about?'

'Well, sort of. There has been a development, but it was Peter I was hoping to talk to about it.'

'Peter?' Jonah queried in a voice that somehow hinted at surprise that Andy might expect his friend to be of more assistance than he in the investigation.

'Did I hear you taking my name in vain?' Peter descended the stairs, followed closely by his wife. 'Hello Andy – and you must be Alice – what can I do for you?'

He ushered them into the lounge and they sat down in two of the elderly-looking armchairs that were positioned randomly about the room. Jonah followed them in and took up a position where he could watch both of their faces. Bernie meanwhile disappeared into the kitchen. Then Peter sat down and looked across at Andy expectantly.

'Forensics have identified a fingerprint on the litterbin behind where the victim was lying.' Andy told him.

'That's good, isn't it?' suggested Peter, when he stopped abruptly after this statement.

'Maybe … the thing is … it belongs to Leroy Gilbert – Stella's brother. I didn't cotton on to who it was, so I went round to his last known address and she came and found us there quizzing their grandmother about where he was. I'm sure she thinks we were harassing her – and, of course, they're both adamant that Leroy had nothing to do with the killing.'

'And I'd agree with them,' Peter said with certainty. 'Why shouldn't he have a perfectly legitimate reason for being there? A fingerprint doesn't prove anything! What does Leroy say about it?'

'I haven't asked him yet. We've arranged to meet him during his lunch hour. I've promised Stella that she can be there too.'

'There you are then! Don't jump to conclusions until you've heard his side of the story.'

'Yes, but … I'm worried he'll think … and I don't want Stella to ….'

'Would you like me to come with you?' Peter asked, as Andy's voice trailed off into incoherence.

'Would you? You know him, don't you? He'll trust you.'

'I don't know about that,' Peter smiled. 'It's his grandmother that I really know – and, of course, Stella is great friends with Lucy. Leroy … well, he was a bit of a wild teenager and kept out of my way when he was living opposite us; and then I've hardly seen him since he moved to Blackbird Leys.'

'But still, you know the family and they trust you.'

'Who's this?' Bernie came in with a tea tray loaded with cups, saucers and a large teapot covered in a yellow-and-brown cosy.

'Leroy Gilbert,' Jonah told her. 'They've found one of his fingerprints at the crime scene and Andy's nervous about interviewing him about it.'

'Well, I don't think for a minute he had anything to do with it,' Bernie declared decisively. 'Why on earth would he? Mind you, I don't know what he could've been doing round the back of Holy

Cross. He doesn't know anyone at the colleges and Goose Lane doesn't really go anywhere else.'

She put down the tray and began pouring out tea for everyone.

'No point speculating,' Peter said firmly. 'Let's just wait and see what he says about it, shall we?'

'Yes.' Andy turned to Alice and dropped the car keys into her hand. 'Drink your tea and then I want you to go back to the nick. I think it'd be overkill having you along when we interview Leroy, as well as Peter and me, and Stella. I don't want him to think we're ganging up on him.'

He picked up his cup and sipped his tea. He looked sideways at Peter, trying to think of the best way to broach his next topic.

'I was … We were thinking about Leroy – about that gang he was involved with – you know! The ones who ….'

'The ones who killed Angie?' Peter finished for him. 'What about them?'

'Are any of them out of jail now? Could any of them be putting pressure on Leroy?'

'I wouldn't have thought so.' Peter looked taken aback. 'I remember being informed ages ago that two of them had been released. It was just a routine notification. I didn't take much notice of it to be honest. The ring-leader got life and I don't remember … or maybe? I don't know.' He shook his head. 'I'm sorry, I just can't remember. I suppose he must be out on licence by now, but ….'

'No,' Bernie put in decisively. 'He's been sent to a secure mental hospital. Don't you remember? He attacked a prison guard and the medical reports showed up some sort of psychosis. We wondered whether he might have been ill all along and just not diagnosed.'

'That's right,' Jonah agreed. 'But the other two could be back in their old haunts, and they may well bear Leroy a grudge.'

'Are you suggesting they could've framed him?' Peter asked sceptically. 'They didn't seem bright enough for that to me. And a fingerprint's a fingerprint. They'd have to have lured him there somehow, and how could they be sure it'd even be found?'

'I was more thinking that they might be pressurising him to … to … well, start going round with them again. Help them out … you know.'

'You mean, they could be involved in something illegal and they've dragged Leroy into it with them?' asked Bernie.

'It's possible, isn't it?' Andy answered. The idea that had been forming in his mind seemed far less plausible now that he had voiced it out loud. He had been imagining them coming out of jail, schooled in all sorts of criminality through mixing with other convicts, and determined to pay back the confederate who had turned against them and been instrumental in putting them behind bars. But how likely was it really that the two inadequate teenagers who had joined in trashing Peter's kitchen all those years ago had turned into the sort of desperate men who were now capable of forcing their former associate to take part in whatever drug-dealing enterprise or protection racket might have been going on in Goose Lane that evening? And, as Peter said, it was even less likely that either of them had the brains to devise an elaborate scheme for getting Leroy sent down for murder. Why would they bother to go to so much trouble after so long? 'I think it would be worth looking them up – just to be sure. You can do that when you get back, Alice. Find out where they're living and what they've been doing since they got out of jail.'

'Have you spoken to Anna yet?' Peter asked Andy as he drove them both to their rendezvous with Stella and Leroy.

'Not yet,' Andy confessed. 'I haven't had time,' he added defensively, knowing that he should have made time to tell his commanding officer about his potential conflict of interest – and recognising that it was his own reluctance to hand over the case to anyone else that had motivated him not to do so. 'This business with Leroy Gilbert cropped up before I had a chance to catch her. I want to do it in person, not over the phone.'

Peter drove on in silence. As they pulled up outside Stella's house, Andy added, 'I'll do it as soon as I get back to the station.'

Stella was watching out for them from behind the net curtains that hung across the bay window at the front of the house. By the time Andy had reached the front door, she was there on the step, dressed in a full-length red coat over black trousers, with a colourful woollen scarf round her neck. She called goodbye to her grandmother over her shoulder and then stepped out of the house, pulling on a knitted hat as protection against the biting November chill. He had never seen her out of her uniform before and noticed for the first time the smoothness of her skin and the liquid clearness of her eyes.

'OK,' she said briskly, 'let's get it over with.'

Andy turned back and hurried down the path to open the front passenger door for her. She gave a start as, bending to get in, she spotted Peter in the driving seat.

'Alice had to take the car,' he told her. 'So, I'm being Andy's chauffeur for a bit.'

Without speaking, Stella sat down next to Peter. Andy got in the back. The car moved off, turning out into Cowley Road, and heading south east across the by-pass to the suburb of Blackbird Leys. In less than ten minutes they were getting out in the car park in Cuddesdon Way, which served the twenty-acre park, described by the City Council as "a green haven in the middle of Blackbird Leys estate, with a tree-lined meandering brook and open grass areas".

'Leroy's here,' Stella said, pointing towards a small white van with a picture of fruit and vegetables on the side of it. 'I hope this isn't going to take long. He only gets thirty minutes for lunch.'

'Don't worry,' Peter assured her, unconsciously taking charge. 'We'll keep it short.'

He got out and starting walking towards the van. Andy and Stella followed a few steps behind, instinctively feeling that Peter was best left to handle this in his own way. Seeing them approaching, Leroy got out and stood leaning against the side of the van. He was as tall as Andy and more solidly-built – muscular, rather than wiry. The hands that gripped a half-eaten ham-and-tomato baguette and a cardboard cup of coffee looked large and strong. The face was set in a belligerent expression – or perhaps defiant would be a better word. Andy couldn't decide. Was this an aggressive front designed to hide an underlying fear? And was that fear of being found out or fear of being falsely accused? One thing was certain: he did not like or trust the police.

'Hi, Leroy!' Peter called out cheerily. 'Can we have a quick word?'

'I thought you were retired.'

'I am. I'm just the taxi driver.' Peter glanced back at his car, then towards the van. 'What's this then?'

'I've been laid off. The shortage of semiconductors means they've cut production and I'm surplus to requirements.'

Peter remembered that Leroy worked at the motor works in Cowley, building the iconic BMW mini.

'I got this job delivering fruit and veg to caterers. It doesn't pay much, but at least it's a job,' Leroy went on. He looked towards Andy. 'Can we get on with it? I need to be somewhere else.'

'All I need to know is why you were in Goose Lane last week,' Andy told him.

'Goose Lane?'

'That's right. Near the back entrance to Holy Cross College.'

'I was delivering some stuff to the kitchens there. You can ask my boss. It'll all be on the system. A couple of trays of veg and a box of oranges. It's a regular order. I go three days a week: Monday, Wednesday and Friday. Why?'

'A man was killed there last Monday – seven-ish. And your fingerprints turned up on the bin next to where he was lying when they found him.'

'And you think I done him in?' Leroy demanded, glaring at Andy.

'No,' Peter intervened. 'We were just wondering if you saw anything – seeing as you were there that day.'

'Well, he wasn't there when I got there. I balanced one of the trays on the litter bin while I closed the door of the van. You can't trust them students not to be getting inside it and messing things up if I leave it open. I'd've seen him if he was there then.'

'Well, that clears up the fingerprint, anyway,' Peter observed brightly. 'You must have touched the bin while you were balancing your tray What time was it you delivered on Monday?'

'About half four. It'll all be in the log, if you want to know exactly. I carried the trays in and handed them over to the supervisor in the kitchen – Mr Armitage. He'll be able to vouch for me.'

'How long were you there for?'

'Fifteen – twenty minutes. It'll all be in the log. We scan the trays in to confirm delivery, and the system time-stamps it automatically.'

'Was there anyone else around in the street?'

'Not that I noticed.'

'And have you ever seen this man?' Andy held up his phone with Jibrilu's photograph displayed.

'No.' Leroy shook his head. 'Never seen him in my life! Is this him? The dead man?'

'That's right,' Andy confirmed.

Leroy stood staring down at the image in silence. Then he jerked his head up and took a bite from his baguette. He looked round at Peter and Andy as he chewed, still defiant but perhaps with less of the underlying insecurity showing. They had no evidence against him and he knew it. 'Is that it?' he asked, swallowing his mouthful.

'Yes. That's it.' Andy pointed at the telephone number on the side of the van. 'If I want to read that log you talked about do I ring that number?'

'Yeah. Just ask for Dave.'

Back at the police station, Andy set Alice the task of checking Leroy's alibi. He had no doubt that the young man's presence in Goose Lane on Monday afternoon was legitimate, but he was determined to dot all the i's and cross all the t's in his first murder case as Senior Investigating Officer. He was also conscious that, when — and if — they found the real murderer, it would be important not to have left any loose ends that could be manipulated by the defence counsel to undermine the prosecution case. The presence of a fingerprint from a known criminal — someone with a history of violence — which had been left unscrutinised, was just the sort of thing that might sow the seeds of "reasonable doubt" in a jury's minds.

After that, he set off down the corridor in search of Anna Davenport. He was just raising his arm to knock on her door when his mobile phone began ringing. It was Yakubu Danjuma. Andy swiped the screen to answer the call, and then turned and walked back to his own office with the instrument held to his ear.

'My visa still hasn't come through,' Yakubu said. 'Is there nothing that you can do?'

'I'm afraid I don't think there is,' Andy sighed. 'The chief Constable is making representations with the Home Office, but …'

After almost half an hour of fruitless discussion, going round and round over the same ground, Andy's patience was growing very thin. How could he get this man off the phone so that he could get on with his work? Didn't he realise that he was impeding the search for his son's killers?

'As I said,' he repeated yet again, 'we're doing our best, but it's all beyond our control, I'm afraid. And the coroner still hasn't released your son's body yet. There were some additional toxicology tests to do apparently.'

'Yes. Jibrilu's body,' Yakubu jumped in eagerly. 'That was another thing. You said before that you could arrange for me to see him – remotely, by a video link. I would like that. It would be some comfort, if I may not get to be there before … If I am not able to attend his funeral.'

'Yes, of course.' Andy grasped eagerly at this opening to get off the phone. 'I can get on to the mortuary right away to discuss it, if you like. Er … but I thought the people from the mosque were doing all that?'

'They told me they needed to wait – until the coroner allows them to take him away. I need to see him *now*.'

'Oh! I see. Yes, well, OK, I'll get on to the mortuary right away then and ring you back.'

Andy ended the call and sat for several seconds gazing round the room, collecting his thoughts. He supposed the mortuary staff must be used to unexpected demands from relatives of the deceased in their care. Nevertheless, now that it came to the point of asking, he felt rather awkward about the proposal. What difference could it make to Yakubu to watch his son's body laid out for viewing in real time, compared with simply seeing a

135

photograph? But then, Andy had never been bereaved, so who was he to question this father's wants and needs?

To his relief, Malcolm, the mortuary manager, took everything in his stride. He could get Jibriliu's body out of cold storage the next day and make him presentable for his father to see, no problem. There was a good WiFi connection in the room where he would be, so Andy could use his phone to conduct the video call. No, it was not a strange request, relatives had asked for much odder things in the past.

Andy spent the rest of the afternoon wrestling with various officials in an attempt to speed up Yakubu's visa application. Eventually, he got through to someone who admitted that there had been a request from the Chief Constable for the process to be fast-tracked. They were doing their best, but Andy had to understand that they still had a big backlog of work as a result of COVID and *everyone* believed their own case warranted special treatment. Yes, he could see Professor Danjuma's application on the system; he would flag it as high priority. Now, was there anything else that he could help Andy with that afternoon?

Andy took the hint and ended the call. He looked at his watch. Time to be making tracks! His "quick word" with Anna would have to wait until tomorrow. Just time to send a text to Yakubu giving him the time of his appointment at the mortuary and telling him that his visa was being fast-tracked and should come through soon, then home to another awkward evening with his mother, in which she would, no doubt, continue to maintain stubborn silence about what had really gone on between her and Yakubu. Conflict of interest? There was a lot more to it than that!

10. ALL IN THE FAMILY

Andy needed to fill up with fuel on the way to the mortuary the next morning. On impulse, he picked up a bunch of purple chrysanthemums from the bucket on the garage forecourt. Flowers were what you brought when you were paying respects to the deceased wasn't it? He put on his face mask – they were no longer compulsory, but the police ought to show a good example – and went inside to pay.

Getting back in the car, Andy felt a rush of misgiving. Why was he doing this? He ought to be in Anna Davenport's office explaining to her why he needed to be taken off the case, instead of …. He should have simply given Yakubu's details to Malcolm and asked him to conduct the video call. He would be better at it. He had experience of dealing with bereaved relatives. Andy would only do or say the wrong thing. But too late now! He had arranged it all with Yakubu. He couldn't back out.

He pulled up in the car park and got out. Turning to close the door, he saw the flowers lying on the front passenger seat. What on earth had induced him to buy those? He slammed the door closed and put the key in the lock. Then he opened it again and leaned in to pick up the bouquet. He'd got them now, no point wasting them.

Malcolm took the flowers without comment and handed them over to an assistant who put them in a vase and placed it on a small table-on-wheels next to the bench on which Jibrilu's body lay.

Andy looked down at Jibrilu's face, which was the only part of his body not covered by a white sheet. They had done a good repair job after the post-mortem. He might almost be asleep, the way his head lay, resting on a small white pillow – such a contrast with his dark skin! – with eyes closed and mouth seeming almost on the verge of a smile.

'I'll leave you to it,' Malcolm said. 'Take as long as you like. We won't need this room again before lunch time.'

He went out, closing the door behind him. Andy was alone with Jibrilu's body. He stood there in silence, studying the man's features. Were they really brothers?

But he was wasting time. Yakubu would be waiting for his call and wondering at the delay. He took out his smartphone and opened the video-call app. Yakubu answered immediately. He had evidently been waiting beside his computer, eager to get his first sight of his son since his untimely death. His face gazed out from Andy's phone against a background of books. Andy guessed that he was in his office at the university where he worked.

'I'm here at the mortuary,' Andy told him. 'They've put your son's body in a private room for you to see him. It's just you and me. Do you want a moment before …?'

'No, please – go ahead!'

'OK. I'll just switch my phone to the other camera, so you'll be able to see him, instead of me.' Andy peered down at the phone to locate the correct button. Ah! There it was. He touched the screen and the small picture of himself, displayed below Yakubu's eager face, was replaced by a chaotic image of the edge of the bench and the floor beneath. He moved the phone slowly, trying get the camera to focus on Jibrilu's face. It was harder to control than he had expected. For a moment, he lost sight of the bench altogether. He turned slowly and the table with the vase of chrysanthemums came into view, then … at last!'

'Can you see him OK?' he asked anxiously. 'It's hard to see on my phone – the picture is so small.'

'Yes. I can see him.'

There was a long silence. Andy stared intently at his phone, trying to hold it steady. On the screen, Yakubu's eyes appeared to be staring back at him, but Andy knew that what he was actually seeing was his son's face on the pillow, part of the sheet covering his body and those stupid purple chrysanths!

'Thank you,' Yakubu said at last. 'Now, can we talk? I brought something to show you too.'

'Oh!' Andy was taken aback, but assumed that this must be something that Yakubu thought might throw some light on the question of who there could be who wished harm on Jibrilu. 'Yes, of course. Go ahead.'

'I'll share my screen,' Yakubu said. 'And perhaps you could switch your camera back now, so that we can see one another.'

Andy continued to watch the small screen on his mobile phone. All he could see was the top of Yakubu's head, presumably looking down at his computer, searching for the correct control with which to display whatever it was for Andy to see. Then suddenly that image vanished and was replaced by another face altogether. It was a head-and-shoulders portrait of a young woman.

Andy stared in amazement. He recognised that face. The same blue eyes smiled out of a photograph on the wall of their sitting room at home – a photograph of a young woman cradling a small brown baby in her arms.

'I see you do recognise Amanda Lepage, after all.' Yakubu's voice penetrated the disorientating fog that had descended on Andy's mind, seeming to come from far away. He nodded silently in reply.

'Your mother, who works in the university library?'

Andy remained silent.

'Yes,' Yakubu nodded with an air of satisfaction, 'I can see it in your eyes. Why did you lie to me?'

'I – I – she … My mother said you were just an acquaintance, someone whose room she cleaned when she was in the sixth form.'

'Oh, we were rather more than that to one another,' Yakubu smiled back. 'You are the proof of that!'

'Aren't you jumping to conclusions there?' Andy asked, getting the words out with difficulty. His mouth seemed suddenly very dry. 'Even if you and she did … you can't just assume … I mean there could have been someone else afterwards.'

'Let's see then. What's your date of birth?'

'I don't have to answer that.' Andy was seized with an intense desire to end this conversation, but his professionalism forced him to remain polite – if only just.

'Spring 1984? Early Summer, perhaps?' Yakubu continued to smile. He was clearly delighted at having his suspicions confirmed, but was this pleasure at having discovered a new son or satisfaction at having caught Andy out in his deceit? 'Yes, I'm right, aren't I? Your face gives you away every time.'

'I'm sorry, we'll have to talk about this another time.' With a great effort, Andy forced himself to speak in the formal way that he used when addressing members of the public in the course of an enquiry. 'I have other things to do. Would you like one final look at your son before we end this call?'

'My *other* son?' Yakubu continued to smile – a rather self-satisfied smile, or was that an ungenerous thought? 'No thank you. I've seen enough. It was kind of you to arrange it for me.'

'No problem. It's my job.'

'And we'll speak again? This afternoon, perhaps? I'm free all day.'

'I'll be in touch,' Andy promised, 'but I do have a lot to do today.'

'I understand.'

'Good bye then.' Andy moved his hand towards the screen to end the call, but Yakubu called out to stop him.

'Just one last thing: the flowers? Who put them there, by Jibrilu's body?'

For a moment, Andy was tempted to ignore the question, pretending to have logged off before hearing it. Then he worked out a way of telling the truth without admitting to his own involvement. 'Just someone from the mortuary,' he said casually. 'I expect it's just routine.'

He must go to Anna now and confess to his conflict of interest. It was impossible any longer to pretend that he was a dispassionate observer of the facts in this case. Whatever his mother might say, it was clear that Yakubu believed that Andy was his son, and that created a problem even if it were not true – which Andy was now convinced it was.

As he drove back to the police station, he went over in his mind all the things that he would need to put in the handover report that he would write for his successor in the role of Senior Investigating Officer. There did not seem to be much to show for a full week of hard graft on the part of his team. They had a good number of suspects, but none of them very convincing. Witnesses had little to say that was pertinent to the case, and there were still several of them who had not yet been interviewed. Esther Orugun, for example: she was the best chance they had of finding someone with a personal motive for harming Jibrilu, and so far she had eluded them. Andy would have liked to interview her himself. It would need to be done sensitively. She was a young black woman in an alien culture, far from home. She might well be reluctant to open up if confronted by, for example, the eagerness for results of Sergeant Williams or Alice's direct uncomplicated approach.

Anna was not in her office when he got back. Her assistant told him that she was at a briefing with the Deputy Chief Constable and would not be back until lunch time. Andy nodded and said that he would call again in the afternoon. He looked at his watch. There was more than an hour of the morning left. He had not been taken off the case yet. There was time to have another go at interviewing the elusive Esther.

As he made his way out, Stella Gilbert emerged from the custody suite, where she had been delivering a driver whom she and Gavin had apprehended still over the limit the morning after the night before. On impulse, he asked her to come with him, explaining that a woman from Nigeria might be nervous of police officers and Stella, being a woman closer to her own age would appear less of a threat than he himself did.

This time, they were in luck. When they knocked on the door of Esther's room, a deep musical voice called back at once, inviting them in.

Andy pushed open the door and stepped inside. Esther Orugun was a handsome woman with high cheekbones and almond-shaped eyes beneath thick elegantly arching brows. She was wearing a bright yellow sweatshirt with the Lichfield College crest printed on the front. Her hair was covered by a headscarf in the same shade. She was sitting at a desk in front of a laptop computer with books stacked high on either side. When she got up to greet them, Andy could see that she was taller than most women, taller even than some men. Or was that just the effect of the way her hair was piled up under her headwrap? She stood with one hand on the back of her chair looking questioningly towards them. When Andy explained why they had come, she started hastily gathering up the papers that were strewn across two easy chairs and a small coffee table in the centre of the room and invited them to sit down. Then she turned the desk chair round to face them and settled herself on it, looking round at them expectantly.

Andy gazed back at his interviewee. He had never seen anyone quite like her. Her skin was dark, like Yakubu's, but smoother and unlined. Her ears, partially covered by her headwrap, had brightly-coloured earrings dangling from their lobes. Her eyes were bright and gentle and her expression was open and honest.

'I suppose I must be your chief suspect,' she said, catching Andy's eye and giving him a sort of half smile.

'What makes you say that?'

'Well, I assume by now someone will have told you about the row we had?' She looked at them each in turn, as if studying their reactions.

'Let's suppose that they haven't,' Andy said, trying not to give away that she had wrong-footed him. 'How about you tell us all about it?'

'It was back at the beginning of October. You know, that seems like a lifetime ago now.' Esther sighed. 'I feel very bad about it now – especially now that he's dead, but at the time … well, like I said, it was back in 0th week.'

'0th week?' queried Stella, who was unfamiliar with this strange Oxonian method of reckoning dates.

'The week before full term begins,' Andy explained. 'The university terms are eight weeks long and they're numbered 1st week, 2nd week and so on. 0th week is the week before 1st week. Most students come up to Oxford during that week.'

'That's right,' Esther nodded. 'But it's different for us postgraduates. I'd been here since the middle of August and Jibrilu arrived the first week in September.'

'And this row, you were telling us about?' prompted Andy.

'Bev – that's Dr Greenhalgh – organised a get-together for all the overseas students, undergraduates as well as post-graduates. She's my supervisor and she's also the tutor for overseas students.

She has this idea that we ought to be one big happy family, helping each other to settle in in a foreign country. I think that's why she put all of us DPhil students together on this weird little staircase cut off from everyone else.'

'It's not just overseas postgrads there, though, is it?' Andy pointed out. 'What about Piers Addison?'

'I suppose there weren't quite enough of us to fill all the rooms,' Esther shrugged. 'Bev told me numbers were down this year, because of COVID. And Piers is from South Africa, so I suppose, if he didn't have anywhere else to go … or maybe Bev thought he'd help us settle in. We were all new this year and he's a third year.'

'And did he?'

Esther laughed out loud. 'Have you met Piers?'

'I have, but I wondered how *you* got on with him – you and the other postgraduates.'

'I try to keep away from him. I think most of the others do too. He asked Marie-Claire out once or twice, but she turned him down, so he gave up.'

'And Jibrilu?' Andy pressed her. 'Did he avoid him too?'

'Jibrilu!' Esther rolled her eyes up to the ceiling. 'Jibrilu seemed to think it was his job to … If he thought something wasn't right, he said so, straight out. He told Marie-Claire her blouse had too many buttons open and her skirt was too short. He told Piers that he shouldn't be taking female students back to his room and letting them stay overnight, and he complained about him making a noise on the staircase when he came home drunk at two o'clock in the morning.'

'And did he criticise you too? Was that what this row was about?'

'No.' Esther suddenly became serious again. 'That was my fault.'

'Oh?'

144

'Bev thought Jibrilu and I were bound to get on because we both came from Nigeria. She obviously didn't think about how big Nigeria is and how different it is in the North from in Lagos, where I live. She invited us both round to dinner at her house – just the two of us.'

'Matchmaking?' suggested Stella, speaking without thinking and then lowering her head and becoming very busy writing in her notebook to cover her confusion at her own temerity.

'Maybe,' Esther smiled. 'I hadn't thought of it like that. I just thought she wanted us to be buddies – you know, mutual support. She tried to get us to talk about what we found different about being in England. She was very concerned that we might be experiencing culture-shock. That set Jibrilu off talking about English women dressing immodestly and talking too loudly. And then, of course, Bev had to put him right by saying that it was all part of working towards equality and that women had to speak up and assert themselves because the patriarchy still held them back, even in this country. Of course, Jibrilu wouldn't accept that, and he wouldn't give way graciously, even though she was a tutor and he was only a student. I just kept quiet and ate my dinner and hoped it would all be over soon.'

'And the row?' Andy persisted.

'That was after we got back to college. Jibrilu was still talking self-righteously about how shocked he was at the behaviour of some of the students at the college. I was still just trying to get back to my room as soon as possible. But then he asked me outright why I didn't back him up. I had to say something, so I tried to explain that I didn't think it was polite to criticise people when we were only visitors to their country, but he insisted that there were some things that were wrong wherever you were and it was our duty to point out to people when they were going against the wishes of Allah, because they were the ones who would come to harm in the end.'

Esther stopped abruptly and stared down at her empty cup on the table in front of her.

'And then?' enquired Andy.

'After that, I don't remember exactly what I said, but I know I accused him of being a Boko Haram extremist who was in favour of kidnapping girls from schools and forcing them into marrying terrorists. We ended up shouting at each other in the quad and lots of people must have seen us there. That's why I thought you'd probably heard about it.'

'No,' Andy told her. 'But your tutor did mention that you'd had relatives killed by Boko Haram.'

'That's right, my aunt Deborah and uncle Samson and their children were all killed when Boko Haram drove a car bomb into their church. It was horrible. I had nightmares for ages afterwards.'

'Yes,' agreed Stella with feeling. 'It's awful when something like that happens to someone you know. Was it a long time ago?'

'Six years, but I still can't get it out of my mind.' Esther shrugged and pulled a face that Andy took to indicate annoyance with herself at this weakness. 'It's not even as if I was there. They lived hundreds of miles away, up in Kaduna province. It's all just in my imagination!'

'To get back to Jibrilu, if you don't mind,' Andy intervened. 'How were things between you after that?'

'I avoided him. Apart from eating in Hall and bumping into each other on our staircase, there wasn't any reason why we should ever meet. In the heat of the moment, the day after the row, I wrote to the college asking to be moved to a different staircase, but they said it wasn't possible. By that time, I'd calmed down and it didn't seem that important anymore, so I dropped it.'

'Would Jibrilu have known about your request?'

'I shouldn't think so. I didn't mention him by name. I just said that I didn't get on with some of the people and I'd like a change. But, by the time they answered, Bev seemed to have got the message that we weren't going to hit it off together. And we were studying different subjects so ....' She shrugged. 'I just let it drop.'

She paused and seemed to be thinking. Andy waited, not wanting to interrupt if she had more to say. His patience was rewarded when she continued, 'I did write a letter of apology – after I told my father about it and he said I should – but I never got round to giving it to him. I've still got it here.'

She swung her chair round and opened one of the drawers under her desk. She took out a white envelope and handed it to Andy. He looked down and saw that Jibrilu's name was written on the outside in neat, rather old-fashioned handwriting.

'It's alright,' Esther told him. 'You can read it if you like. I was going to slip it under his door, but then I started wondering what he'd do when he got it. I – I still didn't really want to talk to him, so I decided to wait until ... I'm going home for Christmas. I thought I'd leave it for him to find after I'd left. Then it'd be three weeks before he could say anything to me, and by then perhaps he'd have forgotten. But now ....'

Her face suddenly changed and her eyes took on a melancholy aspect. 'But now, he'll never know. And I'll have to admit to Baba that I never made it up with him. He told me I mustn't blame all Muslims for what happened to Aunty Deborah, and since she's his sister, I have to listen to him when he says that. I can't forgive the men who killed her – and all my cousins that I used to play with when I was little – but I can see now that I shouldn't have called Jibrilu a terrorist. Baba says that he knows lots of Muslims who don't support Boko Haram. He says they tell him that Boko Haram aren't following Islam at all.'

'Can you think of anyone else who might have fallen out with Jibrilu?' Andy asked. 'Someone else who disagreed with the way he went round criticising, for example?'

'No one in particular. I think he did annoy a lot of people, but not enough for them to want him dead! You don't go round killing

147

someone just because they tell you your blouse is too tight, do you?'

'No, probably not,' Andy agreed. 'OK, now I'd like you to think back to Monday of last week. Did you go to dinner in hall that day?'

'Yes. My parents insisted that I paid for all my meals up-front. I think they were afraid I might not eat properly if I cooked for myself! So, I dine in Hall most nights.'

'And you went down to the hall at what time?'

'Well, I went to compline in chapel first. It's a short service they have every evening just before dinner. It starts at quarter to seven.'

'And before that, you were in your room?'

'Yes, I was working here all afternoon. I had lots of results to write up from some lab work I'd done that morning.'

'So, you were here in your room between four in the afternoon and quarter to seven, and then you went to the chapel and then straight to the hall for dinner?'

'That's right.'

Andy got up and walked over to the desk, which was under the window. He looked out and confirmed that the view was over the Fellows' Garden. Craning his neck, he could just about catch a glimpse of the stained-glass windows of Holy Cross college chapel, but Goose Lane was hidden behind the stone wall that surrounded the garden.

'Was your window open or closed?'

'Closed. It was freezing cold. I had the window closed and the curtains drawn and there was still a draught coming in.'

Nodding, Andy returned to his seat, before asking, 'Did you hear any disturbance at all? Voices in the lane or on the staircase, for instance?'

'No,' Esther shook her head. 'Not that I remember.'

'And did you meet anyone when you were on your way to the chapel? Particularly anyone on this staircase?'

'No, I don't think so, but if it was one of the people who live here, I might not have noticed.'

'OK.' Andy waited while Stella recorded this information in her notebook. Then he smiled at Esther and got to his feet. 'I think that's all for now. Thank you for being so frank with us. We'll leave you in peace now.'

'Mum?' Andy said into his mobile phone as he stood outside the Vere Harmsworth Library on South Parks Road, where his mother was working temporarily while the Radcliffe Science Library underwent redevelopment. 'We need to talk. Can I take you to lunch?'

'Talk? What about? I've got my sandwiches here with me. I haven't got time to go out to lunch.'

'Bring them with you and we'll go and sit on a bench somewhere. It's important.'

'Surely it can wait until this evening.'

'No. It has to be now. I'm right outside the main entrance.'

No reply.

'Mum? Are you still there? Are you listening?'

'Yes, I'm listening, but I don't see what can be so urgent it can't wait for a few hours. Tell me about it over dinner.'

Andy took a deep breath and forced himself to speak calmly. 'No Mum. We've tried that, and you just keep clamming up. And we need to do it before I go to see Anna Davenport this afternoon. Come out and we'll go to the parks.'

Silence.

'I'll give you five minutes, and if you're not out here by then, I'm coming in to get you – with my warrant card.'

'Alright. Just let me grab my coat.' Amanda's voice was tight and brittle, but Andy thought he detected just a hint of relief in it as she terminated the call. Did even she finally recognise that she couldn't keep running away from the truth for ever?

In less than three minutes, she emerged from the building, muffled up against the cold wind in a scarf and with a knitted hat pulled down over her ears. Seeing the plastic lunchbox clasped in her hand, Andy held up an identical one to indicate that he had anticipated her reluctance to waste their packed lunches by indulging in a restaurant meal.

'Thanks Mum. I'm sorry for the strong-arm tactics, but this really is important.'

They walked together to the corner where South Parks Road met St Cross Road, and then past the South Lodge into the University Parks. It did not take long to find an unoccupied bench; very few people were inclined to linger in the chill damp of an English Autumn as it merged into winter. It would be December tomorrow.

'I've been talking to my father,' Andy said, plunging in, determined not to allow his mother to evade his questions this time.

'What on earth do you mean?' Amanda stopped short in the act of prising the lid off her lunchbox. 'You don't have a father.'

'Yakubu Danjuma. I was on a video call with him this morning. It's no good you pretending. He knows!'

'Knows what?'

'That Jibrilu wasn't the only son he had left, after all. That the Amanda Lepage that he knew when he was in Oxford is still here and that she has a mixed-race son. That-'

'And I'm telling you that he was just a passing acquaintance. I cleaned his room!'

'And the rest! Mum, please! He's got a photo of you in subfusc, standing outside the Sheldonian. You must have just matriculated. Why can't you be honest with me?'

'I have been. I *did* clean his room. That *is* how I got to know him.'

'But "just a casual acquaintance"? Come off it, Mum. Why can't you admit that he's my father? We both know it must have been him.'

'He's *not!*' Amanda gripped her cheese and pickle sandwich so hard that yellow juice leaked out and dripped on to her coat. 'He's not your father in any way that means anything! He didn't even hang around for long enough to know that I was pregnant. He strung me along with declarations of undying love and then calmly announced that he was going back to his wives and kid! He had two wives! And still he wanted a bit on the side, a teenager who thought it was wonderful to be going out with a student at the university. We don't need him. We've manged fine without him all these years, haven't we?'

'Yes,' Andy agreed, trying to keep the anger and frustration out of his voice. 'You did a wonderful job of bringing me up on your own. That's not what I'm saying at all! I'm not complaining that you deprived me of my birth father or saying that you should have told him about me or taken me to Africa to get back to my roots. I'm just saying that you've put me in a very difficult position with me being the SIO investigating his son's murder.'

'I can't see why.' Amanda sounded sulky now. 'What if he *is* your father? He still means nothing to you.'

'But that isn't how the defence counsel will see it if I arrest someone for killing the man that they'd be sure to trumpet as my brother! You could end up perverting the course of justice. As it is, I'll just have to go to Anna Davenport and own up to my conflict of interest and ask her to take me off the case.'

'Good. Then you won't have to speak to him again, will you? And we can both just forget all about it.'

'Except that I have to ring him this afternoon, because I promised I'd let him know as soon as the coroner gave permission for Jibrilu's body to be released for burial. He's keen for the funeral to go ahead as soon as possible. And, in any case, he's determined to look you up when he comes, and his visa's bound to come through eventually. Not even British immigration will be able to hold out forever!'

'Surely, once the funeral's over there won't be any point in him coming.'

'Mum! You're just not thinking. Of course, he'll still want to come. He'll want to see where it happened and collect his son's things and talk to the police officer in charge of the case. And-'

'Well, at least that won't be you.'

'And he's also said he wants to see you,' Andy continued with a sigh.

'Well, you can tell him that I won't meet him!' Amanda retorted. 'You can tell him that he's the last person I ever want to meet again. Or, better still, just tell him that he's got it all wrong and I'm not the woman he knew when he was here before and you're not his son and it's all just a big coincidence.'

'Oh Mum! You're being ridiculous! I told you – he knows! He hasn't said so outright, but I know he knows, and he knows that I know, too. And I don't see what the big deal is about meeting him. What can he do that's so terrible?'

'I just don't want to,' Amanda persisted stubbornly, 'and I don't see why I should. Anyway, it's time I was back in work. Say what you like to him, just make sure he knows I'm not meeting him – OK?'

Andy opted for a telephone call, in preference to a video conference, to inform Yakubu that he could now go ahead with organising Jibrilu's funeral. It would be easier to terminate when he had finished conveying the necessary information and Yakubu would not have any opportunity to read Andy's face. He would keep it short and business-like and then go straight round to Anna's office to tell her that she would have to find a new SIO.

Yakubu answered immediately. Andy thought he must have been sitting by his phone waiting for the call. But then, what else did he have to do, all those thousands of miles away from where his son – or one of his sons! – had so recently met his death? Andy imagined him there, sitting at his desk in the university, thumbing through an old family album, looking down at the faces of his dead family. Two wives, and perhaps half a dozen children – Africans always had large families, didn't they? – all gone now! Except for one – one son that he never knew he had.

'Professor Danjuma,' he began, determined to keep the conversation formal and professional. 'I have some news for you. The coroner has released your son's body for burial.'

'That is good news indeed! I will contact the mosque at once and tell them to go ahead. They have everything prepared. Your DCI Khan was most helpful. You must thank him for me.'

'I will. I'm sorry that you had such a long wait. Now, I have a lot of-'

'And I, too, have some good news to relate,' Yakubu cut across Andy's attempt at terminating the call. 'Thanks to your efforts, my visa is to be approved. I must just take some documentation to the British High Commission in Abuja and answer some questions and then they say I will be free to fly to England. I hope to see you next week.'

'Well, perhaps you won't see *me*,' Andy replied cautiously. 'But if you let us know which flight you're arriving on, Thames Valley Police will arrange for someone to meet you and take you to your hotel. That's something else I wanted to tell you,' he went on quickly, sensing that Yakubu was about to interrupt. 'I'm being taken off the case. Another officer will be assigned to lead the investigation. They'll be in touch with you shortly.'

'But why?' Yakubu's bewilderment – distress even – was palpable.

'Conflict of interest. You can't have an officer investigating the murder of his own half-brother.'

'Why not? I would have thought it would make him all the more determined to find the murderer.'

'Exactly! Too determined! The defence would say that the relationship had clouded my judgement and made me charge the first suspect that I found, without bothering to investigate properly. It would be against all the rules. There's no two ways about it, I've got to stand down. DCI Davenport will contact you tomorrow to let you know who you should speak to in future if you want news.'

'I see.'

'So, now I'd better be getting-'

'But you'll keep in touch, won't you? And your mother: ask her to ring me – or a Zoom call! I would so much like to see her face again. Could you give me her number and I'll-?'

'No,' Andy broke in firmly. 'No, Professor Danjuma, that's not possible. She doesn't want to speak to you.'

'You've asked her? She knows I'm coming to Oxford?'

'Yes, she knows, and she doesn't want to see you.'

'But – but that's impossible! Mandy would never say such a thing! We were in love – we *are* in love! I've never loved anyone else! I've got to see her!'

'Never loved anyone else?' Andy's voice was scornful. The arrogance of the man! How did he expect him to believe that? 'When you were already married – twice! How do you think she felt when she found out that you'd lied to her? My mother doesn't owe you anything, and if she doesn't want to meet you again, then I won't let you try!'

'You don't understand,' Yakubu pleaded, dropping his voice almost to a whisper. 'Those two wives – that was just a business arrangement. My father owed a friend a favour, and he had five daughters and very little money. And I was the only son, and it was important for my parents that I gave them an heir. It was all arranged before I knew what was happening. I promise you; I never knew what love was until I came to Oxford and met your mother.'

'A seventeen-year-old schoolgirl who had a part-time job cleaning your room? Love! These days, we'd call it grooming and child-abuse and you'd be locked up and put on the sex-offenders register.'

'You make it sound so sordid,' Yakubu said mournfully, 'but it was not like that at all.'

'So, what was it like, then?' Andy momentarily forgot his plan to keep the call short and business-like.

'It was ….' Yakubu's voice took on a dreamy quality as if he were imagining scenes in his head. 'It was beautiful – like your mother, and it was romantic. We were both so much in love. It must be hard for you to believe that old people like us were once young and passionate, but we were.'

'*You* weren't so young,' Andy countered. 'You were twenty-seven to her seventeen! And you were married, with kids!'

'I asked your mother to marry me. She refused.'

'Because she didn't want to be number three wife! How could you ever have thought she would?'

'I noticed that she hasn't taken another name,' Yakubu commented, treating Andy's question as rhetorical. 'Is she married now? Does she have other children?'

'No – not that it's any of your business what she's done with her life since – since … since you left Oxford.'

'I am sorry.' Yakubu sounded genuinely regretful. 'I did not expect her to … She spoke so harshly the day we parted. I did not realise how much she … I must see her. I must tell her that I never stopped loving her, either!'

'Either?' Andy could hardly believe what he was hearing. 'You don't think she still loves you, do you?'

'Why else would a beautiful woman like her remain unmarried?'

'Why? Why shouldn't she? Why would she want to get married after what you'd put her through? Why would she ever want to have anything to do with men ever again?' Andy blustered to a halt. This was a question that he had never considered before. It had always been just him and Mum, living together as a self-contained unit – with Nana and Gramps stepping in to help out every so often, and occasional visits to Amanda's sisters. It had never occurred to him that his mother might have had a social life of her own, might even have found a partner to share her life with.

'I am looking forward to meeting her again very much.' Yakubu was speaking again. Andy pulled himself together and resumed his formal tone.

'I'm afraid that won't be possible,' he stated in a voice as completely devoid of emotion as he could make it. 'My mother has made it very clear to me that she is not prepared to contemplate any such meeting. Now, I have a lot of work to do, and I'm sure you have preparations that you need to make for your journey to England. So, goodbye, Professor Danjuma. DCI Davenport will be in touch to give you a new contact-point for the investigation into your son's death.'

Andy couldn't face dinner with his mother that evening, so he rang her as soon as his interview with Anna was over and lied that he had to work late to complete the handover of the case. Then he sat at his desk for several minutes, staring into space, before picking up the phone again and dialling Peter's number.

'Andy?' Peter's tone was friendly, but Andy detected an underlying tenseness.

'I'm sorry; am I interrupting something?'

'No, no – well, nothing important. Just let me turn down the gas.' There was a pause and a bang, which Andy interpreted as Peter's phone being put down on a hard surface. He must be in the middle of preparing their evening meal. Soon his voice came through again, still not sounding as if the call were particularly welcome. 'What can I do for you?'

'Oh, nothing really, I just thought I'd let you know I'm off the case. Mum finally came clean and I told Anna about it this afternoon. She's going to break it to the troops tomorrow.'

'Oh! Well, thanks for letting us know. Jonah will be disappointed that he doesn't have a direct line to the SIO any longer, but no doubt he'll be bending Anna's ear about the case as soon as he hears. Has she told you who she's replacing you with?'

'She's going to head up the investigation herself. The idea is that the father is less likely to think he's being short-changed if he's getting a more senior officer investigating his son's death.'

'And when you say "the father" you mean *your* father?'

'Yes, Yakubu. I still can't think of him like that. It's all just so surreal!'

'Give yourself time,' Peter advised. 'It's a lot to take in.'

'But I'm not sure I've got time! Yakubu says his visa's almost through and he's booking a flight for next week. And he's determined to come and see me and Mum. And she's just as determined about having nothing to do with him. They're driving me mad between the two of them!' Andy's voice rose as he attempted to describe his predicament.

'I expect *they* need time for it all to sink in too.' Peter was clearly trying to reassure him, but it felt rather like being fobbed off with platitudes. 'Look, I'm sorry Andy, I've got to go. I've made an omelette and it's not something you can keep warm for hours. I'll be happy to talk, but could you ring me back later?'

'Yes, of course. I'm sorry. Bad timing. I should have thought. Give my regards to Bernie and Jonah.'

Andy put the phone down and sat staring into space. What to do now? He couldn't go home. There was nothing for him to do here, now that he was off the case. No doubt, Anna would find other things for him to tackle tomorrow, but for now he was a free agent. He had better go and find somewhere to eat and then …? He would cross that bridge when he came to it.

11. CASE REVIEW

'Bye-bye, darling. Have a good day at nursery!' Anna kissed her youngest child who was sitting in her high-chair eating her breakfast.

'Calendar!' little Donna protested in response. 'Open the door!'

'She means her Advent Calendar,' her sister Jessica explained for the benefit of their bemused mother. 'You promised she could open a door each day before you went out.'

'But it's not …,' Anna looked down at her watch to check the date. 'Of course, it's the first today. I was thinking it was still November. But how did *she* know?'

'You've always said she's very bright,' Jessica grinned back.

'Nothing to do with you having told her this morning when you got her dressed, I suppose?' Anna put down the driving gloves that she had been in the process of putting on and went over to the high self where they had placed the Advent Calendar.

She got it down and carried it over to Donna, who clapped her hands in delight.

'Can you find the number one?' Jessica asked quickly, before their mother could point out the correct cardboard flap to be lifted this day.

Donna peered at the numbers on the doors. Anna fought with impatience at the delay. She wanted to be in work early this morning. She had a whole new case to get up to speed on and a team of officers who would, no doubt, be agog with speculation about the amazing coincidence of the victim's father turning out also to be the father of the Senior Investigating Officer. She had offered to give them an alternative explanation for his being moved off the case, but Andy had insisted that honesty was the best policy. In all likelihood his relationship with Yakubu Danjuma would come out in the end, whatever they said now, and any other excuse could easily be interpreted as a reflection on his ability to lead the investigation.

Fortunately, Jessica had been working on her younger sister and Donna had little difficulty in remembering that the number one door had a picture of a doll with a blue polka-dot dress on it. She pointed to it, confidently announcing, 'number one!'

'Well done!' Jessica squealed. 'Look Mum! Donna can count!'

Jessica eased open the door and took out the small square of chocolate from behind it. Donna reached out her hand, took it and pushed it into her mouth.

'Well done, Donna,' Anna agreed, kissing her again on the top of her head and then jumping back to avoid a chocolatey embrace from her daughter's small arms. 'But now I really do have to go.'

She picked up her gloves again and went out into the hall, calling goodbye to her husband, Philip, as she passed through. He always remained upstairs until it was time for Jessica to leave for Oxford Brookes University, where she was studying Physiotherapy. At that point, he would take over Donna's care, but until his older daughter left the house, he knew that any attempt to assist would be unwelcome. Jessica accepted his presence in their home as a rather geriatric au pair, but she had never forgiven him for advocating the termination of her mother's unexpected pregnancy – something that he had wanted even before the pre-natal tests had revealed that she had spina bifida. Jessica saw the world in stark black-and-white, and "killing an unborn baby" was very definitely on the dark side in her mind.

Would she ever become reconciled to her father? Anna shook her head in doubt, as she got into her car and set off for the police station. But then, was she any better herself? Philip had forfeited her trust when he made a unilateral decision that the family was moving down to Devon. He claimed that she was never around for him to discuss the plan with her, but that was a lame excuse. He knew that she would not want to leave her work or to submit to the lottery of a transfer to Devon and Cornwall Police.

How could he be so unreasonable? Or was she the unreasonable one? Should she have realised that he had been marking time in his own career while doing the lion's share of the childcare, and he was bound to have been looking forward to the time when Jessica and Piers were old enough to manage without him being at home for them? But he still ought to have discussed it with her before agreeing to go into partnership with that friend of his from uni! Talking wouldn't have cost him anything.

And why didn't he realise that a new baby – albeit an unplanned one – changed everything? He was Donna's father and that came with obligations. He couldn't just wish her away – although he had tried! He should have told Brian that they had to change their plans. But no, he'd made up his mind and nothing was going to stop him!

Is that what Andy's father had been like? Had he planned out his life and then been unwilling to change course after his British girlfriend fell pregnant? Had he expected her to get rid of the baby? Or maybe, as Andy had hinted, he had never known that he was a father? Either way, it seemed that he, like Philip, was now expecting to be given paternal privileges that he had done nothing to earn!

She parked her car and walked briskly up to her office. She had ordered Andy to take some time off. He had several days owing, after throwing himself into the Jibrilu Danjuma case twenty-four seven, and he needed time to think through his new family circumstances. His team, meanwhile, needed someone at the helm, and she had better take that command herself.

She swept into the open plan office and marched straight to the front. Officers looked up from their computer screens or dashed to their desks from huddles of friends standing around with cups of coffee in their hands. Anna turned to face them and silenced all continuing conversation with a look.

'As you were told yesterday,' she began, 'I'm taking over as SIO on the Jibrilu Danjuma case. It's now a week since we identified him and began the investigation into his murder in earnest. So, I think it's time that we reviewed where we're up to and made a plan for what needs to be done next.'

She picked up the notebook where she had summarised the evidence so far and drawn up a list of points that she wanted to go through. 'According to the case file, there has only been one concrete suspect, Leroy Gilbert.' She looked round the room until she located Alice. 'You were checking out his alibi. Did it stack up?'

'Yes, ma'am. His employer showed me the electronic records. It's like Big Brother working there. Every time they make a delivery, they scan in the bar code on the side of the tray and that records what was delivered, the exact time of delivery and the location where they dropped it off. There's also a tracker in the van that records where it is against the time. According to them, he left Holy Cross College at 16.45 on that Monday.'

'And that's too early for him to have been the killer?' asked Anna.

'We-e-ell,' Alice said slowly, careful not to commit herself completely, 'it *is* just about inside the window given by the estimated time of death from the post-mortem, but everything points to it being later than that, really.'

'DI Lepage had a theory that he was in the middle of dressing for dinner when he was killed,' Iestyn put in from his usual place at the back of the room. 'And they don't serve dinner until seven.'

'And we also have the boy who was running away from the scene,' Alice added. 'That was later too.'

'Ah yes!' Anna turned the page of her notes. 'Gabriel Sibanda. Why hasn't he been interviewed yet?'

There was silence and everyone seemed to be looking towards someone else.

'Andy wanted to do that himself,' Alice answered at last. 'He was going to ring the family and arrange to see them. I don't know if he ever did.'

'Alright, I'll see to that myself.' Anna flipped back the page and looked down at her list again. 'Initially, we thought it might be drug-related, but so far no link has been established – is that right?'

'Yes,' confirmed Alice.

'The drugs boys told us there are two rival gangs operating in Oxford at the moment,' Iestyn volunteered, 'but they haven't come up with anything to suggest our man was in either of them. I reckon they just fancy themselves. They can't believe anyone gets killed in the street without a connection to one of their gangs.'

'Especially, if it's a young black man,' Alice nodded in agreement. She had disliked Sergeant Myers intensely. 'I don't rate the drugs connection at all. There's nothing to suggest the victim took drugs or sold them. If it *was* a gang-land killing, he must have just been in the wrong place at the wrong time and got caught in the cross-fire.'

'OK.' Anna jotted down some notes and then looked round the room again. 'What do we think of Esther Orugun? I have her down here as a possible suspect.'

The room fell silent.

'It says here that she was in her room, alone, all afternoon and evening on the day his was killed,' Anna went on. 'So, she had the opportunity to do it.'

'And she has a strong motive for hating Nigerian Muslims,' Alice agreed. 'Even her supervisor thought she might have done it. Andy said he could tell by the way she tried to avoid telling him about her. We tried to interview her a few times, but she was never in.'

'According to his notes, DI Lepage got to speak with her yesterday,' Anna told her. 'That's how he knew that she was in her room at the time. There's no evidence that she left it at all, but no evidence that she *didn't* go down and confront Jibrilu either. Apparently, she said she regrets accusing him of being in cahoots with Boko Haram and was intending to apologise, but she would say that wouldn't she?'

'So, you think we ought to keep her on the suspect list?' suggested Iestyn.

'I think we have to.' Anna frowned down at her notes. 'Unfortunately, we don't have enough evidence to warrant searching her room for the knife or traces of blood, which means it's going to be very difficult to prove it was her. Maybe … Jennifer! I'd like you to do a few searches on social media to see if she has any history of abusive behaviour towards Muslims or referencing anti-Muslim websites or groups.'

'Yes ma'am.' Jennifer Moorehouse smiled. She might only be a civilian, but she knew that she was a key member of the team with IT skills that many of the sworn officers lacked.

'And then we have three students: Hugo Dewar, Victor Lansdown and Piers Addison,' Anna resumed. 'What do we think of them?'

'A bunch of posers,' Alice answered promptly. 'Hugo fancies himself as a Scottish laird and prances around in kilt and sporran. Piers is a white South African who doesn't make any effort to disguise his racism. And Victor thinks he knows all about Nigerians just because his father works for an oil company. They all ooze entitlement and they were very patronising towards me and Andy.'

'OK, so you didn't like them.' Anna smiled to herself at Alice's forthright description of the young men. 'But do we have anything concrete to link them to the murder?'

'Hugo admitted to being out and about at the critical time,' Alice told her. 'But he claims that he came back into Holy Cross College through the main entrance and not the back way. I asked around to see if anyone saw him, but nobody seems to have done. I did find out something interesting about him, though. He's well-known for carrying a knife with him when he goes out.'

'Really?' Anna looked up with interest. 'What sort of knife?'

'A sort of ceremonial one.' Alice fumbled in her notebook to find where she had written down the unfamiliar word. 'It's called a "sgian-dubh". I'm probably pronouncing that all wrong. I looked it up in Wikipedia. It's a Gaelic name for a "small, single-edged knife" which highlanders traditionally stick down their long socks when they're dressed up in their kilts. I can show you a picture.'

She got up and stepped forward holding out her smartphone towards Anna, who looked down to see a photograph of a man's lower leg dressed in a black shoe and cream-coloured woolly sock. Protruding from the top of the sock was the ornamental hilt of what looked to her like a dagger.

'Now, that *is* interesting,' she said thoughtfully.

'We could ask him to hand it over to us for testing,' Alice suggested, relishing the thought of giving the arrogant young man a fright.

'Or we could go and give him some friendly advice about the Criminal Justice Act 1988,' suggested Iestyn.

'Unfortunately, that act specifically allows knives to be carried in public if they form part of a national dress,' Alice told him regretfully, pleased that she had researched this issue, having herself considered an attempt to arrest him for carrying an offensive weapon in public.

'I think we're straying from the point here,' Anna remarked drily. 'I agree that the knife needs looking into, but we need to be wary of showing our cards too soon. He's had plenty of time to clean it up by now, so we'd be looking at minute traces that, if they're there at all, will probably still be there if we wait a few days. Does he have any sort of motive for the attack?'

'Not as such,' Alice admitted. 'But he does have some quite extreme views on overseas students, and all three of them obviously didn't like Jibrilu. They resented him having opinions. Typical "I'm not a racist, but …" sorts of people!'

'That's not enough to arrest them,' Anna pointed out. 'OK, moving on! What about Piers Addison? He lived on the same staircase as the victim, I gather?'

'That's right. He said that Jibrilu kept complaining about him making a noise and criticised him for taking girls back to his room. He *does* seem to have been a bit of a busy-body. I can understand why he got up people's noses.'

'Not much of a motive for murder, though,' Anna commented. It was looking increasingly as if the first week of the investigation had failed to produce any convincing suspects at all.

'But the pathologist said it most likely wasn't intentional!' Iestyn piped up. 'He said it was just bad luck that the blade cut this "femoral artery" that it talks about in the PM report. The killer most likely didn't mean to do serious damage and he may not even have known that he had.'

'Which means we're probably looking for someone who just happened to have a knife with them when they had an altercation with Jibrilu – maybe something quite minor – and used it to threaten him or because they thought he was threatening them,' chipped in Alice.

'Such as Hugo the Highlander?' suggested Anna with a smile.

'Exactly!' Iestyn agreed. 'Or just possibly that youngster that Sergeant Duffield stopped on the High. Young kids often carry knives these days. They think it makes them safer.'

'Gabriel Sibanda,' Anna said thoughtfully. 'I suppose, if he did have a knife with him, he might have lashed out in self-defence, but why would he feel threatened by Jibrilu? Anyway, there's no point discussing that until I've had a chance to speak to him. So, getting back to Piers, where was he when Jibrilu was killed?'

'Hang on!' Alice called out. 'Before we get on to that, did you know that he also has a knife?'

'E-e-er …' Anna checked her notebook. 'It's not in Andy's notes of his interview.'

'No, not the interview with Piers,' Alice explained. 'One of the other students on his staircase told us about it. It's a hunting knife. Apparently, he used to boast about using it to defend himself out in the Bush. He killed lions and cut up antelope to roast over a campfire and all sorts of Boy's Own paper sort of stuff.'

'Mmm.' Ann pursed her lips. 'Yes, that does sound interesting. If other students knew about it, that suggests he sometimes took it out with him, so if he had an argument with Jibrilu, he just might have … but it would be more likely to have taken place on their staircase, not in the lane. Where was he that Monday evening?'

She studied her notes again. 'Ah yes! He said he was out in the afternoon, but he got back to his room before dinner. And he remembers hearing a disturbance in the street, but he didn't look out to see what it was.'

'So, he could have killed Jibrilu on the way back to his room,' Alice pointed out eagerly. 'And then slipped in through the gate that leads to the college gardens.'

'But he said he was at the gym and then shopping,' Anna objected. 'Why would he have his knife with him for that?'

'OK then,' Alice conceded, still determined to make the case against the egregious Piers, 'maybe he heard Jibrilu sounding off about something in the lane and picked up the knife and went out to put the frighteners on him. He got carried away and waved the knife a bit too close and slashed his leg by mistake. Then he gets scared and goes back in and claims he was in his room all the time.'

'But in that case, who did he hear Jibrilu talking to?' Anna asked. 'They'd be a witness. Why haven't they come forward?'

'It could be one of Piers's friends,' suggested Alice. 'That would fit with them being outside the door into Holy Cross.'

'Or it could be that black boy – Gabriel – who ran into Sergeant Duffield,' added Iestyn.

'Yes,' Anna murmured. 'Gabriel Sibanda. I really must get to speak to him today. But, getting back to Piers and his friends, the other one, Victor Lansdown claims to have been at home in Staines that day. Has anyone checked up on that alibi?'

'Yes!' Joshua Pitchfork raised his hand. 'His parents confirmed that he was there from Friday night until early on Tuesday morning.'

'Good.' Anna smiled towards the young DC. 'At least that's one person we can cross off our suspect list. OK. I think that's all for now. I'll leave you all to get on while I phone Professor Danjuma to introduce myself.'

12. AN INTERESTING CONVERSATION

The day passed quickly for Anna. There was so much to do to get up to speed with the Danjuma case, and the numerous other investigations that she was overseeing at the same time also called for her attention. Chief Superintendent Alison Brown called everyone in for a briefing on enforcement of the new COVID regulations, which the government had brought in as a response to the discovery of the omicron variant. A faulty smoke detector set off the fire alarm and they wasted precious time in evacuating the building. Before she knew where she was, it was quarter to four and the appointment that she had arranged with Gabriel Sibanda's mother was approaching.

Snatching a few precious minutes of peace, she sat at her desk preparing herself mentally for the encounter. She planned to go alone, thinking that one police officer would be less intimidating for the boy, but that meant that she would have no-one to take notes while she talked to him. She would need to memorise much of the interview to avoid putting him off by appearing to take down everything he said. Experience with her own children told her that the more seriously they believed that the adults were taking something, the more reluctant they became to reveal information about it. And black teenagers were famously suspicious of the police – unfortunately the feeling was often mutual!

What could she do to put Gabriel at his ease and encourage him to trust her? What did she know about him? Only that he was taking organ lessons from the music tutor at Holy Cross College where his mother was also a fellow, and that the family were Roman Catholics and went to the same church as Peter Johns. She reached for her phone. Perhaps Peter would be able to give her some advice on how to handle the boy. If he knew the family, he might have ideas on how to approach the interview. Back in the days when they worked together, he had always been a sympathetic listener. And, after all, his first wife had been black, so he must have a better idea how their minds worked – or was that a racist thing to think?

Her finger hovered over Peter's name on the phone display. What exactly was she going to ask him? Did she really want to admit that, senior as she now was, she was nervous of making mistakes in interviewing a thirteen-year-old boy, just because he was black? In any case, was it reasonable to disturb him at home so long after he had retired from the police service? She was no longer a detective sergeant learning her trade from her mentor. He had passed on the baton to her and she had to run with it.

She turned to her computer intending to shut it down for the day. She would go straight home after her visit to the Sibanda family in Headington. Andy's account of his interview with Esther was on the screen. As she closed it, Anna glimpsed a name, which prompted her to open the document again. Yes. Andy had taken a uniformed officer with him for that interview: On impulse, Anna rang through to the control centre and asked whether PC Stella Gilbert was on duty that afternoon and where she currently was.

'I hope you don't find this offensive, but I brought you along because I thought our witness might find you a friendlier face than me,' Anna said to Stella as they drove up Headington Hill together.

'The boy we're going to interview has already had a bad experience with the police and I want him to know that we don't all judge him by the colour of his skin. And you may have a better idea how to talk to …'

'I'll do my best, but I don't have much experience with teenagers. My two nieces haven't got to that stage yet.'

Anna didn't know what to say to this. She had been so concerned about the possibility of accidentally offending the sensibilities of an ethnic minority family that she had completely forgotten that her witness was in many ways very similar to her own children. Her son, Marcus, was not much older than this Gabriel whom they were on their way to see. How would he have reacted to being interviewed by the police? The chances were that he'd have put on a show of being laid-back and unconcerned, and then boasted about it to his friends afterwards – unless he thought he was under suspicion. In that case, he'd probably still try to present a nonchalant façade, but afterwards there would be shouting and slamming of doors. He liked to put on a show of cruising through life without a care in the world, which made it all the more difficult to anticipate when the pent-up frustration or anger about some perceived injustice might be about to explode.

Jessica, on the other hand, would have wanted to know all about the case. What had happened? Why was she being questioned? What made them think she had witnessed anything relevant? And she would have wanted to help. She thought justice was important. She thought everything was important.

They parked in front of the Sibanda family home. The curtains were drawn, but Anna could see that the light was on in the front room. A small fir tree in the middle of the tiny front lawn was bright with fairy lights. The security light blazed as they approached the front door, which opened before they got there.

'Good evening!' called a tall woman dressed in jeans and a chunky knitted sweater in a pale blue that matched the headscarf covering her hair. 'I heard the car outside. You must be DCI Davenport.'

'That's right, Dr Sibanda,' Anna nodded. 'And this is PC Gilbert. I hope we're not too early.'

'No, not at all. Come in!' She held open the door while the two police officers stepped inside the hall. Then she pointed to a door on the right. 'Go and sit down while I fetch Gabriel. He's most likely got his headphones on, so he won't hear if I call.'

Anna led the way into the front room, which was furnished with two matching sofas upholstered in green velvet. Against the wall opposite the door stood an upright piano with sheet music piled up on top of it. There was a music stand in the corner to the left of it and three ukuleles hanging on the wall to its right. The whole family clearly shared Gabriel's musicality.

They both sat down on one of the sofas, listening to footsteps on the floor above and then a murmur of voices. Stella gazed round the room, trying to quieten her nerves as she waited for their interviewee to make an appearance. She wasn't sure what Anna was expecting of her. The television screen attached to the wall in a corner by the window was much smaller than the one that her brother, Danny, had insisted that they had at home. Beneath it was a bookcase full of paperback books. Stella couldn't read the titles from where she was sitting, but she recognised the binding of *The Hobbit* and *The Lord of the Rings*.

She got up, wandered over to the piano and started looking at the music. It looked as if someone had been practising a medley of Christmas songs. Without thinking she began to hum the tunes as she spotted *See Him Lying on a Bed of Straw* and *Born in the Night, Mary's Son*.

'Father Damien is hoping that Gabriel will introduce the congregation to a few of the livelier Christmas hymns.' Stella jumped guiltily and spun round to see Dr Sibanda smiling at her from the doorway. She stepped into the room followed by her son, who stood looking nervously round at the two police officers. 'Poor Veronica's repertoire was a bit restricted, I'm afraid. Do you play?'

'I – er – no,' Stella stammered in confusion. 'But I do sing – sort of. We don't have like a regular choir, but we get one up for Christmas every year. We're lucky; one of our organists is quite young. He was organ scholar at St Luke's College and now he's married and settled in Oxford. He conducts the choir – when we have one. One year he made me and Lucy sing a duet: *Every Star Shall Sing a Carol.* It was great fun, but a bit scary too. You'll know Lucy won't you – from St Cyprian's?'

'No, I don't think I do.'

'But you know Peter? He said he met you there. Lucy's his … she's Bernie's daughter. So, Peter's her stepdad, but he's more like her real dad because he died before she was born. She's at Liverpool university now, studying to be a doctor. We were in the same class at school, but she's much cleverer than I am. She wants to be a forensic pathologist. I'm sorry,' Stella looked apologetically towards Anna. 'I'm rambling. I'd better just ….' She sat down next to Anna and got out her notebook.

Anna smiled towards Gabriel and motioned him to sit down on the other sofa. 'Hello, Gabriel. My name is DCI Davenport and this is PC Gilbert. You can call us Anna and Stella. You're not in any trouble. We just need to ask you to tell us about what happened the Monday before last when you were on your way back from your organ lesson. Is that OK?'

Gabriel nodded.

'Right then, could you tell me all about what you did that afternoon, starting from when you left home to go to Holy Cross College?'

'I walked to the bus stop and waited for the bus. It came and I got on it. I got off in the High and walked to Holy Cross.' Gabriel looked round at his mother who smiled back reassuringly.

'Down Goose Lane?' Anna asked.

'Yes. I always go in the back way, because it's right next to the chapel. I went in and then through the little door by the steps up to the organ loft.'

'Was the door – the outer door, I mean – open when you got there?' Anna enquired.

'Yes. It's always open.'

'Good. You're doing very well. Do you know what time it was when you got there – approximately?'

'Ten past four. I know that because Dr Claughton was waiting for me and he told me. The bus was late because of all the traffic.'

'And did you see anyone hanging around in Goose Lane?' Anna asked, glancing down at her notes to confirm that Gabriel had gone inside the building before Leroy Gilbert arrived on the scene. 'You see, we know something went on there that afternoon and we'd be interested to know about anyone who was there – or anything, anything at all, that you saw that seemed odd or different from usual.'

'I don't remember seeing anything.' Gabriel shook his head vehemently. 'I was concentrating on getting to my lesson. I knew I was late and Dr Claughton doesn't like being kept waiting.'

'Alright. Tell us about your lesson. How did it go?'

'OK. I think.'

'Can you remember any of the pieces that you played?'

'Er ... Mendelssohn's sonata number three, and the slow movement from Handel's first concerto and then Mendelssohn again: *Hear My Prayer*. I think that's all.'

'Good. You're doing very well,' Anna nodded, mentally counting off these pieces from the catalogue of sheet music that the Scenes of Crime team had found blowing around in Goose Lane. 'And your lesson went just as usual, did it? No interruptions? No noise from outside in the street? No noise from the kitchens? Banging doors? Voices?'

'No.' Gabriel shook his head. 'But the organ's quite loud. I don't think we'd hear anything going on outside.'

'Yes. OK. So, you finished your lesson – what time would that have been?'

'Half past six,' Gabriel answered confidently. 'We always stop then.'

'OK,' Anna said gently. 'Now, describe to me exactly what you did then.'

'I – I put my music in my case.'

'This one?' At a nod from Anna, Stella took out a photograph from between the leaves of the notebook in which she had been taking down everything that Gabriel said, and held it out towards the boy. He took it and stared down at it. His mother leaned forward to see too.

'It was certainly one just like that,' she answered for him. 'Did you find it there – in Goose Lane – where that student was killed?'

'Yes,' Anna confirmed. 'Most of the music had fallen out – we've got a lot of that too – but there was still a copy of *Hear My Prayer* inside with a Holy Cross College stamp on it.'

'That'll be Gabriel's then. It was nearly new. We gave it to him for his birthday.'

'That's good,' Anna smiled round at them both. 'At least we can stop looking for another organist out that night. OK Gabriel, carry on. What did you do next?'

'Dr Claughton got some more music off the shelves by the organ and told me to have a go with them on the piano at home, and we'd go over them next time. So, I put them in the case too. Then I went out to go home.'

'Were you wearing your coat – or did you have to put that on after you'd finished playing?'

'Oh! Yes, I put it on before I came down the steps. Sorry, I forgot about that.'

'Never mind. You're doing great. You put on your coat and picked up your music case and came down the steps from the organ loft. Did Dr Claughton come with you?'

'No. He started playing the organ. The Messiah – *Unto us a Child is Born.*'

'Very good. Carry on,' Anna prompted as Gabriel hesitated in his story.

'I went out through the little door sort of under the organ,' the boy resumed, looking increasingly nervous as he got closer to the frightening incident in the lane. 'There were some people there, by the door.'

'The door from the chapel?' asked Anna.

'No, the other door, the one for outside. They were standing there smoking.'

'Can you describe them at all?'

'They – they were all wearing the same things,' Gabriel stammered, his eyes opening wide as he remembered the encounter. Anna remained silent, raising her eyebrows questioningly.

'What sort of things?' demanded his mother impatiently.

'Stripey aprons and white hats.'

'Some of the kitchen staff.' Precious Sibanda explained to Anna. 'They often go and stand in that doorway when they want a cigarette. We've often had to reprimand them for it.'

'Can you remember anything else about them?' Anna probed gently. 'Try to picture what it was like in your mind. It might help to close your eyes.'

'There was a lady with a white face and a screechy voice. And some men – three, maybe four of them altogether. One of them had very big hands with all like orange fur on them – like an orang-utan. He made monkey noises at me.'

'Would you know them if you saw them again?'

'I might. I think I'd recognise the woman, and maybe the orang-utan man, but not the others. It was dark and they all crowded round me and wouldn't let me out. I said I'd go back the other way, but they wouldn't let me. They took my music case and it came open and the music started falling out in the road. I was scared, because Dr Claughton always tells me off if I mess any of it up and it was getting all muddy but they wouldn't let me pick it up!'

Gabriel's voice rose in pitch as he recalled the frightening scene. His mother put out her hand and took hold of one of his. 'Why didn't you tell us about this?'

'I don't know.' Gabriel sat staring down at the floor.

'What did they say to you?' Precious Sibanda asked when the silence started to become uncomfortable. 'Did they say *why* they were picking on you?'

'I don't remember,' Gabriel mumbled. 'Something about bongo drums and bananas. And they didn't believe the music belonged to me!' he added indignantly. 'They said I must have stolen it. And there was something about Dr Claughton's organ that they all laughed at, but I didn't get what was funny about it.'

'How dare they?' Precious looked angrily towards Anna. 'This is racial harassment. What are you going to do about it?'

'I intend to find these people and arrest them,' Anna told her calmly. 'We'll need your son to make a statement and we'll make every effort to find out who they are and-'

'You know who they are!' Precious interrupted. 'I told you – they must be some of the kitchen staff. It should be easy enough to find them.'

'Yes, I hear you,' Anna replied patiently, 'and we will be interviewing all the kitchen staff; but right now, I need you to stay calm and let your son tell us as much about what happened as he can remember, so that we can build a good case against them.' She turned back to Gabriel. 'You're doing great. Now, go on: these people surrounded you and you couldn't get out. But you did get away in the end. What happened next?'

'The big hairy one grabbed me and held me up against the wall. That's when I saw his hands. They came at me like – like – like a big hairy ape was after me. He held me there and they all talked about what they were going to do with the music case. One of them said, "hand it in to the porters". I went there when I went for my next lesson, but it wasn't there.'

'That's because they didn't hand it in. We found it in the street,' Anna told him. 'But sorry, I interrupted you – go on.'

'All of a sudden there was someone shouting. I don't know who it was. The orang-utan man turned round to look and his hand wasn't pushing so hard on my shoulder then, so I wriggled out and ran as fast as I could along Goose Lane. Trying to get to my bus.'

'Someone shouted?' queried Anna. 'Who?'

'I don't know! I was too busy running. I was afraid they'd come after me.'

'Can you remember *what* they shouted?'

'Stop! I think. Something like that. He sounded cross.'

'He?'

'It was a man's voice. I'm sure about that. And he was somewhere behind them. That's why they all turned round and stopped staring at me; but I never saw him. It was like … like … Mum took me to a mediaeval mystery play once, and I remember Adam in the Garden of Eden after he ate the apple and this loud voice came from nowhere saying, "Where are you?" It was like that. Like it was God telling them to stop.'

'I see.' Anna sat in silence, thinking about this startling statement. 'Now, I don't want to put words into your mouth,' she went on eventually, 'but is it possible that the voice came from inside a room in Lichfield College? If the window was open, I mean?'

'I suppose so. I didn't think about it. I was just glad he'd let go of me and I could get away.'

'Alright. Never mind. Go on: what happened next?'

'I just ran and ran as fast as I could, until I got to the High, and then …'

'Yes?'

'And then I bumped into a police woman, and she told me to be more careful.'

Anna waited; Gabriel seemed reluctant to continue.

'Go on, Gabriel,' Precious urged impatiently. 'You never told us about this. Why didn't you tell the police officer you'd been attacked?'

'There was this big policeman with her,' Gabriel pleaded, keeping his eyes fixed on Anna, to avoid catching his mother's gaze. 'He wouldn't listen. He made me stand against the wall while he looked in all my pockets.'

'He searched you!' Precious glared angrily towards Anna. 'Did you know about this?'

'Not right away,' Anna answered carefully. 'And we didn't; know Gabriel's name, so we didn't know-'

'I told him my name!' Gabriel intervened angrily. 'He asked me and I told him, but he just laughed at me and joked about me being an angel. He didn't find anything on me, so he let me go. The other one – the woman – came across the road with me and waited until my bus came. I got on it and came home and that's everything,' he finished, speaking quickly as if he hoped the interview would now be over.

'Thank you, Gabriel, that's all very clear.'

'But what are you going to do about it?' demanded Precious. 'I'm going to make an official complaint about that police officer stopping and searching Gabriel. You say you knew about it? What's his name? Why hasn't he been called to account? This looks like a cover-up to me!'

'Mu-um!' pleaded Gabriel, squirming in his seat.

'I'm sorry, Dr Sibanda,' Anna said, as calmly as she could. 'I understand that you're angry. I'd feel exactly the same if my son was stopped and searched by a police officer; and you are completely within your rights to make an official complaint. However, at the moment, my priority has to be finding out who killed Jibrilu Danjuma, and it looks as if the best way for me to do that will be to pursue the people who attacked Gabriel in the back entrance of Holy Cross College. I will also instigate an enquiry into the actions of the police officer who searched your son, and if there were any irregularities in what he did, I'll make sure he is appropriately disciplined.'

'But it'll be his word against Gabriel's,' the indignant mother protested, 'and we all know what the conclusion will be!'

'Our officers all have body-worn cameras,' Anna told her firmly, 'and both officers should have made notes of the incident immediately afterwards. If there are any discrepancies between those records – or if the cameras show up anything irregular – then I assure you we will take action against the officer involved.'

'And his name – for my complaint?'

'I'm afraid I can't tell you now. I need to check the records, to make sure I've got the facts right. I'll be in touch – about that and about the incident in Goose Lane. And we're going to need Gabriel to sign a formal written statement. I'll arrange for someone to take you both down to the police station to do that. Would tomorrow evening be convenient? I may have some news for you on the other matters by then.'

'Very well. Thank you. Yes, tomorrow will be fine, any time after four, so Gabriel's back from school.'

That was a bit awkward at the end,' Stella remarked to Anna as they got back in the car. 'Who was the officer who searched the boy?'

'Neil Duffield,' Anna replied without elaborating.

'Oh. I don't think I know him.'

'I just hope he *did* have good reason to suspect Gabriel was carrying something illegal,' Anna muttered. 'We can do without another racism row. Thank you for coming with me. You did a great job of building a rapport at the beginning. I'm just sorry it turned out the way it did at the end.'

'You didn't mind me rambling on like that? I thought I was just wasting time.'

'Not at all. It all helps to relax the witnesses, and that helps to get them to answer our questions. And under the circumstances, I'm very glad you were there as concrete evidence that we don't have an all-white police service.'

They drove on in silence for several minutes. Then Stella plucked up her courage to say, 'My brothers both get stopped and searched quite often. Danny says it's at least once a month – sometimes more.'

'I wish I could say that surprises me,' Anna sighed. 'I used to think all this talk of "institutional racism" was a load of nonsense, but ... well, I still don't really buy it, but there do seem to be more bad apples in the force than I ever realised before. We need more officers like you to help turn that around.'

'That's what Peter keeps saying – and Lucy! But I don't see what difference I can make.'

'It's all a matter of perception. Once black youngsters start seeing the police as being more like them, they'll be less on the defensive and that may help our officers not to be so suspicious of them. Not that that's any excuse,' Anna added hastily, suddenly realising that her words could imply that she blamed the likes of Danny Gilbert and Gabriel Sibanda for attracting adverse police attention. 'Now, I'll drop you off at home and then go in search of Duffield to give him a piece of my mind.'

13. MISCONDUCT?

Back at the police station, Anna established that Sergeant Duffield was still on duty, patrolling the city centre to give reassurance to shoppers and tourists that the streets were safe. While she was waiting for the call from the control centre to bring him in, she sat behind her desk drinking coffee and pondering on the case.

Gabriel's evidence gave them a whole new line of enquiry, although perhaps Andy should already have thought of questioning the kitchen staff at both colleges, seeing as the murder probably took place during the period when they were there preparing dinner. He should have interviewed Gabriel Sibanda sooner too. He'd known about him since Sunday and it was now Wednesday. This business of finding his father really seemed to have made him take his eye off the ball.

Was it Jibrilu's voice that Gabriel had heard, calling out to the bullies to stop tormenting him? That would certainly have been in character, based on what they knew of him. Several of his fellow students had said that he was in the habit of interfering in what other people were doing. Did he see what was going on from inside his room and shout out through the window? And then, the incident might have prompted him to go out into Goose Lane to speak to the kitchen staff. That was in keeping with what various witnesses had said about him too. He liked pontificating to people about their behaviour. He would have loved giving the "orang-utan man" a dressing down.

A sharp knock on her door was immediately followed by the entrance of Sergeant Neil Duffield, who did not wait for an answer before striding into the room.

'You wanted to see me?' He stood there, feet apart and arms folded, head held high – a confidant stance, defiant almost. Did he know what this summons was about? If so, he evidently intended to brazen it out rather than to admit culpability.

'Yes, sergeant. Close the door please, and come and sit down.' Anna waited until he was seated on one of the two chairs across the desk from her. 'I gather you stopped and searched a thirteen-year-old boy, two weeks ago last Monday?'

'Did I?'

'In the High – about quarter to six?'

'Oh yes! Black youth, ran full-pelt into Tanya Tidworth and winded her. I'd have said he was older than that – sixteen at least.'

'Well, he wasn't. I've just come from speaking to him and his mother. She's planning to put in a formal complaint.'

Duffield's eyes widened in an expression of amazement, whether feigned or real Anna could not be sure, and indignation, which was definitely genuine. He opened his mouth to protest, but Anna continued, 'so I hope you had a good reason for suspecting that he was carrying something illegal. I'd like to see the images from your body camera and your written report of the incident.'

'But that's ridiculous!' Duffield blustered. 'I tell you, he was running like a bat out of hell. He went cannoning straight into Tanya. He'd obviously been up to something and was trying to get away. That's why I told DI Lepage about him. I thought he was probably mixed up in that stabbing in Goose Lane.'

'But that wasn't reported until the following morning, so you didn't know about it when you searched the boy.'

'I didn't mean I thought about that at the time. I just meant I could see he'd been up to something and was trying to get away, like I said. He had a guilty look in his eyes. And he looked terrified when he saw Tanya's uniform. I was sure he must be carrying either drugs or a weapon. Otherwise, why was he running and why was he afraid of the police?'

'Did it not occur to you that he might have been a *victim* of a crime?' Anna asked coldly. 'Or that he might be frightened of the police because of the way kids like him keep getting stopped by them for no reason?'

'Is that what his mother told you?'

'No, it's what PC Gilbert told me about her brothers. And DI Johns. You're old enough to remember him, aren't you? His son used to get stopped for no reason too.'

'This wasn't for no reason,' Duffield protested. 'Tanya asked him why he was running and he refused to answer. It was obvious he was up to no good.'

'Except that he wasn't.' Anna's voice had gone from cold to icy. 'He was running away from a group of people who had robbed him, assaulted him and subjected him to racially-motivated verbal abuse. You should have been helping him, not lining him up against the wall and going through his pockets!'

'If that's true, why didn't he say anything?' Duffield objected. 'Tanya asked him what was wrong. He never said anything! No disrespect, but have you thought he could have made all this up afterwards, to get your sympathy?'

He leaned across the desk and lowered his voice as if speaking confidentially. 'Come on, Anna, you and me both know that young black men are found carrying knives more than any other group in the population. I had every reason to think-'

'Maybe more black men are found carrying knives because more of them get stopped and searched. Come off it, Duffield, this boy didn't make up the way his music case was found lying in Goose Lane when the SOCOs went over the crime scene in the morning.' Anna stared directly at Duffield, who sat back in his chair again and dropped his gaze down at the desk. 'Or all the music out of it, blowing around in the street. Something happened there to make him drop them, and if you'd shown him a little bit of empathy, maybe he would have told you about it in time for you to get there and prevent a man being killed – or at least enabled us to start the investigation into his death twelve hours earlier, while the killers were still in the vicinity. And it's DCI Davenport to you!'

Duffield said nothing. It seemed that he had, at last, worked out that he was in a hole and needed to stop digging. Anna also sat in silence, allowing time for his discomfort to have an effect.

'As I said,' she resumed eventually, 'Gabriel's mother told me that she intended to make a complaint about your treatment of her son. If she does, there will be an enquiry. The first things they will want to see are the footage from your body camera and your written account of the incident. I want both of those on my desk first thing tomorrow morning.'

'The camera wasn't on,' Duffield mumbled, then louder, 'Tanya and I weren't expecting any trouble. We're not supposed to use them during routine patrols.'

'But searching a boy whom you suspected of carrying illegal drugs or weapons is hardly routine patrolling, is it? It would be immensely helpful to your case to have video evidence of exactly what he did to give you grounds for that suspicion, and to confirm that you undertook the search in accordance with the Police and Criminal Evidence Act. Never mind; your written account will just have to do.'

'I haven't had time to type it up yet. It's been all go these last two weeks.'

'No problem, just let me have your pocket book. That'll do fine.' Anna held out her hand.

'I – er – I haven't got it with me. It's OK. I'll get the report finished this evening and you'll have it first thing tomorrow, no problem.'

Anna smiled. She had him rattled at last.

'Good. I'll look forward to reading it – as I'm sure will Dr Sibanda and her lawyers.'

'Dr Sibanda?'

'Gabriel Sibanda's mother. She's a don at Holy Cross College, and his father's a journalist – very well connected in press circles, I believe.'

Duffield's mouth dropped open and he hastily clamped it shut again and adjusted his features to hide his consternation. Anna pressed her advantage.

'So, if they decide to make trouble, they won't find it hard to do it big-time. And you needn't expect anyone else to cover up for you. You picked on a thirteen-year-old boy for no better reason than that he was black and scared, and subjected him to a body search – in public. Have you any idea how that will look if it gets into the papers?'

'I'll have that report on your desk first thing,' Duffield promised. 'I'll get on to it right away.'

'If I were you,' Anna said drily, 'before doing that, I'd go round to the Sibandas and apologise for your behaviour. It's possible – just possible – that they may accept that and hold back on the complaint and the publicity.'

'Yes. Good idea. I'll go right away.'

'And make sure you mean it,' Anna added with emphasis. 'None of that, "I'm sorry if you were upset, but I did nothing wrong" stuff that you get from the politicians. Tell you what: have a go now. Apologise to me for impeding a murder investigation and bringing the police service into disrepute.'

'That's a bit thick!' Duffield was unable to suppress his indignation. 'How was I to know there'd been a murder? I came straight round and told Andy Lepage about it the moment I heard. And I did honestly think the kid was over sixteen and was a potential threat to public order.'

'But don't you see? That's the problem! You saw a black teenager running away from something and immediately assumed that he was a threat. You never even considered that he might have been the one who was in danger. I'm going to look into booking you on some unconscious bias training. Meanwhile …,' Anna sighed. She suddenly felt very weary of this conversation. 'Meanwhile, just get out of my sight! And mind that report's there on my desk when I get in tomorrow morning.'

'Yes, ma'am.' Duffield got to his feet. 'Like I said, I'll get on to it right away.'

Anna waited until the door closed behind him and then reached for her phone. Whatever he may have said, it was quite likely that his first action would *not* be to type up the "contemporaneous" account of the incident recorded – or more likely not recorded – in his pocket book; nor was he likely to be already on his way to visit Gabriel Sibanda and his parents. Anna's assessment of his character suggested that his top priority would be contacting Tanya Tidworth to find out what she had already told Andy and Anna, and to make sure that her account and his were aligned.'

'Hello?' the voice at the other end of the line was hesitant. Tanya was off duty and was not expecting a call.

'PCSO Tanya Tidworth? This is DCI Anna Davenport. I don't think we've met, but you spoke to a colleague of mine a few days ago – DI Lepage?'

'Oh yes, I remember. He wanted to know about the boy that ran into me in the High. He thought it could be connected with that awful incident in Goose Lane.'

'That's right, and it turns out it probably was. We think the boy – Gabriel Sibanda – may have been there shortly before it happened. I'm going to need more details from you about your encounter with him. Can I come round now to talk to you about it?'

'Well, er, could it wait until tomorrow?'

'Not really. I'm sorry; I know you're not on duty, but I really do need to talk to you right away.'

'Oh. OK. Yes. That'll be fine. I'll see you in a few minutes then?'

'Yes. I'll be right over … and, Tanya, if Neil Duffield rings, tell him you can't speak to him. The family are threatening to make a complaint against him and it's really important that there's no suggestion that you and he cooked up a story between you. Do you understand? The least whiff of collusion and the press will be accusing us of a coverup.'

'OK. I understand.

'Come in!' Tanya stood back to allow Anna into the small Victorian terraced house in East Oxford. She was short and plump, with wavy brown hair falling about her face. 'Do you mind if we sit in the kitchen? George and Alfie are watching a Netflix film in the lounge and I don't like to disturb their evening. I promised them they could have it once they'd finished their homework.'

'That's fine,' Anna assured her. 'I know what it's like when you've got teenagers in the house.'

'Go on through – it's the door at the end.' Tanya pointed along the dark hall towards a half-open door at the end furthest from the entrance.

Anna went through and found herself in a small kitchen. There was a window at the far end with a sink under it. The right-hand wall was lined with kitchen units and a gas cooker. On the left, a door presumably led out into the garden. Tanya had placed two dining-room chairs by the wall next to the door, in readiness for this interview. They made the tiny room feel quite crowded.

'Would you like a drink?' she asked, indicating the electric kettle that stood on the counter next to the cooker.

'A coffee would be great,' Anna smiled back. 'I could do with one. It's been a long day.'

She sat down on one of the chairs and watched Tanya busying herself with instant coffee and milk straight from the carton. She guessed that Tanya must be a single mum juggling the demands of raising two boys with the job that kept a roof over their heads and food on the table.

'I have to say, I was uneasy about that boy,' she said as she handed a mug to Anna. 'He looked scared to me – and so young! I was relieved when Neil didn't find anything on him. I wasn't sure he ought to have been searching him without his parents there.'

'It *is* legal to search minors without an appropriate adult present,' Anna told her. 'But only if there's good reason to suspect that they're carrying something illegal – the same as with any stop and search.'

'Neil told me he thought he might be carrying drugs or knives.'

'And if he had reasonable grounds to think that, then he did have the power to search the boy. Now tell me: did you write down an account of the incident as soon as possible after it was over?'

'Not then, no. Neil said, seeing as we didn't find anything, there was no point logging it. He said a lot of police time was wasted on paperwork, when we could be out preventing crime. But, after DI Lepage came asking about it, I wrote it all down then. I've got it here.' She reached out and picked up a manilla folder, which she handed to Anna. 'I didn't know what to do with it. Normally, I'd hand anything like this on to Neil and he'd deal with it, but he'd said not to bother, so ….'

Anna opened the folder and took out three sheets of A4 lined paper filled with neat handwriting. She began to read, taking occasional sips from her coffee as she did so.

'You estimated him as between twelve and fourteen,' she said, looking up. 'But Duffield told me he thought he must have been at least sixteen. Why do you think he got it so wrong?'

'So, he *was* younger? I really thought so, but Neil seemed so sure. I expect it was just his height. He was taller than me. And he did knock me off balance when we collided. But my Alfie's bigger than me too, and he's only twelve.'

'It says here that he told you he was running to catch a bus home. Did he say anything about running away from something that had happened to him?'

'No.' Tanya shook her head vehemently. 'He did seem frightened, but I thought he was probably just scared at being stopped by the police. Neil – Sergeant Duffield – was a bit brusque with him.'

'And then he stood him up against the wall and searched his pockets. I don't see anything here about going through the basis for doing the search or the suspect's right to a written record of the search. *Did* Sergeant Duffield go through those preliminaries before starting the search?'

Tanya did not answer. She sat in silence, staring down into her coffee mug.

'Did he?' Anna repeated quietly.

'No.' Tanya's answer was so quiet that Anna had to strain to hear it, but she had known already what it would be. 'But I'm sure he really did think he'd find something on the boy,' she gabbled, still keeping her eyes lowered. 'He's very experienced. He's very good at spotting when something isn't right.'

'If you suspect everyone, you're bound to hit lucky sometimes,' Anna observed drily. 'I'm sorry, Tanya, this really isn't looking good. But you did the right thing writing it all down,' she added, as Tanya raised her head and looked into her face with scared eyes. 'It would have been better if you'd done it right away, but three days after the event isn't too bad. Now, it's really

191

important that you don't let Duffield persuade you to change what you've said here. I'm going to take this statement away with me now, and I don't want any miraculous new memories surfacing. Do you understand?'

'Yes, ma'am.' Tanya nodded dolefully. 'I'm sorry I didn't do anything before, but I didn't like to say anything at the time – with Neil being a sergeant and everything – and then, afterwards, I thought it was all over and no harm done. I did see the boy over the road to his bus, and I asked him if he was OK, and he said he was.'

'Yes, I know,' Anna sighed. 'I know it's difficult when more senior people do things you're not happy about, but ..., well, I'll do my best for you, but if Dr Sibanda does go ahead with making an official complaint, there will have to be an investigation into what happened, and I don't see how you'll avoid being criticised for not intervening to make sure the search was conducted properly – or at very least reporting Duffield's behaviour afterwards.'

'I really am sorry.' Tanya seemed close to tears. 'I just didn't want to show him up. He is a good police officer. He taught me so much!'

'Well, you've done the right thing now,' Anna tried to comfort her, 'and you wrote this report without waiting to be told, which counts in your favour. It's just a pity that neither of you managed to gain Gabriel's trust. If you had, he might have told you about the people who attacked him in Goose Lane, and you might even have been able to prevent Jibrilu Danjuma's murder.'

'What time do you call this?' demanded Philip when Anna finally made it home that evening. 'Your dinner's in the oven. We've already eaten.'

'I'm sorry. There was a lot to do taking over this new case.' Anna hung up her coat and went through to the kitchen.

Philip snatched up his own coat from a hook in the hall and followed her, shrugging it on to his shoulders as he did so. 'You know Wednesday is my darts night,' he complained, scrabbling in a drawer for his car keys. 'I'm going to be late. It's the quarter final tonight and I'm letting the team down.'

'I know. I *am* sorry, but there were things I just *had* to do. Isn't Jess back yet?'

'She's been and gone. Pre-Christmas disco at the uni, apparently.'

'Well, as I said, I'm sorry you were left holding the baby, but it *was* your choice to come back. Would you prefer me to find us a childminder for Donna, so she doesn't interfere with your social life?'

'Don't be ridiculous. All we need is for you to be a bit more disciplined about your hours. Can't you delegate, now you're a DCI? Or request flexible working?'

Anna sighed. 'You know my job isn't like that. If someone stabbed Marcus to death, you wouldn't be very happy if the SIO told you they couldn't follow up on a lead because they had to get home so that their spouse could go and play darts, would you?'

'I wouldn't need to be told that. Someone else would do it.'

'Yes, because we've got so many detectives just sitting around twiddling their thumbs waiting for something to do! Oh, go on down to the pub, Phil! I'm tired and hungry and I haven't got the energy to argue with you anymore. I thought you said you were late!'

14. FAMILY TIES

Andy pulled his scarf closer round his neck and turned up the collar of his coat against the bitter cold of the December morning. Storm Arwen had passed over causing relatively little impact in Oxford, unlike Scotland and the north of England where homes were still without electricity several days after the wind brought down power lines, uprooted trees and blew roofs off buildings. Now, the wind had abated but it still came in from a cold north-westerly direction, combining with single-figure temperatures to chill within minutes anyone lingering out-of-doors.

He watched as the men from the mosque lowered Jibrilu's body into the prepared grave and then stood back with heads bowed. Why was he there? Was he representing the police? Showing respect for the man whose murderers they had not yet brought to justice? Or was he here to see his brother being laid to rest, in the absence of their father, who had to be content with the live video that was being streamed to him via a stranger's smartphone?

He could hear a murmur of voices, but could not make out any words. Perhaps they were not speaking English. Muslims prayed in Arabic, didn't they? Should he go closer? Should he tell them that he was family? Would Yakubu be hoping to see him there? He was Jibrilu's brother, after all. But they were all brothers, weren't they? At least, that was what Bernie had told him. All Muslims viewed one another as brothers – or sisters, presumably.

There were no women present. Didn't they come to funerals? Or was it because it was someone they didn't know? It was a good turnout of men, though, considering that none of them had known Jibrilu. Or perhaps they had. He should have asked. Yakubu had spoken about his son showing him pictures of the mosque. Perhaps he went there regularly. He ought to mention that possibility to Anna. There might be someone there who would know about any enemies that he had made in Oxford.

There seemed to be a lot of prayers. Were they calling on their God to take care of Jibrilu in whatever afterlife they believed in? Or maybe they were praying for his family? People did that, didn't they, when someone died? Thoughts and prayers, that was what they said, wasn't it? Andy had never been religious, but he did sometimes ask silently for whatever supreme being there might be out there to fix things. Was that prayer?

He had attended a Church of England primary school, which meant that the vicar came in once a week to tell them a Bible story at assembly, and they walked down the road to the church for special occasions such as the Christmas carol service. And he had been to church parade with the scouts. The prayers at those services had all been written down in a book. He could still remember some of them, they had said them over so many times.

When they were in the top class, they had all been encouraged to get confirmed. His mother had come to that service, all dressed up in a hat that he had never seen her wear before – or only in pictures of his Aunt Jenny's wedding. Was the God that he had claimed he believed in then the same God as these men were praying to now? Bernie said that Allah was just the Arabic word for God. But what did "God" mean, anyway? He supposed that he believed in something outside the material world, but what exactly, he wasn't sure. Peter and Bernie and even Jonah all seemed to think it was important – important enough to go to church every Sunday, anyway. But what did it matter really what you believed, so long as you tried to help other people and be a good citizen?

Andy stamped his feet to try to warm them. How much longer should he wait? The figures around the grave were moving now. They were walking towards him. Should he greet them as they passed and tell them who he was? Wasn't that DCI Khan there? So, the police were represented anyway. It would be awkward explaining to him that the deceased was his half-brother. He would probably think that Andy should have handed over the case to Anna sooner. He would probably be right!

Andy turned and slipped out of the cemetery, walking briskly to the side-street where he had left his car. He had seen his half-brother laid to rest. That was enough. Yakubu could not expect him to face the questions of strangers who were unaware that Jibrilu had any family living in Oxford, and with whom he had nothing in common.

Back in his office, he got down to the task of finishing paperwork that had been set aside when the murder was discovered. Anna had told him to take some time off, but this had been weighing on his mind and he was determined to get it finished before catching up on the rest days that he had missed. Besides, he ought to be around in case she needed him to fill her in on any aspects of the case that he had handed over to her so suddenly. She did pop in later for a chat and he was able to mention to her that it might be worth talking to the people at the mosque to find out if Jibrilu had confided in any of them.

He was just tidying his desk in readiness for going home when the telephone rang. It was Yakubu announcing that he was booked on a flight from Lagos arriving on Sunday. Andy expressed polite satisfaction that his visa had come through at last and sympathy that it had not been in time for him to attend the funeral. That gave Yakubu a cue to talk about the ceremony, which had clearly moved him, even though he could only watch on a video link. The mosque had done his son proud, it seemed, with all the right ritual washing and preparation of the body and all the correct prayers. It was a pity that no blood relative had been there in person, he said pointedly, but nevertheless …

Andy fought down feelings of guilt that he had not identified himself or come close enough to be caught on camera. Should he tell Yakubu that he was there? But it might be worse to have come and yet not taken part. Was there some role in the proceedings that the deceased's brother ought to have taken on? No, better to say nothing and allow him to assume that Andy had been too busy with his police work to stand around in a windy cemetery while men he didn't know chanted words he couldn't understand.

He broke the news to his mother that evening, as they sat together in the kitchen eating shepherd's pie and carrots.

'I've said I'll pick him up from Heathrow,' he told her. 'I'd rather do that than have some PC I hardly know doing it and then spreading the word around that he's my father. He's so full of it that I don't trust him not to announce it to everyone he meets.'

'I don't see why men always seem to think it's a wonderful achievement to father a child,' Amanda snorted back. 'That's the trivial part. It's the mothers who do all the work!'

'To be fair, he has lost all his other kids,' Andy protested mildly, 'and in traumatic circumstances.'

'Lost *all* his kids,' she corrected him firmly. 'He needn't think he can come swanning over here and claiming you for his own, when he's never had the least thing to do with us since before you were born!'

'Maybe he would've taken an interest if you'd told him I existed,' Andy felt compelled to point out, despite being entirely on his mother's side in the argument.

'See! There you are! He's doing it already: Setting you against me! Don't listen to him. He's manipulative. He's trying to get his claws into you because he wants someone to replace his real son. Don't let him take you in.'

'I'm not letting anyone take me in,' Andy's voice rose to match his mother's increased agitation. 'I'm just trying to warn you that you can't just pretend anymore. You can't wish him out of existence! He's going to be here soon, and he's going to want to see you.'

'Well, I won't see him! I just won't!'

'OK. I'll tell him, but I don't think he'll give up. What if he comes looking for you at work? He used to be a student here, remember? He's still got his Bod Card[6]; he showed it to me.'

'Tell him, if he does, I'll report him to the police for stalking me.'

'Wouldn't it be a whole lot simpler just to meet him – once – and tell him yourself that you don't want any more to do with him?'

'No. you don't know what I've been through. I don't want to see him or hear his voice or – or – I never, ever want to be in the same room with him again!'

'A video call then, so you can get out as soon as you've said your piece. He's not going to give up until he hears it from your own mouth. He thinks I'm trying to keep him from you. He won't believe me when I say you don't want to meet him.'

---

[6] Students at the University of Oxford are issued with membership of the Bodleian Library, which gives them lifelong access to the university libraries, confirmed by possession of a membership card.

'Arrogant toe-rag! Still thinks he's God's gift to women! Well, I'm not falling for his so-called *charm* this time and I don't want you having anything to do with him either. Why should you run round after him? Let him pay for a taxi from the airport – or get the train!'

'I've told him I'll do it now.'

'Oh well! Please yourself! Just make sure he knows I'm not having anything to do with him.' Amanda gathered the plates together and carried them over to the sink. Returning to the table with a bowl of fresh fruit – their stand-by whenever she had no time to make a dessert – she added, 'The chances are he won't be able to come anyway, the way this new COVID variant's spreading.'

'What d'you mean?'

'With any luck, Nigeria will be on the red list[7] before Sunday. Lots of Africa is already.'

'That's an awful thing to say! Don't forget he's just lost his son. He wasn't able to come to the funeral. At least let him come over and collect his things and see where he died and talk to the people who are investigating what happened.'

'Fine!' Amanda shrugged, picking up an orange and digging her fingernails viciously into the skin to tear the peel off it. 'Just keep him away from me, that's all!'

They finished their meal in a tense silence. Andy wished profoundly that Jibrilu had never come to Oxford. Surely these days he could have done his PhD at a university in his home country? Why would he want to come back to the old colonial power for confirmation of his academic prowess? And if he did

---

[7] During the COVID-19 pandemic, the UK's travel red list was a list of countries from which travel was restricted in order to reduce the spread of the disease.

have to follow in his father's footsteps, why could he not have kept his head down and avoided trouble instead of annoying the likes of Piers Addison and his friends by criticising their morals? Mum would say that he had inherited his arrogance from his father. But was it really arrogance that made Yakubu so determined to renew his acquaintance with her and to claim her son as his own? Might there not be some vestige of real affection for a woman with whom he had been in a relationship for more than two years? And wasn't it only natural to be curious about the son that he hadn't even known that he had?

'Don't bother with the washing up: I'll do it after you've gone out,' Andy told his mother the next morning, as they sat at breakfast together. 'Anna insisted on me taking back some of the time I'm owed, so I'll be off for the rest of the week. 'Are there any other jobs you'd like me to do for you? Any Christmas shopping or anything?'

'I don't think so. I think I've got everything under control.'

'Well, at least let me make dinner tonight.'

'If you like. I was going to get the other half of that stew we had last week out of the freezer, and there's a frozen cheesecake for pudding. I'll get them both out and leave them in the fridge before I go, and then, if you just put the stew in the oven on a low heat at-'

'I meant I could make something from scratch,' Andy interrupted. 'Not that I don't like your stew, but it might be better to keep that for when we're both too busy to cook.'

'If you like,' his mother said, sounding strangely reluctant to let go of the catering arrangements. 'But I don't want you slaving for hours over a hot stove. It's your day off. Why don't you go out somewhere? Enjoy yourself! The weather man said just now it was going to be a fine day. You could go for a cycle ride. Or what about bird watching? You used to go out to Otmoor almost every weekend, but I can't remember the last time you went.'

'Mmm. Yes. I got out of the habit during Lockdown last year and then we've been frantically busy at work ever since things opened up again. Maybe I'll look out my binoculars and ride over there later – after it warms up a bit. You'd better be careful going to work. It's frosty this morning. There may be ice about.'

Once he was alone in the house, Andy's thoughts strayed to the death of Jibrilu Danjuma and the imminent arrival of his father. How was Anna progressing with the investigation? Would she be satisfied with what he had done so far? It had all seemed frustratingly slow, and there were several lines of enquiry that they still hadn't followed up. Would she be asking why there were potential witnesses that had still not been interviewed? Gabriel Sibanda, for example, and his organ teacher. Should he ring her to let her know that he was picking Yakubu up from the airport on Sunday afternoon? Or was that just an excuse he was making to himself to justify asking her for news of a case that was now out of his hands?

He finished drying the breakfast dishes and hung up the tea-towel. Of course, as a member of the victim's family, he had every right to know how the investigation was going. He smiled as this thought hit him. It felt somehow comical to consider himself now on the other side, so to speak – a member of the public demanding justice for a loved-one. Not that Jibrilu could exactly be described as a loved-one, seeing as Andy had never met him! Or his father – Andy's father – their father.

He pondered on Yakubu as he made his way upstairs to his bedroom and started hunting in cupboards and drawers for his bird-watching equipment. Was it fair on his mother to continue to have any contact with him, now that he was no longer obliged to keep him informed about the police investigation? She so clearly wanted him to have nothing to do with his estranged father. And she was quite right in pointing out that he had taken no interest in them until the deaths of his other wives and children had left him with no other family. If she really were the love of his life, as he claimed, why had he made no attempt to get in touch with her in almost forty years?

But would Mum have told him if he had? She had never in his life volunteered any information about his father. It was as if she was pretending that he didn't exist. Could that be because she knew that, if Andy ever tried to find Yakubu, he would be back like a shot wanting to … to what? To take Andy away from her? Was that what she was afraid of? She had dedicated her life to raising him. What right did his absent father have to claim even a part of him?

He became aware of a vibration in his pocket and a buzzing sound that was growing louder. How long had his phone been ringing? He hastily put down the camera that he had been examining, trying to decide whether he had ever downloaded the photographs from an expedition to the South Coast more than two years earlier. Fearful that he would not manage to answer the caller before they gave up, he fumbled with his phone trying to find the right place on the screen to signify acceptance.

To his surprise it was Peter.

'Tell me to get lost if you're busy, but I heard in a roundabout way that you're off the case and on leave, so I was wondering if you'd like that chat you tried to ring me about the other day?'

Peter! Of course! Maybe he would be able to see a way for him to show some decent compassion towards his new-found father without totally alienating his mother. Fancy him remembering that garbled phone call he'd made last week and realising that there might be things he wanted to discuss one-to-one rather than in front of Jonah and Bernie, both of whom tended to have very definite views on everything and limited patience with waverers who could not make up their minds.

'Yes, if it's not putting you out.'

'Not at all! Jonah has been spirited away for the day by his son and daughter-in-law to visit Santa's grotto with his little granddaughter, and Bernie's taking the opportunity to help a couple of elderly friends to get ready for Christmas. So, I'm footloose and fancy free all day. What do you think? How about a walk together? Sometimes it's easier to talk when you're on the move.'

'Good idea. I was just – do you fancy a trip out to Otmoor to look for migrants?'

'Migrants?'

'Birds – wild geese, golden plovers, redwings.'

'Oh! Of course. For a moment you had me picturing people in dinghies trying to cross the Channel! Yes fine. That sounds good. What time …?'

'This morning? As soon as you like. Or were you thinking more …?'

'Now will be fine.'

'OK then, just give me a few minutes to get some things together and make a packed lunch, and I'll pick you up in, say … half an hour?'

'Fine. See you soon.'

'Better wrap up warm; it's quite bleak out there and it can't be much above freezing today *without* the wind-chill factor. And … thanks.'

'They're doing my head in between them,' Andy complained as he and Peter walked briskly side-by-side along the gravel path, which ran beside the flooded grassland that made up the major part of Otmoor Nature Reserve. 'On the one hand, there's Yakubu, all excited at the thought of coming back to Oxford and meeting us both; and then there's Mum refusing to have anything to do with him and resenting me even talking to him. They're both being stubborn as mules and neither of them will listen to sense!'

'I suppose it's been a shock for both of them,' Peter reflected charitably.

'Not as big as for me! Either of them could've got in touch with the other any time since Yakubu went back to Nigeria. I was completely in the dark! That's what annoys me about him. If Mum was really the love of his life, the way he claims she was, why didn't he come looking for her sooner? Why wait until he's got no other family left? It's as if – as if he only wants me as a replacement for Jibrilu. I'm not sure I like the idea of being the sub that only gets to play when the rest of the team drop out.'

'Or maybe he thought he couldn't get back with your mum while Jibrilu was alive,' suggested Peter. 'He might have been worried about the effect on him of learning about his father having an affair so soon after marrying his mother. Or he could have thought he couldn't expect your mum to become mother to his son.'

They walked on in companionable silence, while Andy thought about that.

'But then again, how can I be sure that he *didn't* try to contact Mum earlier?' he resumed after a few minutes. 'The way she's behaving now, I'm quite sure she wouldn't have told me if he had. I just don't feel I can trust her anymore! What else may she be keeping from me? And I can't understand her attitude. I keep telling her that the only way she's going to get him off her back is if she agrees to talk to him and tells him herself that she doesn't want to see any more of him; but she just keeps saying she isn't even prepared to speak on the phone. It's ridiculous! What does she think he can do to her?'

'It's not always easy to stay rational in these sorts of situations,' Peter said cautiously. 'I suppose I was a bit like your mum when my half-sister turned up all of a sudden.'

'Really? Why?' Andy asked eagerly, then, more guardedly, 'I mean, if you don't mind talking about it.'

'At the time I just wanted them to leave me alone. I'd got on fine for over fifty years. I just didn't want them coming in a disrupting my life. Looking back, I suppose I was frightened of what they might be expecting of me. And I told myself that I was worried about the effect it might have on my kids, suddenly being presented with a new aunty and grandmother. They'd already lost their mum. They didn't need any more upheaval.' He sighed. 'But looking back, I think I felt that my identity was being threatened. I'd always prided myself on not needing to have any family. Or the children's home where I grew up was my family. I know everyone would have you believe that I ought to have been excited at the thought of finding my mother at last, but it all just seemed … well, unnecessarily disruptive. I'm not keen on excitement. I quite like boring.'

'Me too,' Andy grinned. 'I think that's more or less how I feel. Mum and I were doing alright. I never felt the need for a dad. I think – hang on! Isn't that a marsh harrier?'

Peter looked in the direction of Andy's pointing arm and saw a large raptor swooping over the reed bed and grassland. Andy excitedly snatched up the binoculars that he had hanging round his neck and trained them on the bird. 'Yes, I'm sure of it. Did you know? Back in 1971 there was only one pair in the whole of the UK, but there are probably nearly four hundred now, thanks to conservation measures. Go on! Have a look!'

He passed the binoculars over to Peter, who dutifully pointed them in the direction of the bird of prey, which was still patrolling back and forth in its hunt for food.

'I'm afraid I wouldn't have known it was anything special,' he confessed. 'I'd probably have had it down as a buzzard. Anything bigger than a kestrel, I tend to assume is a buzzard – apart from red kites, of course; I do know what they look like. This one has a wide wingspan a bit like that, but I've never seen a bird of prey flying so low.'

'It *is* about the size of a buzzard,' Andy conceded, but the coloration is quite different. 'See the grey on its wings? And their distinctive V-shape? But there *are* a lot more buzzards about, so you're probably right more often than not,' he added with a grin.

They stood watching the elegant bird swooping in apparently effortless flight. Then, all of a sudden, it twisted round, looking momentarily ungainly as it disappeared into the reed bed. A few moments later, it reappeared with something clutched in its talons. Just as quickly, Andy had his binoculars up to his eyes again. 'It's got something!' he told Peter excitedly. 'A small mammal of some sort, I think. No! It's a bird – quite big – a moorhen, I think.'

The marsh harrier disappeared into a clump of tall reeds, presumably looking for somewhere discrete to consume its prey. Andy and Peter resumed their walk.

'And when you did finally meet her, what was it like? Your birth mother, I mean?' Andy asked.

'Dreadful!' Peter shuddered and then laughed. 'You couldn't have made it up! There was I, with two mixed-race kids; and there was she …! She couldn't hide her disgust when she saw the photos of Hannah and Eddie that she insisted I showed her. She'd been so pleased at the idea of having grandchildren, and then so disappointed when they weren't what she was expecting. Bernie and I just walked out of her house and came back to Oxford and never had any more to do with her – even though she was dying of cancer.'

'How dreadful!' Andy hardly knew what to say. 'And your kids? How did they …?'

'Luckily, I hadn't told them about her turning up. They never knew anything until long after she was dead. I wasn't going to tell them even then, but then, out of the blue, I got a letter from my half-sister, Jane.'

'And …?'

'She was getting married. She wanted me to come to the wedding.'

'Whew!' Andy whistled. 'That must have been a difficult one. Did you go?'

'In the end. I nearly didn't, but between them Lucy, and Father Damien from St Cyprian's wore me down. And then, after I'd said "yes" Jane showed me a photo of her intended!'

'And …?' his friend prompted, after Peter's dramatic pause had gone on for longer than he felt comfortable with.

'He was a Ugandan. His family fell foul of Idi Amin back in the seventies and they came over here to get away. He was "black as the ace of spades" as our mother would have put it!'

'Wow! I bet you never saw that one coming!'

They came to a bench and sat down. Andy took a small rucksack off his back and, reaching into it, drew out an insulated flask.

'Hot soup?' he enquired. 'I could certainly do with something to warm my hands up!'

'Great!' Peter nodded. 'I didn't think to bring a hot drink. I can see you've been here before.'

'Once or twice!' Andy grinned back. He poured tomato soup into two plastic mugs and handed one to Peter. 'It's where I come to get out from under Mum's feet. She always seems to be busy with housework when she's not out at work. I offer to help sometimes, but she likes to do things herself. She says it's quicker than teaching me how to do them right!'

They sipped their soup in silence. It was from a tin, Peter could tell. Amanda Lepage wouldn't have time to make it from scratch, and yet she would probably see it as a slight if Andy were to take it upon himself to experiment with cookery. It had been a bit like that with his first wife, Angie. She was grateful to him when he hoovered the floor or cleaned the bath, but putting wholesome, well-cooked food on the plates of their growing family had been her preserve.

It was very different with Bernie! She had jumped at his suggestion of retiring and becoming a house-husband. She didn't leap to the assumption that he had offered to get their meals because he had a low opinion of her own culinary ability. And she certainly didn't care if he volunteered to take over cleaning duties because she could not be trusted to notice when dusting or mopping was needed. If he wanted the limescale around the taps on the washbasin removed, let him do it himself; it wasn't doing anyone any harm that she could see!

This commercially-produced soup wasn't bad, anyway. Perhaps it was an indulgence on his part to make his own. And he probably wouldn't have bothered to dream up the recipe if they hadn't had too many tomatoes in the garden for them to eat in salads and on pizzas – thanks to Jonah driving them on to make the most of the extensive grounds.

'I suppose that's why she doesn't want Yakubu coming back into her life,' Andy murmured, bringing Peter abruptly out of his musings. 'I hadn't worked it out until now, but I've been the only thing in her life for ... well, forever. She gave up her degree to look after me when I was born; and then she did an Open University course so she could get a better job and buy a house for us to live in; and she still hardly ever goes out, apart from just occasionally with people from work.' He laughed a short, mirthless laugh. 'Yakubu thinks she never married because she's still pining for him! I don't think it's occurred to him that she's never had the chance to meet anyone, what with having to work full-time to pay the mortgage and then come home to get my meals. In any case, I don't suppose she was exactly a great catch, with a mixed-race kid hanging round her neck like the proverbial albatross!'

'I'm sure that isn't how she sees you,' Peter protested gently. 'There are plenty of reasons why she might not have wanted another relationship.'

'It doesn't matter what the reasons were. The point is: she gave up everything for me, and however this all pans out, I've got to see to it that she doesn't get hurt.'

'I'm not sure it's going to be within your power to do that,' Peter cautioned. 'Don't-'

'I feel sorry for Yakubu, losing his whole family like that,' Andy continued, as if Peter had not spoken, 'but that doesn't give him a right to come here and start interfering in *our* life. I grew up hating him for what he did to Mum. But then, I started to think, maybe it was just a sort of culture clash. Maybe he really did think she'd go back to Nigeria and be his third wife! So, I just pushed him right out of my mind for years and years. And now ...!' he sighed. 'Now I just don't know! He always seems so plausible when I'm talking to him, but then, right afterwards, I get this feeling that he's manipulating me. Is his sob-story about losing his whole family in a house fire even true? I know he deceived Mum all those years ago. Maybe he's a congenital liar and ... And then I talk to Mum, and she's just so stubborn and dogmatic about not even speaking to him that I want to scream at her to grow up and stop acting like a child. And then, afterwards, I start to wonder if I'm the one who's being childish. I just don't know what to do for the best!'

15. MURDER ON THE MENU

Anna, meanwhile, was intent on following up Gabriel's story and trying to identify his attackers. Taking Alice with her, she timed her arrival at Holy Cross to coincide with the start of the evening shift for the kitchen staff. As they approached the door from Goose Lane, a young woman with a white-painted face dropped a cigarette end on the pavement and ground it out with her shoe before following them into the dark passageway.

They had phoned ahead and the manager was waiting for them. He stepped forward the moment they entered the kitchen, holding up a piece of A4 paper.

'Good evening! You must be DCI Davenport and …?'

'DC Ray,' Anna answered. 'Yes. I gather you got my message, Mr …?'

'Armitage – Greg Armitage – I manage the catering department. I've got the list you asked for here: it's got the names of all the staff who were on duty on the evening of Monday the twenty-second. Now let me take you somewhere a bit more private.'

He led the way into a small room behind the main kitchen: a store for mops and brooms, its walls lined with cupboards bearing brightly coloured signs warning that they contained substances hazardous to health. He closed the door behind them and turned to Anna, smiling apologetically.

'Not very comfortable, I'm afraid, but we can speak here. I gather you've had a complaint against some of my staff. Can I ask what exactly?'

'A young boy was accosted on his way out of the chapel after having an organ lesson with Dr Claughton,' Anna told him. 'He was subjected to verbal abuse and then pinned to the wall while some of his property was taken. His description of what his assailants were wearing suggests that they were working in the kitchens here. They were standing outside in Goose Lane, smoking. Do your staff often do that?'

'I'm afraid so. We have a strict *No Smoking* rule in the kitchens, of course, for food hygiene reasons. So, staff who can't manage to go a whole shift without a fag do tend to congregate out there.'

'Could you highlight the smokers on this list?' Alice asked, passing the piece of paper back to him and handing him a pen. 'Just put a mark by each of them, so we know where to start.'

Armitage took the paper and rested it up against one of the cupboards so that he could annotate it as she had asked. When he handed it back, she could see that he had put ticks next to five names.

'Thank you. Are they all on duty tonight?'

'Yes, I think so.' Armitage took back the paper and looked down at the list. 'Yes – I'm sure they are. Do you want me to get them in here to speak to you?'

'Yes please – one at a time. And don't mention the incident with the boy. Tell them we're just asking about anything unusual they may have seen going on in the lane that evening.'

'I understand.' Armitage nodded and turned to go. Then, as he put out his hand to grasp the door handle, he suddenly spun round again. 'Of course! That's the same night that student was killed, isn't it? And you were here, weren't you?' He looked towards Alice. 'You were with that other inspector guy – the black officer who looked like he could do with a bit if feeding up. I get it now! OK. I'll send them in.'

Their first interviewee was a plump motherly woman who gave her name as Edwina Farrell. Mentally comparing her with the descriptions of his attackers that Gabriel had given to Andy, Anna ruled her out from the start.

'Thank you for speaking to us,' she said with a friendly smile. 'We won't keep you long. We're just asking anyone who may have been out in Goose Lane at all on the evening of Monday the twenty-second of November to think back and see if they can remember anything going on out there round about the time when you were preparing the dinner here. We've had reports of a disturbance round about that time. Did you see or hear anything?'

'The twenty-second? That's the day that young man was killed, isn't it? Val and Doreen told me about it. I sometimes do breakfast too, so I know them quite well. Val was terribly shaken up about finding him like that. When I saw in the papers it happened the night before, I did think back in case I'd seen something – without realising it was important – you know. But I couldn't think of anything.'

'Mr Armitage told us that staff sometimes nip out for a smoke and stand out in Goose Lane. Did you notice anyone do that that night?'

'Not that night particularly, but if you're interested in that you'd better speak to Courtney – Courtney Middleton. She's only seventeen, but she smokes like a chimney. She's always popping out for a fag, and there's two young men who're always following her out when she goes. Apprentice chefs they are. It's the latest thing. I think the college gets money for taking them on or something. Anyway, they've got these two youngsters who both think they're going to be the next Jamie Oliver. What with showing off their fancy ideas and chasing round after Courtney, they don't get much work done. We'd be better off without them, in my opinion. It's me and Betty do everything. These young ones don't know what real work is!'

'So, if a group of kitchen staff were seen congregating around the door into Goose Lane, your money would be on them being Courtney Middleton and these two apprentices?' queried Alice, before Mrs Farrell could catch her breath to continue.

'That's right. Courtney Middleton, Tyler Briggs and Logan Wyatt. The lads weren't so bad before she came, but she seems to have turned their heads. I can't see what they see in her myself – all painted white like a china doll and piercings all over her body! She's still at school, doing her A' levels. She works here part-time, four evenings a week. She started out just covering at weekends over the summer. Then, when term started, she started doing Mondays and Thursdays as well. I suppose she must need the money, with her forty-a-day habit and what she must spend on her appearance. She was going on the other day about a tattoo she'd had done on her backside. Of course, Tyler and Logan took a great interest in that! They always get a lot more work done the days she's not here.'

'Thank you,' Anna leapt in at Mrs Farrell's next breathing space. 'You've been very helpful. Just one final question: did you happen to notice a boy – a young teenager – going in or out of the little door from the chapel that evening?'

'You mean Gabriel? No, these days, he's always here before me. We used sometimes to meet on the bus, but he started coming earlier to get a longer lesson. But he was definitely there that day, because I heard the organ playing as I came through the passage. I could tell it was a lesson, because it kept stopping and then going back and playing the same bit over again. Not that I could hear anything wrong with it the first time. I think that Dr Claughton must be a bit of a fuss-pot, but I suppose you have to be when you're teaching someone. I just wish Mr Armitage would be a bit more fussy about the way Tyler and Logan carry on – seeing as they're supposed to be learning on the job!'

'So, you know Gabriel Sibanda?' asked Alice.

'Well, not really. We just got off the bus together a few times, and walked here together. I asked him what he was here for, and he told me about his organ lessons with Dr Claughton. I like to hear an organ playing – especially the good old tunes. There was a Christmas concert in the chapel the other day, and Dr Claughton played some beautiful things. The choir was good too – really raised my spirits! And goodness knows, we could do with a bit of Christmas cheer after the last eighteen months or so! But, as I was saying, it's been a while since I saw Gabriel to speak to, because he's always here before me now, and he's gone again before I get out at the end of my shift.'

'Thank you.' Anna walked over to the door and opened it. 'You've been very helpful, Mrs Farrell. We won't keep you any longer. Could you ask Mr Armitage to send Miss Middleton in next?'

'Miss …? Oh, Courtney! Yes, yes of course. I'll do that.'

A few minutes later the door opened again and a young woman walked in. As Mrs Farrell had described, her face was covered in a pale foundation which made her dark eye-lashes, enhanced by a liberal application of mascara, and red-painted lips stand out starkly. Also prominent was a black star on the side of her nose.

'Mr Armitage said you wanted to see me.'

'Courtney Middleton?' Anna asked, although she was in no doubt.

'That's right.' The young woman nodded her head and a pair of pendulous earrings jangled quietly. Her attention drawn by the sound, Anna looked and saw that each ear had four piercings containing a variety of rings and studs in different designs.

'I'm DCI Davenport and this is DC Ray. We're hoping you may be able to help us with finding out about some incidents that took place just outside of here in Goose Lane on the evening of the twenty-second of November. That is a week ago last Monday. You were working here that evening?'

'Yeah, but I didn't see anything.'

'I've been told you sometimes nip out to the Goose Lane door for a cigarette. Do you remember doing so that evening?'

'I might've done.'

'We've had reports of a disturbance in the Lane sometime between six-thirty and seven o'clock. Did you see or hear anything?'

'No.'

'No shouting?'

'No.'

'Did anyone go in or out through the Goose Lane door while you were there?'

'Not that I noticed.'

'We have a witness who remembers seeing you with a group of friends, standing in the doorway. He had to ask you to move so he could get past. Do you remember that?'

'No.'

'You're quite sure about that?' Anna asked coldly. 'Only, he gave us a very convincing description of you.'

'I don't remember anyone pushing past us the Monday before last,' Courtney insisted. 'Can I go now?'

'OK.' Anna nodded. 'Ask Mr Armitage to send your friend Tyler in.'

'Who says he's my friend?' demanded Courtney belligerently.

'Just tell Mr Armitage we want to see him next, please,' Anna sighed. It was beginning to look as if this was going to be a long night.

Once Courtney had left, Alice pushed the door closed and turned to Anna. 'She's obviously lying through her teeth. She's the woman with the white face that Gabriel told Andy about, sure as anything! How about getting him to identify her?'

'We could try that later, but I'd rather not let it come down to her word against his. Let's see what her friends have to say first.'

There was a knock on the door. Alice opened it and let in a tall, lanky young man with a thick thatch of red hair, on top of which his white hat balanced precariously, doing very little towards preserving hygiene in the kitchen. Anna studied his hands, which dangled at his sides on the ends of unusually long arms. Sure enough, they were large, and the backs were covered with long, red hairs. This was evidently Gabriel's orang-utan man. The boy clearly had a knack for picking out the salient features of the people he met. His observational skills would make him a good police officer.

She introduced herself and Alice, and invited the young man to confirm that he was apprentice chef, Tyler Briggs. He nodded briefly, then stood staring over her head. Anna reflected how much more satisfactory it would be if they had been provided with a room large enough to accommodate chairs for them all to sit on, instead of this cluttered store cupboard. Andy would have found it easier to interview this witness. At least he was tall enough to look him in the eye. After her lack of success with Courtney, she decided on a more direct approach.

'A week ago last Monday, you and some of your colleagues accosted a boy as he was going out of the Goose Lane entrance. Why did you do that?'

'Who says I did?' demanded the youth, glancing down briefly and then resuming his distant stare.

'We have a witness who described you extremely well. We know that you were working here that evening and we also know that you often go outside to smoke during your shift. Our witness says that you pushed the boy up against the wall and held him there. What had he done to make you do that?'

'I know my rights. I don't have to answer your questions. If you're charging me with something, you've got to arrest me and I'm not answering any questions without my solicitor there.'

'Look Tyler,' Alice cut in. 'This isn't about you and that boy. We're investigating a murder, and we think you were there shortly before it happened. What we want to know is: did you see anything out there in the lane that was unusual in any way? Another witness told us they heard shouting. Did you hear anything?'

'No. Well, yes, maybe. Just as we were coming back in, someone did shout something from the other side of the road.'

'Good. Now we're getting somewhere,' said Anna. 'Now, about the shouting. Was it a man's voice or a woman's?'

'A man, defo. Deep, like he was big.'

'And what did he shout?'

'I didn't catch the words. Like I said, we were on our way back in.'

'I see. And now, getting back to the boy. He remembers you very well. He told me he'd recognise you if he saw you again, and he described you so well I'd have known you anywhere. Are you sure you wouldn't like to tell me your side of the story and save us the bother of rustling up a dozen more redheads to line you up with for a formal identification?'

'No comment.'

'Very well, if that's how you prefer to do it, Alice! Could you caution Mr Briggs while I go and fetch Miss Middleton back in. We'll take them both back to the station and take some pictures for identification purposes.'

'Hey!' Tyler looked at her directly for the first time. Anna looked back. Good. She had got him rattled. 'You can't be serious!' he protested. 'OK. We had a bit of fun with him, but it weren't anything serious. We were just having a laugh. We didn't hurt him or anything!'

'Alright,' Anna smiled. 'Tell me about it.'

'We were standing by the door, like you said, chatting and having a fag.'

'*We* being?' queried Alice, who was taking notes again.

'Me and Courtney and Logan.'

'Just the three of you?' asked Anna.

'Yeah. That's right. Like I said, we were minding our own business, having a bit of a laugh together, when this kid comes along, trying to push past us. He looked too young to be a student, so we asked him what he was doing there. We're supposed to do that,' he added defensively. 'Security. Can't have just anyone coming inside and wandering around. He looked like he might have been pinching things, so we had a look in his bag – just to see what he'd got, like.'

'And what did you find in the bag?' asked Anna.

'Just some paper with music on it. He said it was his, but it had "Holy Cross College Chapel" stamped on it, so we knew he was lying. We took the bag and told him we'd hand it in at the porters' lodge. Then he ran off and we went back inside. Like I said, we never hurt him. If he says we did, he's lying.'

'And did you hand it in?' asked Anna.

'Hand what in?'

'The music and the case. You said you were going to hand it in at the porters' lodge.'

'No. Not in the end.' Anna could see that the young man was thinking fast, trying frantically to come up with a plausible explanation. 'He wouldn't hand it over. We took hold of it, but he fought back – like a mad thing. It fell in the mud, but he just kept on fighting. It must've got kicked into a corner somewhere. We were too busy trying to stop him hitting and biting us. By the time he'd run off, we'd forgotten about the bag. And Armitage was calling us back in. So, we went inside.'

'And the shouting?' asked Alice. 'Was that before or after the boy ran away?'

'After, I suppose. When we were going in, like I said. Maybe they were shouting at the kid.'

'Yes,' agreed Anna. 'Perhaps they were. Thank you, Mr Briggs. We won't keep you any longer. If you could just ask Mr Armitage to send in Mr Wyatt?'

Logan Wyatt was shorter than Tyler, but more heavily-built and muscular. His shaved head and tattooed hands gave him an aggressive appearance, which was belied by a nervous expression and a mincing walk. 'Mr Armitage said you wanted to see me?'

'That's right,' Anna confirmed. 'I'm DCI Davenport and this is DC Ray. We're interested in what went on in Goose Lane between six and seven the Monday before last. You were out there for a while with Mr Briggs and Miss Middleton, I gather?'

'I may've been. I don't remember.'

'Then let me refresh your memory,' Anna offered. 'You were standing together in the doorway when a boy came out of the chapel and tried to get past you. According to Mr Briggs, you were suspicious of him because he didn't look like a student and you asked him what he was doing there. Is it starting to come back to you now?'

'Er, yeah. I remember that. Tyler didn't like the way he was cheeking us, so he ...' He trailed off, evidently unsure how much his friend had admitted to.

'He what?' prompted Alice.

'He ... er ... he got hold of him – not hard, like, just to show him who was boss. And then Courtney grabbed his bag – he had this funny leather bag he was holding.'

'Why did she do that?' asked Anna.

'Because … because … because we thought he must've stolen it! It wasn't the sort of thing a kid like that would have, was it? I mean – it was all new, shiny leather and papers inside with music printed on them.'

'A kid like what?' asked Alice menacingly. 'What was it about him that made it so impossible he could own a music case?'

'Like – like … well, only posh kids have that sort of thing.'

'Perhaps he *is* a posh kid,' suggested Anna mildly. 'His mother is a tutor at this college, and her friend Dr Claughton is teaching him to play the organ. Does that make him posh?'

'But, but …,' Logan stuttered. 'But he was …'

'Black?' suggested Alice.

'Yeah, I suppose.'

'OK. Go on,' said Anna. 'What next?'

''Er … well, there was this guy started shouting. So, Tyler let go of the kid and he run off. And then we went back inside and got on with our work. And that was it like.'

'What was the man like?' demanded Alice. 'And what did he shout?'

'A big black guy. He come over and started shouting and swearing at us like we was doing something wrong.'

'You were,' Alice pointed out coldly. 'You'd just assaulted a young boy and stolen his music case.'

'We never! He started it! We were only having a bit of fun with him. We were going to give him the bag back. And we never took it away. We left it there for him to come back and get it.'

'We'll have to wait and see what the magistrate thinks about that,' Alice told him menacingly. 'Meanwhile, perhaps you could have another go at describing the man who shouted at you. He was black – what else?'

'Dunno.' Logan shrugged. 'That's all I remember.' Then, after a short pause, 'and big – taller than Tyler. But, like I said, as soon as he came, we went back inside. We didn't want any trouble.'

'So, none of you got out a knife you'd brought from the kitchen and threatened him with it?' suggested Alice. 'To frighten him off?'

'No! We just went back in and closed the door.'

'Logan and Tyler could be telling the truth,' Anna said to Alice after they had completed all their interviews with the kitchen staff. 'They've given us an explanation of why Jibrilu was out there in the lane in his shirtsleeves on a cold November night, but that doesn't automatically mean that one of them killed him.'

'A bit of a coincidence though, isn't it?' replied Alice. 'Especially considering what easy access they all had to the sort of knife that was used. One of them could've had one in the pocket of their apron and taken it out to defend themselves when Jibrilu came over, all self-righteous, telling them to lay off Gabriel.'

'It's going to be hard to prove, though.' Anna leaned back against a cupboard labelled, "bleach, disinfectant, drain-clearer". 'How can we possibly tell which knife to send off for testing? There are probably dozens of them in there. I saw at least six as we came through just now! They'll all have been washed by now, anyway. The same goes for their aprons and clothes.'

'How about their shoes?' suggested Alice. '*They* can't have been boil-washed!'

'Yes,' Anna murmured. 'Yes, you might have something there. And Logan and Tyler were both wearing canvas trainers. They won't have been polished like you might do with leather shoes. OK, here's what we'll do. We'll take away one of each kind of knife that they have in the kitchen – for Mike Carson to have a look at and say if they could have been the murder weapon. And we'll take Tyler, Logan and Courtney's aprons, just in case there are still traces of Jibrilu's blood on them. You never know, just having us take them may put the wind up them enough to spark a

221

confession. And we'll take all their shoes too. And then, tomorrow, we'll have them all in to the station for questioning under caution. Even if they didn't do it, I'm pretty sure they know more than they're telling us.'

'Surely they must've done it!' protested Alice. 'It all fits. Three bullies attacking a young black boy. Jibrilu comes over to tell them off. They resent his interference and pull out a knife and – there you are!'

'Or they get frightened and one of them takes out the knife in self-defence,' Anna nodded. 'I know. It does all fit very nicely, but I'm thinking about those other knives we've come across in this investigation. What if they're telling the truth when they say they went back inside as soon as Jibrilu came on the scene. What's to stop Piers Addison turning up with his hunting knife and deciding to teach him a lesson for having the effrontery to challenge a group of white people? Or Hugo Dewar could have been there with his ceremonial highland dagger. Either way, you never know, Courtney or Logan or Tyler may have seen them, and they may magically remember if they think that otherwise they're going to be charged with murder themselves.'

'I've had a look at those knives you gave me,' Mike Carson's musical brogue came over the telephone the next day, 'and almost any of them could've done it. Because it was a slash rather than a stab, the shape of the wound doesn't give us a clear idea of the shape of the weapon. Do you want me to send them on for testing?'

'No. There's no point,' Anna told him. 'Those are just the tip of the iceberg. There are a whole lot more knives in that kitchen, and there's no knowing which one might have been the one. Besides, the manager took me through the cleaning process. The dishwasher subjects all the cutlery to high pressure washing with

95-degree water and a powerful disinfectant. It's much the same with the aprons they use: all boil-washed weekly. Any tests that we did for blood would almost certainly come up negative, and that would just be grist to the mill for the defence team. A good counsel would easily convince a jury that the absence of evidence is the same as evidence of innocence. To be honest, I'm pinning my hopes on a confession. With three suspects, only one of whom can have actually wielded the knife, there's a good chance one of them will give way eventually, if only in order to pin the actual killing on one of the others.'

'OK. I'll send them all back to you then, shall I?'

'Yes. Thanks Mike.'

Anna put down the phone and sat for a few minutes thinking through the day ahead. Uniformed officers had been dispatched to bring in Courtney, Logan and Tyler for questioning and a magistrate was being sought to provide warrants for searching their homes. It wasn't clear what they would be looking for, since both the assault on Gabriel and the killing of Jibrilu appeared to be spur-of-the-moment incidents. But you never knew: one or more of them could be involved in white-supremacism. Or they could even have taken the murder weapon home with them, absent-mindedly or with a misguided intention of disposing of it.

'Now, Courtney,' Anna said again, looking at her across the table of the interview room. 'Logan has already told us that a man came across the road and took part in an altercation with you. I'm just asking you to tell us what you saw of him.'

'And I just told you – I *didn't* see him.' Courtney did not look up from examining a chip in the nail varnish on her immaculately-shaped fingernails. 'I must've gone back in before he came over.'

'The same way you didn't notice a boy coming out of the chapel?' asked Alice. 'Even though your friends say you grabbed his bag?'

'I never!' Courtney looked up at last, her eyes flaming. 'That was Logan.'

'So, you *do* remember!' Alice's tone was triumphant. 'Now we're getting somewhere. 'Let's go back to the beginning, shall we? Tell us all about it.'

Courtney glanced nervously towards the solicitor who sat silently beside her. He nodded almost imperceptibly.

'OK.' Courtney looked across at Anna. 'Look, do you think I could have a fag first?'

'Sorry. There's no smoking in here.'

'The sooner you tell us everything, the sooner we'll be able to let you go,' Alice added.

'OK.' Courtney took a sip from the plastic beaker of water that stood on the table in front of her. 'Like I told you before, we were all standing in the doorway – that's me, Tyler and Logan – having a quick fag in between prepping the veg and getting the starters out on the tables. It was grapefruit. We'd got them all ready in the fridge. And this kid comes wandering along the corridor wanting to get past into the lane.'

'Go on,' Anna prompted, after waiting several seconds for her to continue. 'What next?'

'Logan asked him what he was doing there. It's what we're told to do,' she added defensively. 'There's been trouble with intruders getting in the college. We're supposed to report anyone who looks suspicious to the porters.'

'So why didn't you?' asked Alice.

'We would've done, only he ran off after Logan and Tyler had words with him.'

'And by "words" you mean …?' queried Anna.

'Like I said, they asked him what he was doing there and he said he'd been playing with Dr Claughton's organ, which made us all laugh. And then there was a bit of banter and then he ran off.'

'And did you or either of the others lay hands on the boy at all?' asked Anna, 'to stop him going back inside the college, for example, or to prevent him running away?'

'No.' Courtney hesitated and glanced towards the solicitor again. 'Well, yes. Tyler may have sort of-'

There was a knock at the door and Jennifer Moorehouse came in. 'Ma'am? There's someone from the lab on the phone. I think you might want to take the call. It's about those shoes you sent to them.'

'OK. Thanks Jenny.' Anna turned to address Courtney and her solicitor. 'We'll take a breather for a few minutes. Just have a think about your position. We've got a witness who can testify that you were there and that you subjected him to racial harassment. If you don't tell us what really happened, you could be convicted of a whole lot more than that. Don't you think it'd be far better to tell us the truth? I don't think you were the one with the knife. Why should you go down as an accessory to murder, when you could get the benefit of helping us to nail Tyler or Logan for it instead?'

'We've done a Kastle-Meyer test on those shoes you gave us,' the lab technician said, pausing afterwards as if he had conveyed dramatic news.

'And that is?' asked Anna, none the wiser.

'It's a presumptive test for blood. The laces on one of the shoes came up positive.'

'So, there was blood on the shoes? Which pair was it?'

'It was the one labelled *Logan Wyatt*, but, as I said, this was just a presumptive test.'

'You mean, you're not sure?'

'That's right. The Kastle-Meyer test can throw up false positives. And even if it *is* blood, we don't know yet if it's human. It could've dripped off a raw steak, for instance. And it could be human, but not from the victim. The wearer of the shoes, for example, could've cut his hand and then transferred his own blood to the laces when he tied them up.' Anna got the impression that the technician was quite enjoying giving her this lecture in forensic science. 'I was ringing to ask if you want us to do a confirmatory test for blood, and then, if that's positive to go on to a DNA analysis. My boss needs you to sanction the expenditure.'

'Yes, go on. It's important we know for sure. Get on with the tests, and send me your report as soon as they're done.'

Anna ended the call and went straight back to the interview room where Courtney was waiting. Alice had just arrived back too, with cups of tea and a plate of Rich Tea biscuits on a tray.

'I thought these might help,' she explained, turning to face Anna, as she entered. 'Shall I get some for you too?'

'No thanks.' Ann sat down and leaned across to the switch to start the video-recording again. 'Interview resumed at eleven-thirty a.m.'

She looked towards Courtney, who had just taken a bite from one of the biscuits. 'I've just been speaking to the forensic science lab. They've been looking at your shoes – and more importantly, at Logan's shoes. They've found traces of blood on them. *I* think it came off the knife that he stabbed Jibrilu Danjuma with after he intervened to stop you harassing Gabriel Sibanda. *Now* are you still sure that you didn't see anyone shouting at you to stop bullying the boy, and then coming over to have it out with Logan and Tyler?'

'I – I – I want to talk to my solicitor.' Courtney looked nervously towards the lawyer, who gave another of his infinitesimal nods.

'OK.' Anna got to her feet. 'You can have ten minutes. She stopped the recording and swept out of the room.

'What now?' asked Alice, as soon as the door was closed behind them. 'Do we confront Logan?'

'No, not yet,' Anna replied thoughtfully. 'I have a feeling Courtney is about to spill the beans. 'I'm hopeful that her solicitor will advise her to shop Logan for the murder, with a view to avoiding the worst consequences for harassing Gabriel. Then, *after* we've got Courtney's version of events, we can confront Logan, and with any luck he'll confess.'

'What if he says it was one of the others? It could come down to his word against Courtney's.'

'Then we talk to Tyler and see if he can break the deadlock. And in any case, we need to interview the whole kitchen staff again to find out if any of them saw one those three slip a knife into their pocket before going out. Now I'm going to grab a coffee and check my emails before we go back in and see what Courtney has to say for herself after she's had a chance to consider her position.'

In hoping for an immediate accusation from Courtney followed by a confession from Logan, Anna was disappointed. After the ten-minute break, Courtney appeared more composed and confident. She answered each of Anna's questions with a cool, "no comment". The solicitor had clearly informed her of her right to silence and, most likely, had been clever enough to realise that the forensic evidence was weak and would not be sufficient by itself to convict any of them for murder.

Logan was similarly reticent. In fact, he now appeared to remember rather less about the encounters with Gabriel and Jibrilu than he had the day before. Anna sent them both back to the cells in the hope that a few more hours of incarceration would produce a change of heart in one or both of them.

'Well now,' she said to Alice when they re-convened after lunch, 'Let's see what our orang-utan man has to say for himself. If he won't talk, then I think we're going to have to rely on Gabriel identifying them as the people who assaulted him and then going for some sort of joint enterprise charge in respect of the murder.'

'I'm sure he'll be able to pick out Tyler,' Alice said confidently. 'His description of him was spot-on.'

'Yes,' Anna nodded. 'I think we're going to be pretty safe as far as the threatening behaviour charge is concerned. It's pinning the murder on any one of them that's going to be tricky. Just because the blood dripped on Logan's shoes, that doesn't mean that he had the knife. If they all refuse to talk, the CPS[8] may not even let it go to court. OK, let's go.'

They entered the interview room where Tyler sat, accompanied by a bored-looking middle-aged man with a bald head and glasses. Anna recognised him as one if the solicitors upon whom they called when suspects demanded legal representation, but could not name a lawyer of their own. He had a newspaper on the table in front of him, which he folded up and put away in a black attaché case when she and Alice sat down.

'Good afternoon, Mr ...,' Anna hesitated over the name, which she had been convinced she knew. The solicitor opened his mouth to enlighten her, but with relief she remembered it in time. 'Gordon,' she continued. 'I take it that you are familiar with the charges that your client faces?'

---

[8] The Crown Prosecution Service is responsible for prosecuting criminal cases in England and Wales. It is independent of the police and government. It may decline to take to court cases that are unlikely to result in conviction or where the public interest would not be served by a successful prosecution.

'I am,' he replied, still deadpan. 'And we'd both be grateful if you could apply a degree of urgency to your proceedings. We have been waiting here for over twenty minutes.'

'My apologies,' Anna replied coolly. 'I was called to review some new evidence.' She turned to address Tyler, who looked down to avoid eye contact. 'Blood spatter on the shoes that we sent to the lab. Evidence that one of you stabbed Jibrilu Danjuma that night in Goose Lane. He came across to protest at the way you were bullying Gabriel Sibanda, and one of you took out a knife from their pocket and killed him with it. Isn't that what happened?'

'No!' Tyler slammed both fists down on the table, half rising to his feet and then slumping back into his chair. 'No,' he continued in a muttered undertone. 'It wasn't like that. It was self-defence. And no one was supposed to get hurt.'

'Tell me about it.' Anna spoke softly, coaxingly, leaning forward and gazing down on Tyler's bowed head. He looked up, his eyes wide and frightened, like a cornered animal. Despite his size, he looked young, almost as vulnerable as Gabriel Sibanda had seemed. She was suddenly convinced that Jibrilu's death had been a terrible accident. Not that whoever had wielded the knife wasn't culpable, but it hadn't been pre-meditated or intended.

'Come on,' she urged gently. 'I've got kids of my own about your age. I know how easy it is to get carried away when you're in a group together. Especially if there's a girl there you want to impress. Tell us what happened, and we'll see that you're treated fairly.'

There was a long silence. The solicitor leaned back in his seat with his arms folded across his chest and closed his eyes. Anna became conscious of her own breathing as she waited for Tyler to speak.

'It – it was Logan had the knife,' he said at last, his voice hoarse and indistinct. Alice got up and poured water from a jug on a shelf at the side of the room into a plastic beaker, which she set down on the table in front of him. He took a gulp, sputtered on it, wiped his mouth with the back of his hand and put the cup back down on the table. Then he swallowed hard twice and went on. 'We'd been chopping carrots for the dinner. He must've dropped it in his pocket before we went out. I dunno why.'

'OK,' Anna said encouragingly. 'So, you finished chopping the carrots and then went out for a smoke – just you and Logan and Courtney, is that right?'

'Well, Courtney went out and Logan followed her, and then …'

'And then you went too,' Anna finished for him, feeling suddenly enlightened. 'You didn't want Logan and Courtney to be alone together – is that it?'

'Sort of,' Tyler muttered, bowing his head even lower, enabling Anna to see the red flush on the tops of his ears, between greasy locks of his hair. 'We went out to that little door that goes to Goose Lane. There were a couple of students there. They're not allowed to smoke inside the college either. They finished their fags and went through to the quad, and then we lit up. There was music coming from the chapel – loud – and someone singing something. Then, the next thing we knew, there was this black kid wanting to get past.'

He stopped and took another gulp of water. Anna waited for him to go on.

'He talked weird – like in them old films they have on at Christmas.'

'How d'you mean?' asked Alice.

'He said, "Excuse me. May I come past?" No one really talks like that, do they? Logan thought it was hilarious. And he was carrying this funny leather bag – like he had a handbag. We all thought he must be a bit … you know. Courtney said something about it and that made Logan laugh even more. Then the kid says he's been having a lesson with Dr Claughton – on his organ. And *that* set Courtney off laughing. Playing with Dr Claughton's organ!'

'I'm not laughing,' Anna told him coldly as he burst into raucous, rather hysterical giggles. 'Gabriel says you stole his music and pinned him up against the wall. Is that what happened?'

'We never stole anything! We thought *he* must've stolen it from in the college. Where would a kid like him get that sort of thing?'

'Probably the same place he got those good manners that you found so amusing,' Anna told him icily. Glancing at Mr Gordon, she saw that the solicitor was sitting up straighter in his chair and looking rather more alert than previously. She even thought that she could detect a glimmer of amusement in his eyes. 'It's a pity that your parents don't seem to have been quite so careful over your upbringing. But don't let me interrupt you. What happened next?'

'This guy started shouting at us. I don't know who he thought he was. He came running over shouting at us to leave the kid alone. He'd run off, but this guy still kept on at us, telling us to pick up all the pieces of paper that'd dropped out of the bag, and calling us names and threatening to report us.'

'Can you describe him?' asked Anna. 'What did he look like?'

'He was big – taller than me and Logan. And black. In the dark, all you could see was his eyes, all flashing white in the street light. And his shirt. That showed up white too. He grabbed hold of my arm, and it hurt. I've got a bruise – look here! This is where he had hold of me.' Tyler pushed up his sleeve above the elbow and held out his arm for Anna's inspection.

She looked down. Sure enough, there were dull yellow and brown marks from where someone had gripped the skinny forearm tightly.

'That's when Logan got out the knife. He waved it in front of the guy's face and told him to let go of me. He shouted back. I don't know what he said. I think it was in a foreign language. And then he let go my arm and grabbed at Logan. I didn't see what happened then. The next thing I knew he was lying on the floor holding his leg in both hands. We all just belted back inside and got on with making the dinner. We never knew the guy was hurt! Even next day, when we came to work and we heard about someone being found dead, we never thought it was him.'

'You weren't there to get the breakfast in the morning?' queried Alice.

'No. We only do dinners – and sometimes lunch, if there's something special on. We work six six-hour shifts: four till ten Monday to Saturday.'

'I see.' Anna looked at him thoughtfully. She was inclined to believe that he was telling the truth now. 'And what happened to the knife – the one that Logan waved at Mr Danjuma?'

'He must've dropped it back in his pocket. We forgot all about it until we were getting changed at the end of the shift. He found it in his apron and put it in the dishwasher with the rest of the knives.'

'You didn't notice any blood on it at all? Or on the apron?'

'*I* didn't, and Logan didn't say anything, if he did. He just put it in the laundry bag with all the other aprons. We've got to have fresh aprons every day. Mr Armitage insists. It's hygiene. We've got to make sure we keep our number 5 rating.'

'I see.' Anna watched as Tyler took another draught of water and then put down the cup and looked across at her as if to indicate that he had finished his story now and was waiting to be allowed home. 'And afterwards. Did you and Logan discuss what happened at all?'

The young man shook his head, but did not catch her eye.

'Tyler!' Anna leaned closer, speaking low, but with a hint of menace in her voice. 'You might as well tell me. Did Logan ask you not to tell us about the man, and about him having a knife?'

'No! He didn't have to. We all knew if we said anything you'd think it was us who did him in. But we didn't! I never touched him and Logan only waved the knife about a bit. We never killed him!'

'Maybe that's not what you meant to do.' Anna sat back in her chair again, 'but you admitted just now that he was holding his leg when you left him, after Logan slashed at him with the knife. He bled to death from a cut in his leg. Logan's knife severed an artery.'

'How was we to know?' Tyler demanded, looking up, wild-eyed. 'Logan said he never even knew he'd touched him. We never saw any blood! He was still alive when we left him – alive and shouting at us. It was self-defence! He started it!'

'But you left him collapsed in the street and went back in to finish preparing dinner!' Alice said contemptuously.

'He was alive, I tell you! I never touched him. *He* attacked *me*!'

16. FAMILY REUNION

Andy stood in the line of taxi-drivers in the arrivals hall, self-consciously holding up the sheet of card on which he had written "Prof Danjuma" in blue marker-pen. There was something ridiculous about waiting there for Yakubu to appear through the door leading from Immigration. Who else ever needed to hold up a card with a name on it in order to be sure of being recognised by his own father?

He peered at the people streaming past: white businessmen with briefcases, probably involved in the oil industry; young black couples with tired children riding on top of suitcases on luggage trolleys, perhaps returning from visits to grandparents; older people – some of them grey-haired men whom Andy momentarily thought might be Yakubu – grandparents on their way to join the younger generation for Christmas, maybe. There were so many, the flight must have been full. But then it was the last flight from Lagos before the latest new travel restrictions came into force. A few hours later and Yakubu would have been prevented from coming to England by new rules aimed at reducing the spread of the new omicron variant of the COVID-19 virus.

That would have suited Mum, of course. She wouldn't have minded if Nigeria had been put permanently on the "red list" of countries from where only British and Irish citizens, and others with permanent residence in the UK, were permitted to enter the country. Anything that would prevent the return of her former lover – what a strange concept for Andy to get his head around! – was welcome news to her.

The crowd was thinning now. Most of the taxi-drivers had identified their passengers and left with them for the car park. Where had Yakubu got to? Was there a problem with his visa? Would he be detained as an illegal migrant? Or bundled on to a plane back to Nigeria? No, more likely there was a problem with his luggage. Perhaps it had been put on the wrong plane at Lagos after the internal flight from Abuja. Or maybe it had been damaged by the luggage handlers. Or could it have contained something illegal and Yakubu be under arrest!

But no, there he was, making his way slowly, leaning on a walking stick in one hand and pulling a modest-sized trolley case in the other. He looked older and more bent than he had on screen, but Andy did not need the cardboard sign to prevent them missing one another. The old man had spotted him too now. He speeded up his walk and a smile broke out on his face. Andy stepped forward, weaving through the last few straggling passengers standing in groups or wandering slowly around looking for signs to their transfer bus or the taxi-rank.

'I'll take that,' he said, holding out his hand towards the trolley case.

Yakubu handed it over and then clapped Andy on the back with the hand that was now freed up. 'At last!' His voice sounded hoarse with emotion. Andy hoped that he was not going to make a scene. Africans could be very lacking in reserve when it came to expressing their feelings. He could do without public histrionics on top of everything else he was dealing with at present!

'I'm afraid it's a bit of a walk to the car, sir,' he apologised, looking down at Yakubu's stick. 'Will you be OK? I can rustle up a wheelchair easily enough, if that would be better.'

'No, no, my boy. Your old Dad isn't as decrepit as all that! I'm just a little stiff after sitting so long on the plane. Go on! Lead the way!'

Andy turned and set off back towards the car park, walking slowly, trying to match his pace to that of the old man, who put out his hand and took his arm for additional support. Together they made their way out of the terminal building and into the fresh air.

'I'll take you straight to your hotel, sir,' Andy told Yakubu. 'You'll have to self-isolate there for ten days. I've arranged for someone to come round there tomorrow to give you your first PCR test, so you won't have to go out to a testing centre.'

'Ten days! But I have been vaccinated. I thought that meant I could leave quarantine as soon as my test result came back. I sent you the details. What is the problem?'

'Your second jab was too recent,' Andy told him. 'It has to be more than 14 days before you arrive in England.'

'Aagh! And I paid a lot of money for that second vaccination. I was told it would speed things up.' The weight of Yakubu's hand on Andy's arm seemed to increase as this unwelcome news sunk in. 'So, it will be ten days before I can visit Jibrilu's grave or see where he died?'

'I'm afraid so.' Andy felt irrationally guilty for being compelled to enforce rules that put public health ahead of the needs and desires of individuals, however distressing their circumstances.

'But you'll come and visit me? You *and* your mother?' Yakubu's voice brightened at the thought. Andy's guilt feelings increased as he was forced to dash even this small hope.

'No,' he said firmly. 'Self-isolation means exactly that. You have to stay in your room and no visitors are allowed. I've spoken to the hotel. They'll send meals up to you. Once a day, you can come out and go for a walk in the garden while they clean your room. Apart from that, you have to stay in there all the time.'

'In my room?' Yakubu seemed to be struggling to take this information in. 'And I can see no one?'

'There'll be a telephone in your room, sir,' Andy told him, trying to soften the blow. 'And Wi-Fi. I can lend you a laptop, if you haven't got one, so you can use email and do video calls. DCI Davenport will speak to you tomorrow, when you've had time to get settled in. She has some news to give you about Jibrilu's death.'

'News? What news?'

'They've made some arrests. They have three people charged and in custody.'

'And they killed Jibrilu? Why? What happened?'

'DCI Davenport will tell you all about it when she rings.'

'But you must know. Tell me who these men are and what they had against my son!'

'As far as I know,' Andy said cautiously, 'they didn't intend to kill him. It was two young men showing off to a girl they both wanted to impress. Your Jibrilu intervened when they started making fun of a teenage boy who was coming out from a music lesson in the college, and one of them swiped at him with a knife. They worked in the college kitchens – that's how he came to have a knife on him. That's all I know about it,' he added firmly. 'You'll have to ask DCI Davenport if you want more details.'

He led the way past rows of cars to where his own small hatchback was parked.

'Here we are,' he announced, leaving the trolley case standing behind the vehicle and reaching out to open the passenger door. 'If you would just get in here, sir,' he added, holding out his arm to help Yakubu inside, 'I'll put your luggage in the boot and then we'll get on the road.'

'Please! You must stop calling me that,' Yakubu protested. 'I *am* your father after all. And what about you? I think I heard your colleague say *Andy*. Is that what-'

'*Inspector* will do fine. And I would prefer to continue to address you as *Professor Danjuma*, sir. I think it's better to keep things on a professional footing. After all, we have only just met.'

'But I'm your father!' Yakubu protested. 'And surely our professional relationship ended when you were taken off the investigation into Jibrilu's murder? Please! If you won't call me "father", at least let us be on first-name terms. Call me Yakubu, and what about you? What does your mother call you?'

Andy hesitated. It would feel like a betrayal if he were to tell Yakubu the truth. While he had long since given up the unequal battle against friends, colleagues and passing strangers alike who all instinctively shortened his given name to *Andy*, apparently without thinking about it, his mother invariably continue to refer to him as "Andrew". Ridiculous as it would sound if he were to put it into words, to reveal that to his father would be like confiding in him a secret pet name known only to the two of them.

'Everyone calls me Andy,' he said a last. 'You can use that if you like, but I'd rather stick to *sir* and *Professor Danjuma*. That's what my mother would want,' he added, well aware that he was sticking a metaphorical knife into Yakubu's ribs and twisting it round. But why not? Mum was the injured party here, not this over-familiar academic who had exploited her vulnerability and even now seemed unable to appreciate that fact.

'I'm afraid it'll be quite a long drive at this time of day, even on a Sunday,' he apologised a few minutes later as they queued to turn out of the car park into the road. 'The traffic's always bad on the M25 in the afternoon, but at least there won't be all the commuters heading home along the M40, with it being the weekend.'

While Andy concentrated on driving, Yakubu kept up a stream of one-sided conversation covering his memories of Oxford life back in the eighties, his delight at discovering his new son, and his eager anticipation that he would soon meet the love of his life again. At first, Andy tried to acknowledge his words with the odd nod or grunt, but soon he abandoned the pretence of listening and retreated into his own thoughts.

How was it that Yakubu still would not listen when he was told that Mum had no feelings for him any more – or more accurately, that her feelings towards him were entirely hostile? Why was he so obsessed with the new son that he had only become aware of in the last few days, and not more taken up with grieving for his real son – the one whom he had brought up single-handed and incited to go to Oxford and thence to his death? How was he, Andy, going to manage the inevitable meeting between this imposter father and his mother? When an irresistible force meets an immovable object, the impact is bound to cause destruction, but there must be something he could do by way of damage limitation.

They were approaching the ring-road when he emerged from his own contemplation and realised that Yakubu was speaking earnestly to him, justifying his behaviour towards "my Mandy" and begging Andy to intercede with her on his behalf.

'It was different in my country back then,' he was saying. 'It was my duty to marry and have children. Marriage was for the family. It wasn't about love – not the sort of love that I had for my Mandy! We had a daughter, Samirah; but it was a difficult birth, and afterwards my wife could not have any more children. I needed an heir. It was expected of me. And Zubaydah had a sister, Jamilah, so I married her too. It was what our parents wanted and it was good for Zubaydah, who was ill and couldn't look after the baby. Jamilah helped her, and she was company for her while I was away in Oxford. I loved my wives, but in a dutiful way – the way I loved my sisters.'

'Except you didn't have children with your sisters, I hope,' Andy grunted.

'No, of course not. I did not mean that. I meant … I was trying to say that it is possible to have affection for someone without having that – that special spark of – of – of *passion*. It was so different when I met Mandy. That was when I discovered what Love really is. I didn't want to leave her, but I had responsibilities. My father was ill. I had to go back to support my mother and sisters.'

'And your two wives and goodness knows how many children!' Andy interjected.

'Only one. It was many years before Jamilah and I had any children. We had begun to think she was … After my father died, my mother kept talking about another wife. When I told her that I thought two was enough, she proposed that I divorce one of them. To me that was unthinkable! Samirah was still young and she needed her mother – both of her mothers. I told my mother that, insha'allah, we would have a son, but that I could not turn them out just to satisfy her impatience.'

'Your loyalty to your wives is touching,' Andy sneered. 'It's a pity you didn't remember your obligations to them when you were busy seducing my mother!'

At this, Yakubu gave a short gasping intake of breath. Glancing briefly at his passenger, before fixing his gaze firmly back on the road, Andy was surprised to see a trickle of moisture running down his cheeks. There were several seconds of tense silence before he resumed his story, the emotion clearly discernible in his voice.

'And then at last, Jibrilu was born! I could hardly believe my good fortune. My mother was delighted, and Jamilah was … I had never seen her so happy! And then, just a few months later, they all died – Zubaydah, Jamilah, Samirah, my mother and my two youngest sisters, my whole family, all but Jibrilu.'

'I'm sorry,' Andy mumbled, almost without thinking. In his work, he was often called upon to express sympathy with bereaved families.

'I was away from home,' Yakubu went on. 'I was at a conference in Benin City. I got a call saying that the house had caught fire in the night. My family were all asleep upstairs. The neighbours tried to get in to rescue them, but they were driven back by the smoke and flames. I thought they had all died, but then they told me that Jamilah had thrown the baby out of a window and one of the neighbours had caught him and he was safe, alḥamdulillah.'

'It must have been a terrible shock to hear that he had been killed,' Andy said dutifully, glad that they were not far from the hotel now.

'Yes. It was terrible,' Yakubu agreed. 'We had grown so close. It was a wrench even to allow him to go to Oxford, but I knew it was what he needed for his career. And I had hopes, even then … I never forgot about my Mandy. I wrote many letters to her after I returned to Nigeria. But she never replied. When Jibrilu got his place at Lichfield College, I thought that perhaps, if I came to see her in person, she would …'

'Too late for that now,' Andy told him bluntly. 'Now, this is your hotel. I'll just take your bag in for you and check that they've got your reservation OK, and then I'll leave you to settle in. I expect DCI Davenport will be in touch tomorrow.'

'And you will talk to your mother for me?' Yakubu pleaded. 'Explain to her that I never stopped loving her. I know that I let her down-'

'You can say that again!' Andy snorted as he went round to the boot to get out the case.

'I let everyone down,' Yakubu continued dolefully. 'My parents, who so wanted me to leave an heir; Zubaydah and Jamilah who never got the love I ought to have had for them; Jibrilu dying so far from home; you, my son, growing up without a father-'

'Mum and I did fine, thanks,' Andy said coldly. 'We didn't need you and we still don't. I'm afraid you're wasting your time trying to get her to speak to you. She's moved on, and so should you.'

He walked up the steps to the glass door at the front of the hotel. It slid open automatically as he approached. He walked across to the reception desk and introduced himself and Yakubu to the middle-aged woman who was standing there. She smiled sympathetically when she heard the purpose of Yakubu's visit to Oxford and then checked his reservation on a computer before asking him for his passport, which Yakubu handed over to her in silence.

'Thank you, sir. I'll just take a photocopy and then you can have this back. If you could just fill in this form, while I'm doing that …?'

As she pushed open a door at the back of the reception desk Andy turned to go. 'Good bye then. As I said, DCI Davenport will be in touch.'

'No, wait!' Yakubu dropped the pen that the receptionist had given to him on the desk and took hold of Andy by the arm. 'Promise me that you will ask your mother to speak to me. Please! I know I don't deserve it, but I would like a chance to make amends.'

Andy pulled his arm away, minded to walk out without responding. But then his eyes met Yakubu's. They were full of pain. He was probably a manipulative old man who was skilled in playing on people's emotions, but he was also a bereaved father whose son had recently been killed in a senseless knife attack.

'Alright,' he said at last. 'I'll ask her, but don't get your hopes up. If she says "no" that has to be the end of it.'

'Yes, yes, I understand. Thank you so much. Just a telephone call would be … or a video call would be better. I just need to-'

The receptionist was back with his passport. Yakubu broke off suddenly. He took Andy's hand and shook it. 'Thank you. You are very kind. Goodbye, Inspector Lepage.'

'Thank you for collecting Professor Danjuma from the airport,' Anna said when Andy reported to her the following morning. 'How is he?'

'Angry that he still has to self-isolate for ten days when he paid a big bribe back in Nigeria to get his second vaccination so that he wouldn't,' Andy grinned back. 'But I told him he was lucky to be able to get here at all, seeing as Nigeria went back on the red list today.'

'And how are you and your mother coping with it all?'

Andy hesitated. It was hard to know where to begin or what it would be fair on his mother to reveal about her feelings.

'I'm sorry,' Anna apologised, sensing his discomfort. 'Scrub that. It's none of my business. I just thought it must be difficult for her, having him turn up again after so long. It's … it's taking longer than you'd think adjusting to having Philip back after he left, and he was only away for three years.'

'She's a bit in denial about it,' Andy admitted. 'And Professor Danjuma seems to be in denial about the problem. He keeps asking me to arrange for them to meet and Mum keeps saying the day Hell freezes over will be too soon, and …'

'And you're piggy-in-the-middle trying to keep everyone happy,' Anna finished for him. 'Well, if you need more time off to get your head round things, you only need to ask.'

'Thanks, ma'am, but I'd rather be working. I more or less promised Professor Danjuma that you'd ring him today. I hope that's OK.'

'Yes, that's fine. I want to talk to him. I need to make sure he understands that, just because we've got his son's killers in custody and charged, that doesn't mean it's all over. It could be months before the case is heard. The backlog in the crown courts doesn't seem to be getting any shorter. OK, I'll take things from here. Now …' Anna dropped her gaze and began searching among various scraps of paper on her desk.

Eventually, she found what she wanted and handed it to Andy. He looked down and saw that the paper had a name, address, and phone number on it.

'This came through overnight,' she explained. 'It's a robbery with violence. The victim was walking home from an evening at the pub. PC Gilbert will be able to fill you in. She attended when they called 999, but the perpetrators were long gone by then. Her shift ended a few minutes ago, but you may just catch her if you're quick.'

Relieved to have something to take his mind off his domestic worries, Andy threw himself into tackling this new case. Robbery might not make the headlines in the same way as murder, but its victims were nevertheless often deeply traumatised by the experience. It was a gross understatement to say that it was unnerving to discover that streets that you had walked many times before could harbour thugs lurking in the shadows with knives and fists at the ready, waiting for unsuspecting strangers to walk past.

In this case, the victim was a muscular man in his mid-forties, who clearly found it deeply embarrassing to have been sufficiently intimidated by his assailants that he had handed over his wallet and mobile phone to them without putting up a fight. Andy suspected that he would not even have reported the incident if his partner had not insisted on it. She did most of the talking, while he paced the front room of their small house muttering repeatedly that they had jumped him from behind.

When he got back to the station, intent on writing up the details of the robbery and setting the wheels in motion to check the whereabouts of one or two known criminals who might easily have been responsible for it, Andy found two more incident reports on his desk awaiting his attention. With his team still tied up in finalising the cases against Logan, Tyler and Courtney for submission to the Crown Prosecution Service, everything new that came in was being directed to him. In his present frame of mind, that suited Andy just fine. He needed to be busy.

As he put his key in the lock when he got home that evening, Andy remembered, with a sinking feeling, his promise to Yakubu to do his best to arrange a video call between his estranged parents. He had not yet managed to find an opportune moment to broach the subject with his mother, but the disagreeable task could not be put off for ever. Better to get it over with.

He could hear the radio on in the kitchen. Mum was in there, bending down to check on something in the oven.

'I'm home,' Andy announced.

'Good. Dinner's nearly ready. I just need to set the table.'

'I could do that,' Andy volunteered. 'I wanted to-'

'No, it'll be easier if I do it. Go and get your coat off and wash your hands. It'll only be five minutes.'

Andy backed out of the room. This was obviously not a good time for raising tricky questions with her. Perhaps she would be more receptive over dinner.

As they ate her bacon risotto – a favourite food of Andy's – Mum kept up a steady flow of light conversation: anecdotes about the antics of academics in the library, news from Aunty Pauline on a visit to her daughter in Dubai, comments on the latest figures for coronavirus infections …. It was as if she knew that he was hoping to broach a difficult subject and was trying to head him off. Perhaps there would be a better opportunity later, when they were settled together in front of the television.

But no! It turned out that Mum was off out to Aunty Jennifer's in Islip. In fact, since Andrew was back home on time for once, why didn't he come too? It was his cousin Ellie's eighteenth birthday tomorrow. The present and card that she'd bought were from both of them. And Ellie and Jennifer would be so pleased to see him.

So they went, and Aunty Jennifer did seem pleased to see her nephew. Whether Ellie was equally delighted to entertain her aunt and cousin was a moot point. In fact, she disappeared after about half an hour, having arranged to meet her boyfriend for an evening out in Oxford. Her mother's protestations that she had school the following day, were ignored. She was an adult now – or she would be in a few hours' time. She could make her own decisions!

'Teenagers!' Aunty Jennifer sighed as she watched her daughter go. Then she turned towards her sister and smiled. 'But I suppose we were just the same. I remember all the rows there were when Mum found out you were seeing a postgraduate student while you were still at school. And then, when you brought him back to see them for the first time! At least Ben is Ellie's age. And they're both pretty responsible about their schoolwork most of the time. She just doesn't like having us ruling her life. I should have tried to organise things so that she was the one who invited you over.'

They didn't leave for home until late. Andy toyed with the idea of introducing the subject of a video call with Yakubu in the car on the way back, but he felt too tired to cope with the inevitable arguments and protests that this would provoke. Perhaps there would be time to talk about it over breakfast tomorrow.

He got up early and made coffee and toast while Mum was still in the bathroom. It was a risky strategy, because she sometimes saw his attempts at helping with their domestic routine as some sort of criticism of her home-making skills. He was relieved to see her smile as she entered the kitchen and saw the table laid ready.

'That coffee smells good,' she said happily. 'Thanks. Now, sit down and I'll pour you some.'

Andy obeyed. He waited until the coffee jug was safely back on the table and Mum was sitting down spreading butter on her toast before speaking again.

'I need to talk to you about Professor Danjuma,' he began nervously.

'I don't see why!' She was immediately on the defensive. 'It's got nothing to do with me. And I don't see how you're involved any more either.'

'I promised him I'd ask you to speak to him on Zoom. He's stuck in his hotel room until he's out of quarantine and he's lonely.'

'Surely he must have people back in Nigeria he can talk to, if he wants company.'

'It's not just that, you know it isn't! He's been promising himself he's going to see you again ever since his son came up to Oxford.'

'Then why didn't you put him right? It can't be that hard to explain.'

Andy sighed. 'I'm sorry Mum, but it's no good sticking your head in the sand. He's not going to give up, whatever I say. He'll only believe you're serious about not wanting anything to do with him if you tell him yourself. He probably thinks *I'm* the one trying to keep you apart.'

Silence.

'Look,' Andy went on, 'he's probably going to be out of self-isolation on Monday. If you don't agree to speak to him before that, he'll come to look for you. You don't want him turning up at work, do you? Or at Nana and Gramps? They're still living in the same house you grew up in, aren't they? And he's been there – Aunty Jennifer said so last night. What would they think if he suddenly turned up on their doorstep?'

'OK, OK,' she muttered, running her hands through her hair, and then sitting with them on her head, gazing down distractedly at the table. 'Give me his email address and I'll drop him a line.'

'Thanks Mum. I'll email it across to you.' On impulse, Andy got up and went round the table to give her a hug and a peck on the cheek. 'It won't make any difference – to us, I mean. Honestly, I'm not about to run off to Nigeria to find my roots or anything daft like that!'

'I thought I ought to tell you,' Anna said, later that week when Andy reported to her private office for one of their regular briefings. 'There's been a small setback in the Jibrilu Danjuma murder case.'

'Oh?'

'You remember the blood they found on Logan Wyatt's shoelaces?'

'Yes?'

'It turns out it's not human after all.'

'So … does that mean you'll have to drop the charges?'

'With confessions from all three of them? Not likely! And Gabriel Sibanda came up trumps and identified all three of them as his attackers, which makes them guilty of racially-aggravated assault whatever else. And once the jury accepts that, why wouldn't they convict them of killing Jibrilu too?'

'Just so long as they don't withdraw their confessions once this new evidence is shared with the defence team,' Andy suggested. 'They could start claiming that we forced the confessions out of them.'

'Mmm,' Anna nodded. 'The Chief Super has already thought of that. She's asked for the tapes so she can review the conduct of the interviews. I *think* we're squeaky clean, but you never know, do you? One person's intensive questioning is another person's intimidation! We had to push them hard or they'd have stuck to their story that they went back inside without even seeing Jibrilu.'

'What are you going to tell Professor Danjuma?'

'Fortunately, I didn't go into all the details when I briefed him about the arrests. So, he doesn't know about the blood on the shoelaces – unless you told him?' she added apprehensively.

'No. I just said you had some suspects in custody. I'm not even sure if I knew about the blood when I saw him.'

'That's good!' Anna was clearly relieved. 'With any luck, we can keep the business of the blood out of the public domain. Just so long as the defence lawyers don't try to make something of us using it to persuade their clients to admit to having a knife and using it to threaten the victim. Now, what about you? Do you have any plans for when Professor Danjuma is out of quarantine?'

'He wants to see the place where Jibrilu was killed.' Andy told her. 'So, I suppose I'll have to take him there. Apart from that, I'll be trying to keep away from him. My mother still isn't happy about me having anything to do with him, which is making things very difficult. She has agreed to have a Zoom meeting with him on Friday, which is progress, I suppose. Perhaps she'll calm down a bit after that's out of the way.'

Friday dawned bright with a touch of frost on the grass and on the windscreen of Andy's car. With term over and the omicron variant of COVID now causing a rapid upsurge in cases, his mother was working at home. She had arranged a video-call with Yakubu for her lunch break. Andy carefully avoided mentioning it as he prepared to leave for work, hoping silently that she would not back out at the last minute. It would be all too easy for her to allow (or encourage) a Teams meeting to over-run and prevent her keeping the appointment.

It was, therefore, with an initial feeling of relief that he received the telephone call from his father that afternoon, confirming that he and "Mandy" had met together for the full forty minutes allowed on a free Zoom call. But his heart sank as

Yakubu spoke eagerly about his joy at renewing his acquaintance with his sweetheart and his plans for their future together as a family. Mum would never have changed her tune so rapidly or completely. Yakubu must have got hold of the wrong end of several sticks!

After vainly trying to dampen Yakubu's enthusiasm with words of caution verging on discouragement, Andy eventually pleaded work as an excuse to end the call. He sat at his desk staring down at the paperwork that he was supposed to be completing before going home for a weekend off duty. He tried to focus his mind on ticking the correct boxes and filling in the right details, but it was difficult to concentrate. This stuff didn't really need a DI anyway. He decided to delegate the task to Toby Hitchin. He was keen to learn more about working in CID. Let him do it by entering up the details of this week's caseload into the computer.

He still had time owing from the long hours that he had spent in the early days of the recent murder enquiry, but he was reluctant to go home. Mum would probably be upset by her encounter with Yakubu, which she would probably believe could have been avoided if Andy had been firmer with him. And he needed more time to get his head around the strange story that Yakubu had related to him just now. He put on his coat and went for a walk in Christchurch Meadow, hoping that the fresh air would clear his head.

But no amount of thinking made any difference to his confusion. Could it really be true that Mum had experienced a complete change of heart and was now just as keen as Yakubu was for them all to meet up? It seemed unlikely in the extreme, but was Yakubu deluding himself or deliberately misleading Andy in the hope of bouncing him into further contact? Should he feel sorry for his father because he had lost his whole family or angry that he appeared to be trying to make him and Mum into replacements for them?

And again and again, round and round in his mind, that million-dollar question: was it possible that she really had agreed to get back together with the lover who had abandoned her nearly forty years before?

Back home that evening, his mother quickly disabused him of this notion. In answer to his mild enquiry as to how the Zoom meeting had gone, she launched into a tirade of abuse against Yakubu. He had not changed in the least, she declared. He was still the same arrogant rat-bag he'd always been. It was time he learned that he wasn't God's gift to women. If he imagined that he could just walk back in and act like the dutiful husband and father, he had another think coming!

Andy listened in silence. This certainly agreed more with what he had been expecting, but was it possible that it was a case of "the lady doth protest too much"? If this were how she had spoken to Yakubu, how could he possibly have got things so wrong? And why had he, Andy, been so weak and stupid as to agree to discuss with his mother arrangements for them all to meet in person once Yakubu was released from self-isolation?

Eventually, he summoned up the courage to remind his mother that, all being well, Yakubu would have a negative test result on Monday and be free to leave his hotel.

'As far as I'm concerned,' she snorted in response to this, 'he can go wherever he likes – the further the better! Just so long as he keeps away from us, that's all.'

17. ANGELS

'Yes,' Andy told Yakubu, 'the prosecution is going ahead, but it could take some time before the case is heard; and there's a good chance it'll end up being manslaughter, rather than murder. But then, the nature of Jibrilu's injuries were such that that was always on the cards. I do honestly think they never intended to do him serious harm. Now, the place where it happened is just along here.'

He led the way along Goose Lane, past the gate into the Fellows' Garden of Lichfield College to the back door of Holy Cross.

'They were standing around here, taking a cigarette break,' he explained, pointing at the worn flagstones across the threshold. When Gabriel Sibanda, the boy I was telling you about, came up behind them, they wouldn't let him through. One of them pinned him up against the wall – just there!'

'But why?' asked Yakubu. 'What had he done to them?'

'Nothing. They just seem to have enjoyed tormenting him. I think maybe they didn't like seeing a black boy who was .... I think he didn't fit in with their sense of – of – of the way things ought to be – the correct social order, if you like.'

'How do you mean?'

'A black boy shouldn't have been so clearly more affluent and more cultured than they were. They taunted him about playing bongo drums and eating bananas. It's alright for a black boy to be a boxer or a footballer, but playing the organ and carrying sheet music around in a leather case wasn't acceptable in their minds. But that's only a guess,' Andy added quickly. 'I can't get inside their heads any better than you can. Maybe they just enjoyed picking on people generally. Anyway, fortunately Gabriel made an excellent witness. He gave us good descriptions of two of them, and managed to pick all three out from a set of photographs. So, however the murder/manslaughter charge goes, we've definitely got them for racially-aggravated assault and abuse – and robbery too, seeing as they took his music case.'

He turned and pointed across the road.

'That's the window of Jibrilu's room. He saw what was going on and shouted out at them to stop. Then he jumped out of it and ran over to make sure they did. Gabriel ran off scared, and Jibrilu started telling the bullies what he thought of their behaviour. They claim they were scared of him and that's why one of them took out a knife, but it was three against one, so I can't see a jury being convinced by that argument.'

Yakubu stood in silence, gazing across the street at the low, lead-lighted window in the pale stone wall of Lichfield College. Then he turned slowly, his eyes lowered as if he were tracking his son's footsteps across the road.

'And this is where he died?' he asked at last, gesturing down at the cobbles.

'Yes. Well, here.' Andy indicated the corner where Val and Doreen had discovered the body. 'They found him just here, partly hidden by the bin.'

Yakubu nodded slowly. Then he walked over to the spot and knelt down. He seemed to be saying words under his breath but Andy could not catch what they were. Perhaps they were not in English. Then he bowed lower. His head was almost touching the ground. Was he kissing the place where his son had died? Andy stepped back and took up a place by the wall of the college. Even watching this odd ritual felt like an intrusion on Yakubu's grief.

'Thank you.' Yakubu's voice came as a shock. He was back next to Andy, standing tall and looking him in the face. 'I needed to see the place. And now …? Do we go inside?'

'Yes. They're all in there. I can hear the organ playing.'

They stepped through the door into the dark passageway through the college. Immediately the music became louder. It reached a climax and then there was a pause.

'This way.' Andy led Yakubu to the small door into the chapel. As he opened it, the organ began playing again. They both went through, closing the door behind them. The chapel seemed to be deserted. No, not quite: Moses Sibanda was sitting at the far end of one of the long sideways-facing pews.

Then a woman's voice attracted their attention. Precious Sibanda was standing at the lectern, hidden at first by the stairs that led up to the organ loft, but now visible as they came further into the chapel.

'The Angel Gabriel from heaven came,' she sang, the pure tones seeming to soar high into the lofty roof of the building.

Looking up, Andy could just see the top of Gabriel's head above the wooden parapet of the organ loft as he accompanied his mother. Standing behind him, looking over his shoulder was a tall man in an academic gown – Dr Claughton, presumably. He turned at the sound of their footsteps on the tiled floor. Seeing them making their way quietly to seats near the front of the chapel he turned back and bent over his pupil to whisper something in his ear. Then he came silently down the wooden staircase and crept out through the small door beneath the organ loft. He evidently knew why they were there and wanted to leave the family to speak with Andy and his father alone.

Gabriel continued playing and Precious continued to sing. Andy and his father sat side-by-side listening to the haunting melody. When it drew to a close with a final "Gloria!" from Precious and a resonant chord from the organ, there was silence for a second or two before Gabriel began hastily pushing closed stops in preparation for turning off the organ. Precious stepped forward and greeted them.

'Professor Danjuma! Thank you for coming.'

'No indeed!' Yakubu replied. 'It is I who should be thanking you. Your son must have been one of the last people to see my son alive. I would very much like to hear about it from his own lips – if that will not be too much to ask?'

'Of course not. We are so grateful to your son for rescuing Gabriel. If he had not intervened, who knows? It could have been Gabriel whom they …. I'm sorry, that must sound callous. I didn't mean that it was any better that your son was ….' She put out her arm and placed her hand gently on his shoulder for a moment. 'We are all so sorry for your loss. If there is anything we can do to help …? Was he your only child?'

'He was when he died,' Yakubu replied. 'But I had lost a daughter before this, and …,' he added, glancing towards Andy, 'his death has been instrumental in me finding another son that I never knew I had. Insha'Allah, I will find some way of making amends to him and his mother for the damage I did to them forty years ago.'

Precious turned to Andy with a questioning look on her face. He gave a quick shake of his head and a wry smile. 'It's a long story.'

'It sounds a fascinating one!' Moses Sibanda had come up to them now and was shaking Yakubu's hand warmly. 'I'm sure that I could find a publisher, if you would like me to help you write it.'

'Moses!' his wife reproved him. 'This is not the time. Besides, not everyone wants their name in the papers.'

'You're right. I'm sorry. I have a journalist's eye for a sensation, I'm afraid. But we came here to thank you – or to thank your son, Professor Danjuma. We may owe Gabriel's life to him.' Moses turned and called to his son, who was now standing by the parapet of the organ loft, looking down on them nervously from above. 'Come down Gabriel, and tell Professor Danjuma what happened.'

Gabriel obediently descended the stairs and began his account of the frightening incident. Yakubu listened intently, smiling at his description of the orang-utan man, and frowning when Gabriel told him about being pinned against the wall while the white-faced woman taunted him.

'I didn't really see him,' he finished apologetically. 'I just heard him shouting and then it must've been him running back the other way when I was running away. I was too scared to stop. I'm sorry, maybe if I'd stayed a bit longer …'

'Gabriel, we've told you before-,' Precious began, but Yakubu interrupted her.

'No,' he said firmly, laying his two hands gently on Gabriel's shoulders. 'There was nothing you could have done. The doctors say he died within minutes. You could not have got help in time to save him. What is to be will be.'

'Yes, sir. Thank you,' Gabriel mumbled dutifully.

'And I am sure that this is something that was meant to be,' Yakubu went on. 'Did you know that you and my son have the same name?'

Gabriel shook his head.

'It is true! Jibrilu is "Gabriel" in our language. Jibril is the angel who told Maryam that she would be the mother of Isa Masih – Jesus the Messiah of the Jews – and he also revealed the holy Qur'an to Allah's Messenger, Mohammed, salla Allahu alayhi wa sallam. You are both named after a very great angel indeed!'

'Thank you for telling us that, Professor Danjuma. It's very interesting.' Precious smiled at Yakubu and then pointed upwards. They all looked up at the beams that supported the roof. At first

Andy could not understand. Then he made out the shapes of dozens of angels carved into the wood. 'I am quite sure,' Precious continued, 'that your Jibrilu is with the angels in heaven now.'

'Insha'Allah he has a place reserved for him in Jannah,' Yakubu nodded. 'He was a good boy, although he was too quick to judgement sometimes, and sometimes too impetuous – like his father, I am afraid.' He looked towards Gabriel again. 'May I shake your hand? I would like to thank you for testifying to the police. It is because of you that my son's killers have been found.'

Andy watched as Gabriel held out his hand nervously and Yakubu grasped it. For the first time, he felt a small shiver of pride in his new father. Turning away to avoid staring, he glimpsed a figure standing at the back of the chapel, just inside the main entrance from the quadrangle. He stared in amazement. It was Mum! Had she been there all the time, listening? Then, a moment later, she was gone. He heard the door close behind her and rapid footsteps on the paving outside.

THANK YOU

Thank you for taking the time to read Just Another Knife Crime. If you enjoyed it, please consider telling your friends or posting a short review. Word of mouth is an author's best friend and much appreciated. Thank you,

Judy

ACKNOWLEDGEMENTS

I would like to thank many Facebook friends, especially those from the *Pesky Methodist* group, for their support and encouragement and for suggesting on ideas for my books.

I am grateful to Gillian Gilbert for reading the manuscript, giving helpful comments, and pointing out typographical errors.

I am indebted to the authors of a wide range of internet resources, which I have used for researching the background to this book. These include:

Police and Criminal Evidence

- www.gov.uk/biometric-data-records
- www.gov.uk/police-powers-to-stop-and-search-your-rights

Knife injuries and knife crime

- Security Magazine
- Stack Exchange
- Physio-pedia
- Ingenia.org.uk

Nigeria

- Behindthename.com
- Legit.ng
- visareservation.com

DISCLAIMER

This book is a work of fiction. Any references to real people, events, establishments, organisations or locales are intended only to provide a sense of authenticity and are used fictitiously. All the characters and events are entirely invented by the author. Any resemblances to persons living or dead are purely coincidental.

Many of the locations and institutions that feature in this book are real. Their inhabitants and employees, however, are purely fictional. In particular:

- Neither Holy Cross nor Lichfield Colleges exist;
- None of the police officers depicted here are based on real people in Thames Valley Police or any other police service.

MORE BOOKS FROM JUDY FORD

Many of the characters in this book feature in the fourteen **Bernie Fazakerley Mysteries**:

1. **Two Little Dickie Birds**: a murder mystery for DI Peter Johns and his Sergeant, Paul Godwin.

2. **Murder of a Martian**: Peter and Jonah solve a double murder and Peter meets Martin Riess for the first time.

3. **Grave Offence**: Peter investigates an assault and a suspicious death, while Jonah is in rehab in the spinal injuries centre.

4. **Awayday**: a traditional detective story set among the dons of Lichfield College.

5. **Death on the Algarve:** a mystery for Bernie and her friends to tackle while on holiday in Portugal.

6. **Mystery over the Mersey**: a murder mystery set in Liverpool.

7. **Sorrowful Mystery**: Jonah investigates a child abduction and Peter embarks on a new journey of faith.

8. **In my Liverpool Home**: Bernie and her friends return to Liverpool to investigate a suspicious death in Aunty Dot's Care Home.

9. **Organ Failure**: a body is discovered under the organ in St Cyprian's Church and Jonah is called in to investigate.

10. **Rainbow Warrior**: One of their friends is injured in a hit-and-run incident and Jonah is convinced that this is attempted murder.

11. **Admission of Innocence**: Father Damien calls Peter and Jonah out of retirement to solve a murder case and prevent a miscarriage of justice.

12. **Lethal Mix**: Three of Lucy's student friends are injured in an anti-Muslim hate crime in Liverpool. Jonah, Peter and

Bernie assist Merseyside Police to bring their attacker to justice.

13. **A Secret Gardener?** Bernie's friend Martin discovers a body in the Fellows' Garden of his Oxford College.

14. **Crowd of Witnesses**: Jonah decides to write his memoirs, beginning with a murder investigation from 1982.

Andy Lepage's colleagues from Thames Valley police also appear in five other novels:

- **Changing Scenes of Life**: Jonah Porter's life story, told through the medium of his favourite hymns.

- **Despise not your Mother**: the story of Bernie's quest to learn about her first husband's past.

- **Weed Killers**, **Lost in Lockdown**, and **Victim Statements** form a trilogy of novels about the aftermath of the murders of two young men.

And there's a book of short stories, in which Peter Johns narrates his side of the story:

- **My Life of Crime**: the collected memoirs of DI Peter Johns. This includes some episodes that appear in other books, but told from a new perspective, as well as some completely new stories.

You can find all these on Judy Ford's **Amazon Author page**.

Visit the Bernie Fazakerley Publications **Facebook page**.

Follow Judy Ford on **Twitter**: @JudyFordAuthor.

GLOSSARY OF ARABIC WORDS AND PHRASES

Alayhi al-Salaam – Peace be upon him. This phrase, or its abbreviation "a.s.", is often used by Muslims after the names of prophets as a sign of respect. The English abbreviation, pbuh, is also sometimes used.

Insha'Allah – God willing

Jannah – The Muslim equivalent of heaven or paradise, where the righteous are rewarded after the Day of Judgement.

Salla Allahu alayhi wa sallam – Peace and blessings of Allah be upon him. Muslims often say this phrase (often abbreviated "saw" or "pbuh") after saying the name of a prophet of Islam.

GLOSSARY OF UK POLICE RANKS

Uniformed police

Chief Constable (CC) – Has overall charge of a regional police force, such as Thames Valley Police, which covers Oxford and a large surrounding area.

Deputy Chief Constable (DCC) – The senior discipline authority for each force. 2nd in command to the CC.

Assistant Chief Constable (ACC) – 4 in the Thames Valley Police Service, each responsible for a policy area.

Chief Superintendent ('Chief Super') – Head of a policing area or department.

Police Superintendent – Responsible for a local area within a police force.

Chief Inspector (CI) – Responsible for overseeing a team in a local area.

Police Inspector – Senior operational officer overseeing officers on duty 24/7.

Police Sergeant – Supervises a team of officers.

Police Constable (PC) – 'Bobby on the beat'. Likely to be the first to arrive in response to an emergency call.

Police Community Support Officer (PCSO) – A uniformed civilian member of the police service.

Crime Investigation Department (CID) – Plain clothes officers

Detective Superintendent (DS) – Responsible for crime investigation in a local area.

Detective Chief Inspector (DCI) – Responsible for overseeing a crime investigation team in a local area. May be the Senior Investigating Officer heading up a criminal investigation.

Detective Inspector (DI) – Oversees crime investigation 24/7. May be the Senior Investigating Officer heading up a criminal investigation.

Detective Sergeant (DS) – Supervises a team of CID officers.

Detective Constable (DC) – One of a team of officers investigating crimes.

These descriptions are based on information from the following sources:

[1] Mental Health Cop blog, by Inspector Michael Brown, Mental Health co-ordinator, College of Policing.
https://mentalhealthcop.wordpress.com/, accessed 31st March 2017.
[2] Thames Valley Police website,
https://www.thamesvalley.police.uk , accessed 31st March 2017.

GLOSSARY OF OXFORD JARGON

This glossary is by no means exhaustive. A fuller list of Oxford terminology may be found on the University website.

The Bod – student slang for the Bodleian Library.

The Broad – Broad Street, one of the main streets in the centre of Oxford.

Coming up – Arriving at Oxford at the beginning of term

Fellow – A member of staff holding a Fellowship at one of the colleges. Fellowships may be Tutorial (teaching) or Research.

Finals – Also known as "Schools". Both terms are abbreviations of "Final Honours School". These are the examinations taken by undergraduate students at the end of their final year of study.

Going down – Leaving Oxford at the end of term

Gown – Members of the university are entitled to wear gowns that indicate their level of scholarship. The term may also be used to refer to the university community as a whole, as in "Town and Gown" which expresses the, sometimes uneasy, relationship between the residents of Oxford and the members of the university,

Hall – the dining hall of a college. This term may also be used to denote the evening meal ('dinner') served there. 'Formal Hall' means that staff and students are required to dress formally in gowns when attending.

The High – short for "the High Street", the main thoroughfare through Oxford town centre running from Carfax Tower to Magdalen Bridge.

High Table – The table in a college dining hall, often on a dais, at which the Head of House and Fellows dine.

GLOSSARY OF OXFORD JARGON

Hilary Term – The second term of the university year, which starts in January.

Isis – The part of the River Thames that runs through Oxford.

Master – The principal of a college. Each Oxford college is headed by a senior Fellow. Each college uses its own terminology for this. Titles include: Master, Principal, President, Rector, Dean, Warden, Provost.

Matriculation – Matriculation confers membership of the University on those students who are enrolled at the University of Oxford and following a degree-level course.

Michaelmas Term – The first term of the university year, which starts in October.

Schools – Also known as "Finals". Both terms are abbreviations of "Final Honours School". These are the examinations taken by undergraduate students at the end of their final year of study.

Scout – A college servant responsible for cleaning. Each scout is usually assigned to a specific part of the college. A student may refer to "my scout" meaning the scout responsible for cleaning his or her room.

Sheldonian Theatre – The main ceremonial hall used by the University for events such as Matriculation and degree ceremonies.

Staircase – The older Oxford colleges are designed on a 'staircase' system, in which a group of rooms is accessed by a staircase that opens on to one of the quadrangles around which the college is built. Typically, rooms are identified by a combination of the name of the quad, the number of the staircase and the room number within the staircase group.

GLOSSARY OF OXFORD JARGON

Subfusc – Formal attire worn by students and academics on formal occasions, including matriculation, examinations and graduation.

Trinity Term – The third term of the university year, which starts in April.

Tutor – A member of staff (or a postgraduate student) who gives tutorials to undergraduate students.

Tutorial – A session in which one or two (or occasionally more) students are taught by a Tutorial Fellow or some other person appointed by their college. Typically, this involves students preparing work in advance and talking about it during the tutorial.

Tutorial Fellow – A member of staff holding a Tutorial Fellowship at one of the colleges

MAP OF OXFORD

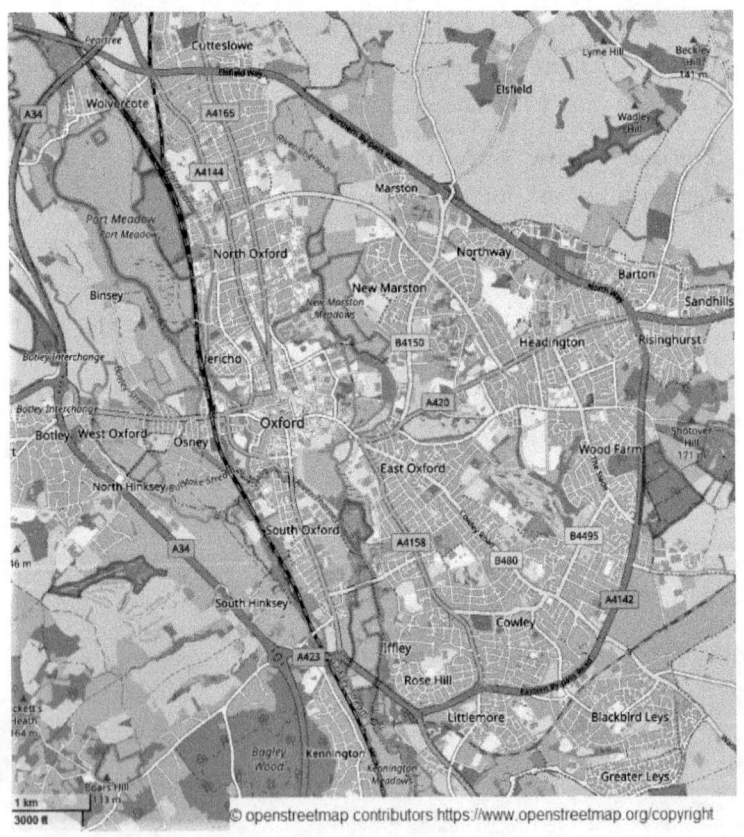

ABOUT THE AUTHOR

Like her main character, Bernie Fazakerley, Judy Ford is an Oxford graduate and a mathematician. Unlike Bernie, Judy grew up in a middle-class family in the South London stockbroker belt. After moving to the North West and working in Liverpool, Judy fell in love with the Scouse people and created Bernie to reflect their unique qualities. She has worked in academia and in the NHS.

As a Methodist Local Preacher, Judy often tells her congregation, "I see my role as asking the questions and leaving you to think out your own answers." She carries this philosophy forward into her writing and she hopes that readers will find themselves challenged to think as well as being entertained.

www.ingramcontent.com/pod-product-compliance
Lightning Source LLC
Chambersburg PA
CBHW060403180626
46817CB00007B/2500